Les has played in rock bands, sold everything from shoes to double glazing. He's been a policeman, trainee train driver, a chauffeur, a weighbridge operator, an office manager, a builder, worked in a psychiatric hospital, been a stand-up comedian and actor and now writes and directs plays. This is his first novel.

Dedication

To my family and friends who always believed in me.

Les Clarke

Kevin Doyle R.I.P

AUSTIN MACAULEY
PUBLISHERS LTD.

Copyright © Les Clarke (2017)

The right of Les Clarke to be identified as author of this work has been asserted by him in accordance with section 77 and 78 of the Copyright, Designs and Patents Act 1988.

All rights reserved. No part of this publication may be reproduced, stored in a retrieval system, or transmitted in any form or by any means, electronic, mechanical, photocopying, recording, or otherwise, without the prior permission of the publishers.

Any person who commits any unauthorized act in relation to this publication may be liable to criminal prosecution and civil claims for damages.

A CIP catalogue record for this title is available from the British Library.

ISBN 978-1-78629-876-8 (Paperback)
ISBN 978-1-78629-877-5 (Hardback)
ISBN 978-1-78629-878-2 (E-Book)
www.austinmacauley.com

First Published (2017)
Austin Macauley Publishers Ltd.
25 Canada Square
Canary Wharf
London
E14 5LQ

Chapter One

Kevin Doyle was thirty-one years old and a complete waste of space. He hadn't 'worked' in years, no one in their right mind would think of employing him with his record of petty crime. He lived on benefits, did a bit of this and a bit of that and had been known to do some driving when *certain* people needed a driver who could keep his mouth shut. Doyle could certainly do that. He'd seen first-hand what happened to people that couldn't!

Doyle was one of those people that knew people and he got by ...

But today he wasn't working, today was different. For some reason completely out of the blue and for no excuse other than for the fact it was a gorgeous sunny day, Doyle had decided to do something he hadn't done in years, and that was to *go fishing!* Just like that. No planning, no preparing, just straight off-the-cuff, he wanted to go fishing.

He used to fish quite regularly years ago, I suppose if you'd asked him he might have said it was his hobby, but life and circumstance had got in the way and his fishing tackle had stayed locked away in his garden shed for years until today.

So he'd taken what was left of a loaf of bread from the bin in the kitchen, dug a few worms from the garden and chucked his rods and tackle into the back of his van and driven down to a pond he knew a few miles away. It wasn't a particularly large pond and not many people fished it as it was quite well-hidden and off the beaten track, accessed only by a dirt road that ran alongside a farm.

Doyle used to go to school with the son of the owner a million years ago, and thinking back on it, he probably hadn't seen Jamie for getting on for twelve years or so now, and Doyle did have a sudden thought that perhaps in that time the farm might have changed hands and been sold and have new owners. *Oh well, sod it* he thought, he'd cross that bridge when he came to it if and when it ever cropped up.

Remembering back though, more often than not, Jamie and he would be the only ones fishing there, Doyle rather hoped that aspect hadn't changed. He liked the solitude of fishing and if he found the place was packed he'd just get back in the van and go back home.

Doyle had parked up and had a scout about; and was chuffed to find that there was no one else there. The plants and rushes around most of the pond were pretty overgrown, so it looked like no one came there very often. Which was great, just how he liked it, peaceful.

Doyle retrieved his gear from the van, sussed out a suitable swim and tackled up. Fifteen minutes later his rod was on the water, he was sat down with a fag, the sun was shining, he was chilled, and all was well with the world. An hour later however the novelty had started to wear off. He'd caught one small perch that wouldn't even fill a sandwich and had had two more bites and that was that. He hadn't had a touch now for nearly fifty minutes and he was on the verge of calling it a day when he decided he'd have a cast under the branches of an overhanging tree.

He'd noticed a steady stream of bubbles rising and he reckoned there could be some carp or tench down there.

Doyle started to reel in his line when his hook snagged on something. *Oh great here we go* he thought, and no matter how he manoeuvred his rod, he couldn't free his line. The hook was well and truly caught on something and whatever it was, he wasn't going to be able to dislodge it without losing his tackle.

Doyle held the rod low and parallel with the water and started to walk backwards, expecting that at any moment the line would snap and he'd lose his rig and everything. He applied more pressure and he felt the line start to move, whatever he'd hooked, it was coming to the surface.

He carried on walking backwards and reeling in the line and then a corner of something broke the surface of the water. It looked like a curtain, but no, it was quite long and bulky; it looked more like a shop mannequin, the kind of thing they use to display the latest fashions on, and then the smell hit him.

"Jesus Christ!" he said pulling a face and turning his head away from the stink. It was then he realised it wasn't a shop dummy at all; it was the body of a woman wearing a dark blue evening dress. Her body was bloated and macerated and crayfish were clinging to her and feasting on her loose flesh.

Doyle dropped his rod and staggered back half-stumbling in his haste to get away from the repulsive sight of the dead body, but as the body began to roll over and sink, he noticed a glint of something gold around her neck.

Old instincts die hard and Doyle grabbed the rod and put the pressure back on, reeling the body back to the surface. He was suddenly fearful his line would snap with the weight and he would lose his newfound prize, so he snatched up his landing net. He held it by the net and used the pole to help drag the body into the side of the bank. The smell was overpowering and he forced himself not to gag and be sick. He breathed in through his mouth and managed to get the body right into the side of the pond. He dug the pole of the landing net into the riverbed to hold it still and prevent it from floating away, luckily close to the bank the water was only about three feet deep.

Doyle cast anxious looks all around but he couldn't see anyone else and he'd heard no other cars or seen anyone else since he'd arrived. Doyle stared down at the woman; both fascinated and repulsed at the collection of large and small amphibians scurrying about on her body and in and out of her dress. But Doyle had been right about the gold, only she wasn't wearing one gold necklace, she was wearing two! He knelt down and managed to undo the clasps. They were quality, he could tell that by their weight and design and she was also wearing a thick gold bracelet on her right wrist, which he also undid and dropped onto the bank.

On her other wrist, she wore a watch. It looked expensive but the water had got into it and the face had clouded over, it wasn't worth the hassle, so he left it. He picked up his spare rod rest and tentatively lifted her hand clear of the water. She was wearing some classy rings, boy was she ever! Apart from a gold wedding ring, she wore a large ring that had a ruby set in the middle surrounded by diamonds. That had to be worth shedloads! Plus, she had two rings on her middle finger that looked expensive as well. What a result this was turning out to be, fuck the fishing!

Doyle pulled at the rings and the flesh started to come away from her fingers. He screwed his face up at the mess. There was no blood, just the shedding of the soft tissue of skin that had been made sodden by being immersed in water for so long. He managed to get both rings off her middle finger but the big ruby ring and the wedding ring remained firmly stuck.

This was no time for sentiment; someone could come along at any time. He reached into his tackle box and found the cutters he used for his metal traces. He wet his lips and psyched himself up and then grabbed her finger and snipped away at the flesh and bone with the cutters. The flesh was like jelly and squished, and the jaws on the cutters were only small so he had to whittle away at the bones in stages, but in a short while the finger broke free and he scooped the rings off the stub and threw the remains of the finger out into the middle of the pond.

Christ the ruby ring was a beaut, God knows what it was worth? Apart from the ruby in the centre, there were six equal-sized diamonds surrounding the main stone, and despite its watery ordeal, it still caught the sun and reflected the light in a glorious and expensive way.

Time to go!

Doyle used his cutters to sever the fishing line, then freed the landing net handle and used it to push the body away from the bank. It gave a sort of roll and then half sank.

Doyle grabbed the bit of rag he'd used to hold the fish and wrapped the jewellery in it and buried it in his tackle box under his spare reel and lines and floats etc. He didn't break down his rod or chair or landing net. He just scooped up all of his tackle and half-ran with it held haphazardly in his arms to his van, where it was dumped unceremoniously onto the floor in the rear and the doors slammed shut behind it.

Doyle started the van and slowly did a three-point turn. He forced himself to act naturally and not speed off and draw attention to himself should anyone see him. In about ten minutes' time he'd be back home, he'd only caught the one little fish but instead he'd netted himself a pot of gold!

Chapter Two

Martin Conner's phone vibrated and he pulled it out of his pocket and answered it.

"Yeah."

"It's me, Kev," he said striving to keep the excitement out of his voice.

"Kev who?" Conner asked irritably.

"Doyle, Kevin Doyle, you know!"

"Oh," Conner replied, none too happy to get the call.

"I've got something you might be interested in," he said keeping his voice as steady as he could.

"Don't think so mate, but thanks anyway," Conner moved the phone away from his ear and was about to end the call when Doyle yelled at him.

"It's gold! I've got some gold to sell!"

Conner held the phone back up to his ear. "And where would a tosser like you get gold from then?"

"Can't say, but it's the real thing, honest …"

"Yeah, yeah," Conner said disinterested.

"Straight up, it's fucking mint! None of your bling, it's the business." Doyle gushed.

Conner cut in, "Is it hot?"

"Hot? No, that's the last thing it is. No it ain't hot I promise ya." He smiled at the irony. "It's good stuff you won't believe it when you see it. I got seven bits for you."

"Sounds like you've been busy." Conner thought for a moment. "Alright … eight o'clock rear car park of The Crown. If you're late, or you're trying to sell me some shit, I'll break your fucking legs for ya."

"I'll be there! You'll love it, honest." Doyle felt his stomach drop at the thought of getting on the wrong side of Conner; he'd seen his handiwork before and he sure as hell didn't want to be on the receiving end of it. The line went dead.

Doyle had just over an hour to kill, he fancied a drink, and he felt he'd earned it. He might as well go down the Crown now and get a bevy or two in while he was waiting. Sounded good to him, but first he thought he'd give his brother a bell. They hadn't spoken for a couple of weeks and Chris would be impressed that it was him calling and not the other way around for a change.

Chris Doyle was the older of the two brothers by three years. But unlike Kevin, Chris had made something of himself and had never been in trouble with the law or anyone else for that matter. He ran an IT company and was always busy. He was the one that always seemed to be bailing Kev out of trouble. He'd paid for his rehab when he was at his lowest ebb lost in a drug-induced world and sleeping rough. And on two occasions he'd found employment for Kevin, neither of the jobs had worked out and Chris never bothered again, reluctantly content to let Kev get by as best he could. Sometimes no matter how hard you tried to help someone it was just never enough. They were still quite close though, although they rarely actually saw one another; they did keep in touch by phone fairly regularly.

Chris answered the call on the second ring and felt an anxious twinge when he recognised the caller.

"Yo Bruv, to what do I owe the pleasure? You alright?" Chris rather expected a tale of woe but was surprised to hear his brother in fine spirits.

"Yeah I'm cool, I'm great yeah. How about you, you alright?" Kev began to rub his thumb over his first two fingers, a nervous habit he'd had for years and could never seem to stop doing.

"Yeah I'm just getting changed."

Kevin slapped his palm against his forehead remembering. "Shit yeah I forgot sorry!"

"No it's OK, I've got a few minutes yet, did you want something?" It would be very rare for Kevin to phone out of the blue and *not* want something. A phone call would normally mean he was in trouble or he was short of money. Chris waited for the story to unfold and took a quick look at the wall clock checking the time.

"No … no I'm fine honest. I've just had a great day that's all. I've made a bob or two today and I'm just out for a drink to celebrate and I thought I'd give my brother a call, you know like you do. But I'm cool really."

"Well that's great to hear Kev, and look keep in touch yeah, but I'm sorry mate I've really got to go. I'll ring you next week and I'm really chuffed to hear from you and that you've had a great day, that's brill. Later."

"Yeah and you, laters." Kevin disconnected the call, he felt a little deflated. He'd have liked to have talked for longer but he'd forgotten it was Tuesday. Chris was always busy on Tuesdays and Thursdays.

Chris put the phone back into his kit bag and pulled the black obi tight around the waist of his Gi and opened the door and entered the dojo. He bowed and walked out in front of the class. Another younger man who was also wearing a black belt bowed to Chris and then turned to the class.

"Sensei ne rei!" The students bowed to Chris and Chris returned the bow.

"Hajime!" Chris said firmly and the class began to execute a series of moves. Chris however was not fully focused and his mind kept slipping back to his brother's phone call, he had a sinking feeling that his brother's sense of wellbeing was going to be short-lived.

Chapter Three

Doyle had already cleaned the items and they were now encased in his one clean handkerchief and stuffed down the bottom of his trouser pocket. He had no idea what the jewellery was worth, but all the bits were Hallmarked so he knew they were class. Conner would no doubt try to rip him off but he didn't know anyone else to fence the gear off to, and Conner would know how to get rid of it without any problems.

Doyle had another sniff under his armpit. Whenever he was nervous he always started to sweat and no matter how much deodorant he sprayed on, he could always smell it. Not to worry, there was plenty of time to have another squirt before he left to meet Conner, then he really would start to sweat!

Doyle parked his van in the back car park of The Crown and entered the pub. He nodded at a few people he knew and got himself a pint and stayed at the bar, checking to see who was in and if there was anyone he needed to avoid. There were a few people out there who had old scores to settle with Kevin Doyle but it looked like his luck was holding out so far tonight.

Two pints later, Doyle went into the toilet and relieved himself and then splashed water on his face and stared at his image in the grubby chipped mirror. Christ, he looked old. Maybe he'd make enough off this deal to piss off somewhere for a week or two, God knows he could do with a holiday in the sun somewhere, he couldn't even remember the last time he'd been away apart from a stretch in Pentonville, but he wouldn't want to talk about that. He sniffed under his arm, he was getting worked up and nervous again and he'd started to sweat. Let's just get this deal over with so I can get out and go home he thought.

He walked out of the pub and back into the rear car park. There was no sign of Conner. Doyle checked his watch: there was still three minutes to go. Suddenly there was a screech of tyres and a Beemer drove fast into the car park throwing up a shower of shale as it went past Doyle. It slammed to a halt and a few seconds later Conner got out.

Conner was a big man, tall and bulky with a streak of meanness you did not want to know about. He took a final drag on his cigarette and threw the butt on the ground and twisted his shoe on it to put it out. Doyle shambled across to meet him, conscious of the smell he was giving off. His heart was pounding and his mouth had gone dry.

"This better be good Doyle," Conner said looking the weedy little specimen up and down, "Christ you stink!" Conner said screwing up his face, "don't you ever wash?"

"It's nerves … when I get nervous I sweat I can't help it, it's not my fault."

"Well come on then!" Conner barked at him, "I ain't got all night. What cha got for me then, and it better be good now you've got me out here."

Doyle fumbled in his trouser pocket and pulled out the hankie, Conner was not impressed.

"That snotrag better be clean or you'll be using it to mop up your blood!" Conner said firmly.

"Yeah, yeah course it is," Doyle said rapidly. He unwrapped the hankie and held it open in the palm of his hand towards Conner.

Conner looked and flicked the items about with his index finger. He reached into his pocket and brought out a loupe, a jeweller's eyepiece, and jammed it in his eye and picked out two of the rings.

"It's good stuff," Doyle said encouragingly.

Conner stopped and looked at the man. "Just keep it shut while I'm looking, alright?"

"Yeah, yeah, course, sorry!" Doyle said and shrugged and stuck his hands in his pockets and looked down at the ground.

He was right though Conner thought, this *is* good stuff. He picked up the ring with the ruby and the diamonds. Doyle couldn't help himself.

"That's a beaut, that's gotta be worth a fair bit all them diamonds an' that ..." Doyle stopped talking when Conner raised his head and gave him a look that froze the blood in his veins.

"When I say *shut it*, I mean, *shut it!* I won't tell you again."

Doyle nodded his head rapidly and promptly stopped speaking, Conner went back to work. Doyle was right, it was a beaut, 24 carat, pure gold and the diamonds were genuine. All the pieces oozed class; Conner knew he would make a killing on this little lot and no mistake. He checked out the necklaces and the bracelet, they were all either 24 or 22 carat, whoever had owned them must be stinking rich, what a find this was turning out to be!

Conner wrapped the jewellery back up in the hankie and slid it into his pocket; Doyle watched his prize collection disappear and wasn't sure quite what to do about it.

Conner reached into his pocket and pulled out a roll of banknotes held together with an elastic band, he counted out two hundred pounds and held it out to Doyle.

"There ya go," he said "and thanks for the call you done good."

"No wait hang on a minute, that ain't right!" Doyle protested, "two hundred quid for that lot! I've looked at it, it's all Hallmarked, it ain't crap, it's gotta be worth a lot more than that!"

Conner remained calm but took a step closer to Doyle; the smell was coming off Doyle like vapour. "What d'you know about Hallmarks then, eh?"

"I know it means they're classy, that they're real gold …"

"Bollocks!" Conner said cutting in. "Not one of those Hallmarks are real, they're all fake.

Someone's just got a little engraving set and carved some initials on them to make them look authentic. I've got books at home with all the Hallmarks you can get that tell ya who made them and where, and I can assure you that what it says on this gear don't amount to diddly. The only bit that's worth anything and not that much, is the ring with the ruby in it, and they ain't diamonds round it either, they're zircon or some cheap shit like that …"

Doyle butted in, "but the weight of them necklaces, feel the weight, it's class stuff …"

"You ain't got a fucking clue what you're talking about!" Conner countered. "Course it's heavy, at its best, it's 9 carat, the rest is made up of copper, zinc and silver, it's one step above bling that's all. It just looks good but that don't mean it is good, and I'm doing you a favour by taking the lot off your hands in one go." He waggled the notes in front of Doyle. "So just take it cos you'll get fuck all else outta me 'cept a kick up the arse!" He flung the notes on the ground and started to walk back towards his car.

"Bastard!" Doyle yelled at him, "you've ripped me off you bastard I ain't that stupid!"

Conner stopped and turned and started to come back towards Doyle at speed, Doyle panicked and turned and ran as fast as he could towards the entrance to the car park risking a quick glance over his shoulder, and as he did, Conner's laughter filled his ears. Doyle felt like crying, he'd been duped and there was nothing he could do about it. His prize was lost. Doyle was too busy making his getaway to notice Conner bend down and scoop up the banknotes and stuff them back in his pocket; grinning from ear to ear. Conner got back in his motor and lit up another fag.

What a great start to the night he thought!

Chapter Four

Jimmy Cook and Alex Morgan were two typical thirteen-year-olds, not particularly naughty but always larking about and getting up to mischief. They were pushing and shoving each other about as they made their way down the dirt road that lead to the pond at the back of Asker's farm. Jimmy had just bought a green laser pen off eBay and he was excited about trying it out. Someone at school said that if you shone the beam into a duck's eye, it would flip over onto its back, flap its wings about like crazy and die, and Jimmy wanted to test it out and see if it was true. And the only place he knew anywhere near that might have ducks was Asker's pond.

"You seen any ducks here before then?" Alex asked recovering his footing as Jimmy got in a good shove.

"Can't remember I ain't been down here for years. They've probably filled it in by now or put a fence round it for health and safety!"

They both laughed and then Alex darted in quickly at Jimmy hoping to push him off the slight rise of the road and dump him in the ditch alongside, but Jimmy saw it coming and at the last moment stepped aside. Alex's momentum carried him forward and he ended up in a heap down in the ditch. Jimmy collapsed in fits of laughter looking down at his best friend in the mud-filled ditch and felt sure he'd wet himself if he laughed any more.

"Oh you bastard!" Alex wailed, "It's all wet down here!" Alex half-rose and then slipped back over in the ditch, Jimmy clutched his ribs and roared with laughter and the tears ran down his cheeks.

"It's not funny!" Alex moaned scrambling to his feet again and hauling himself up the bank and back onto the road. His trousers and shoes were caked in mud. "Look at the state of me?" He said holding his arms out to the sides, "Me trainers are soaked!"

"You should have taken 'em off before you went for a paddle then!" Jimmy said then burst into fits of laughter again.

Alex bent down and scraped a handful of mud off his trainer and threw it at Jimmy hitting him on the chest.

"Oi you wanker! Pack it in!" Jimmy said trying to wipe the mud off but making it ten times worse, spreading it further across the front of his top. "Now look what you done!"

They both heard a noise and instantly stopped what they were doing.

"D'you hear that?" Jimmy asked suddenly alert. "That sounded like a duck to me, bingo! Come on let's go!" He said excitedly getting to his feet and together they semi-crept closer to the water's edge, shielded at first by the rushes and vegetation that ran around the side of the pond.

Alex saw the duck first. It was a mallard making its way slowly and majestically across the pond.

"There it is!" He whispered and pointed.

"Yeah gotcha!" Jimmy replied scrambling the laser out of his pocket. "Looks like he's going across to the other side, we'll shoot round this way and meet up with him when he gets there." He gently punched Alex on the arm. "I can't wait to see this!"

"No, nor can I!" Alex replied and together they moved in a half-crouch making their way around the pond.

Jimmy noticed the odd shape in the water first and reached out with his arm to stop Alex and pointed down at it. "What the hell is that? Look just there, what d'you reckon that is then?"

Alex looked but he couldn't quite make it out. "Dunno … could be some old curtains or something someone's dumped in there."

"It don't look like curtains to me, come on let's take a look." Jimmy moved fast down through the reeds and stopped at the water's edge. "Holy shit it's a body! Look it's a body!" He yelled at Alex who was following close behind slightly hindered by the fact the wet had soaked through his trousers and jockeys.

"No way," Alex said arriving seconds later. He gazed down at the shape half-submerged in the water and then he too could see that it was in fact a woman's body. "Oh shit you're right it is a body! Well how did it get in there then?"

"Well you can bet she didn't come down here for a swim!" He started to look around. "Come on we need to find a stick or something to drag her into the side."

Alex stood transfixed, his discomfort forgotten as he gazed down at the blue dress and the exposed leg of the woman.

"Come on!" Jimmy said poking about in the bushes looking for something suitable to use. He focused in on a small tree that was growing up amongst the reeds and plants alongside the pond. He grabbed the tree and tried bending it over, it stubbornly resisted his attempts. "Come on Alex give me a hand over here will you I can't do it all by myself!"

Alex wandered over towards Jimmy, still not quite taking in what they'd discovered. How did a body get in the pond and did someone put it there or did she fall in? His mind was a jumble, he just couldn't think beyond what he had seen. He'd never seen a real dead body before, he'd only ever seen dead actors in films and games and things.

"Alex come on help me will you!" Jimmy insisted, still gripping the tree with both hands.

Alex finally snapped out of his reverie and hurried to Jimmy's side and together they bent the sapling over double until it cracked and split and then Jimmy was jumping up and down on the bent branch as it broke away from the thin trunk of the young tree. Jimmy kept forcing the branch up and down until finally it broke free and Jimmy was left with a piece of branch about five feet long.

"Let's do it!" He said triumphantly as he made his way back to the water's edge and their gruesome discovery, clutching his newly acquired piece of tree like a lance.

Jimmy reached out but even with the stick his reach was too short. "Shit!" He said, "I can't just reach it, here give me your hand and then I can reach out a bit further I'm not far off."

Alex stood right by the water's edge and gripped Jimmy's hand as Jimmy stretched out as far as he could. He continually slapped the stick at the water in front of the body making a small wave that eventually caused the body to move forward a little. Then the stick touched the body and Jimmy applied pressure and the stick half-rolled the body over and it moved closer to them. Jimmy managed to snag the stick in the cloth of her dress and let go of Alex's hand and used both hands on the stick to drag the body closer to the bank.

"Oh Christ!" Alex said covering his nose with his hand, "What a stink oh God!" He turned away as Jimmy brought the body right into the bank.

Jimmy laughed out loud. "Look at that! Fucking hell there's millions of things eating her up look!" The two boys stared in fascination as they watched two crayfish working their claws at the woman's flesh amidst hundreds of small shrimps and strange little black and red wriggling things, like tiny worms sliding all over her body and in and out of her dress.

"Look at her hand!" Alex said pointing. "They've like chewed one of her fingers right off, oh God!" He turned away gagging, the smell was overpowering and he fought to hold down the feeling that he was about to be sick.

Jimmy continued prodding at the body with his stick. The sodden cloth pulled apart as he pulled at it. "Here Ally look she ain't got no bra on!" He continued ripping the cloth of her dress and it just disintegrated and fell away and left her breast partially exposed. Jimmy laughed and poked at it. It was soft and spongy like jelly, and parts of it began to peel away with the pressure. Jimmy pulled a face and dropped the stick. He had to admit the smell was getting to him as well.

"What we going to do with it like?" Alex asked keeping his hand firmly fixed across his nose.

"I dunno, do I? I only came here for the ducks."

Alex fumbled out his mobile. "I'm going to phone the police, we might get a reward or something for finding it …"

Jimmy grabbed his hand. "Don't be a muppet! It ain't a lost dog we found, it's a dead woman and we shouldn't even be in here. Come on let's get out of here." He started to move away.

"But it could be someone's mum, she might have children," Alex protested, "we should tell someone."

"I ain't getting involved; you know we'll only get into trouble over it. I'm going home sod it, I was never here." He picked up speed and started back down the road away from the pond.

"Jimmy wait!" Alex shouted after him but he just kept walking and then Alex looked back at the woman. He felt a deep sadness for her and thought of his own mum who was probably still at work and how he would feel if it was his mum that was lying drowned in a pond and no one knew where she was. He watched Jimmy disappearing in the distance and he came to a decision and pressed the numbers for the emergency services. The call was answered almost immediately and Alex froze suddenly uncertain quite what to do or say.

"Hello caller, what emergency service do you require?" A few seconds passed in which Alex started to shake. "Caller are you still there? Are you injured or are you in danger?"

"There's a body," Alex blurted out, "she's dead. It's a woman!"

"Where are you calling from?"

"She's at Asker's pond in the water." Alex cut off the call and shoved the mobile back in his pocket and started to move away from the pond without daring to look back, desperate to get away and catch up with Jimmy who would be miles ahead by now. His brain was racing, Jimmy wouldn't be happy about what he'd done but he thought it was the right thing to do and he hadn't given his name so they wouldn't know who it was that phoned. He was back on the dirt road now and he started to pick up speed desperate to reach the safety of his own room and try to get the sight and smell of the poor woman out of his system. All he kept thinking of was that he was glad it wasn't his mum lying there in the dirty water of a pond being eaten by millions of insects. He shuddered at the thought and broke into a run.

Chapter Five

An hour and forty-five minutes after Alex's phone call, Asker's pond had become the main centre of attraction. There was a white tent set up right by the water's edge and a police van and two police cars both with their lights still rotating, cast their colours around and across the still water of the pond. There was also another white van parked up alongside the tent with its rear doors open. Blue and yellow tape was suspended across the road and an officer with a clipboard stood there watching the comings and goings and noting down anyone that came and went. Out in the middle of the pond was a small inflatable boat and divers were in the water searching the murky depths for anything else that might be connected with the body that now lay on a table encased in a body bag within the tent.

Ten minutes later two detectives rang the doorbell at Alex's house. The police had checked the mobile number the call had been made from with the service provider, and they in turn had supplied Alex's details.

Alex's mum answered the door and was shocked when the two men identified themselves as detectives from the local police station and showed their warrant cards. She felt her heart start to beat a little quicker. What the hell had Alex been up to now! She recovered herself and asked. "How may I help you?"

"We're looking for Alex Morgan, is he at home?"

Her heart went thump and her legs almost gave way. "Yes, yes he's home he's up in his room. He's lying down, he's not feeling very well."

"We need to talk to him if we may please Mrs Morgan it is important, is it alright to come in?" The detective moved past the woman without waiting for a reply and stepped into the hall.

Mrs Morgan looked at the first detective waiting patiently in the hall and opened the door fully to the other detective who briskly followed his colleague into the house. Mrs Morgan had a quick look both ways up the road and then shut the door.

"Can you tell me what this all about please? What's Alex supposed to have done? He's a good boy you know, oh I know you probably hear that all the time but it's true he's never been in any real trouble..."

The detective cut her off. "He's not in any trouble Mrs Morgan but we're hoping he can help us with our enquiries."

She didn't like the sound of that at all. That was 'police speak,' she'd watched enough cop shows on the telly to know that was a phrase that covered a multitude of sins and she wasn't going to let them get away with it.

"You can't see him until I've phoned a solicitor," she said a lot more confident than she felt.

The two detectives exchanged glances, they hadn't expected that.

The older of the two detectives spoke next. "I think we've kind of got off on the wrong foot here Mrs Morgan. Alex isn't in any kind of trouble, he made a '999' call today to the police and reported an incident and we'd just like to have a word with him about what he witnessed, that's all. There's certainly no need for a solicitor."

She held her hands together to try and stem the shakes that were coursing through her body. "Really?" she asked. "You're not going to suddenly arrest him or anything?"

"No Mrs Morgan I can assure that's not why we're here. We just need a word to verify a few facts and get some more details from him that's all."

"Oh, right I see. OK then," she said reassured. "If you just wait in there," she indicated the lounge, "I'll go up and get him for you."

The two men filed past her into the lounge and as she climbed the stairs to Alex's room, a sense of weariness and unease starting to build up inside of her.

Chapter Six

Steven Talbot was a very successful 'businessman.' He was primarily a property developer and was the biggest property owner in the county, not to mention the other pies he had his fingers in that helped swell his annual income to somewhere just short of 1.6 mill in the last financial year. He took out his mobile and pressed some numbers and then put the phone in the amplified holder on his antique oak desk and sat back and waited.

"He-llo?" The voice said evenly.

"It's me," Talbot said.

The voice on the other end of the line almost snapped to attention. "Sorry Mr Talbot I didn't recognise the number."

"Different phone, it's a pay as you go, you know what I'm like."

Carson's mind was racing, he wasn't expecting the call, he'd hoped that somehow he'd got away with the massive cock-up and Talbot would never get to hear about it. He knew this was going to be bad news, the worst, and he was dreading what the outcome of it would be.

Carson tried to sound casual, "What can I do for you?" he asked, as he slumped down in the battered armchair in the lounge of his little flat, his mind started to race.

Talbot's voice was like steel, "I've just had a call from one of my people down the nick."

Carson felt his blood run cold, oh Christ here we go he thought.

"It seems they've found a woman's body in a pond. Now you better not tell me it's Lizzie Calder or I will personally nail your bollocks to the fucking wall!"

Carson's world just collapsed and he lost the ability to speak. He opened his mouth to try and explain but nothing would come out, it was like he'd been struck dumb, such was the fear he felt.

"You listening to me you moron!" Talbot bellowed down the phone.

Carson dropped the phone and it fell into his lap. He sat there shaking and unmoving.

"Carson! Pick up the phone and speak to me or I'll be paying you a visit with a can of petrol and a lighter! Talk to me you useless prick!"

Carson fumbled for the phone and held it to his ear. "It wasn't meant to happen like that, it was a mistake ..."

Talbot cut him off in mid-sentence. "You got that right! Is it Lizzie Calder?"

Carson tried to calm himself down before he answered. "Yes," he whispered.

"How the fuck did that happen!" Talbot roared springing up from his chair. "That's not what I asked you to do. Put the frighteners on her I said so her old man would change his mind, I didn't want the woman killed did I! You know when the Old Bill start digging they're going to find a link that leads right back to me. You know that, don't you? When Calder finds out she's dead, which he will do in a very short space of time, he'll probably even tell them himself!" Talbot paced about his office the anger coursing through his veins making him clench and unclench his fists. "Whoever's responsible, I want him stripped and tied to a chair in the lockup by the time I get there."

"It's awkward," Carson offered weakly.

"What the fuck does that mean?" Talbot demanded leaning forward with his palms flat on the desk yelling into the speaker at the man.

"They weren't our boys. You had Ritchie and Kennedy up at Kingston's night club sorting the problems out up there and Curtis and Gregg were stuck up in Southampton picking up that shipment off the ferry and …"

Talbot interrupted, "Just tell me what happened maybe there's some way round it." He slumped back down in his chair and ran his fingers up through his hair trying to calm down.

"You wanted it doing quick and I had no one close at hand to cover it so I used a couple of Reardon's boys …"

"You did what! Without clearing it with me? What are you fucking stupid or something!"

Tommy Reardon was the closest thing to a rival that Talbot had. He ran a string of pubs and clubs and owned brothels and brought drugs down from Liverpool on a regular basis, each was aware of the others 'business interests' but they never openly challenged each other, instead they operated side by side with an unwritten understanding that they would never encroach on each other's turf or business. Talbot knew that Carson was pally with Reardon and there was a time when he thought Reardon was trying to poach him away but following a phone call and an assurance that that wasn't the case, Talbot let them get on with it. Now it looked like Carson had dropped him right in the shit with Reardon and given him a giant edge over him knowing he'd supplied the muscle that had murdered the wife of someone he was putting pressure on to sell him some property. Jesus what a fucking mess!

"I didn't know this was going to happen, did I?" Carson offered limply. "Christ, you can imagine how I felt when they told me what they'd done. And it was their idea to dump the body in the pond not mine, turns out they'd used the place before …"

Talbot was on his feet again. "What! You're telling me that she's not the first body they've dumped in that pond?"

"It turns out there was some bloke owed Reardon about thirty grand for some big stakes gambling debt, and he hadn't paid him, so they took him out to Guy's Wood, and before they'd even laid a hand on him, the bloke pissed himself and had a heart attack on the spot and snuffed it."

"Then they should have just taken him back home, propped him up in his armchair and legged it, and no one would have been any the wiser! Jesus. This is getting worse by the minute this is. So how come they killed her then?"

"I wasn't there, but one of them said that when they broke in, she set the dog on them and then she hit one of them with a poker. Whilst one was scrapping with the dog the other one got the poker off her and hit her with it and it cracked her skull open."

Talbot let out a long sigh. "Oh Jesus Christ. You know this is all gonna end in tears, don't you? If push comes to shove I'm gonna need the names of those two bozos and we're going to have to offer 'em up, we ain't got a lot of choice in the matter."

"Christ boss, Reardon ain't going to take too kindly to that …"

"You think he wouldn't do the same to me if the boot was on the other foot! Course he would, this shit ain't landing on my doorstep. Now I want the names of those boys and you need to get some eyes on 'em. I wanna know where they are twenty-four seven. Do not let them out of your sight or your name may get mentioned. Now am I making myself clear?"

Carson felt sick. "Yes boss," he managed to answer weakly then there was a click and the line went dead. His body released all the tension and he slumped back in the chair barely able to believe he wasn't about to get hospitalised. Well not yet anyway …

Chapter Seven

Talbot paced about the room, what to do, what to do! He knew Lizzie hadn't been seen around for a few days, but he thought that after his boys had paid her a visit, that Calder was playing it safe and had sent her away whilst he looked at his options. He never dreamt for a single minute that they'd topped her and dumped her body in a pond!

None of this was meant to happen. John Calder owned a block of flats and businesses in an area that Talbot had started to develop, but despite Talbot making him a fair offer for his properties, Calder had refused to sell. This was a spanner in the works to Talbot who had banged out a couple of really big back-handers to officials very high up in the local council, not to mention the other palms he'd had to grease to even get the project started, and the consortium that were spoon-feeding part of the massive outlay were getting restless as the building side of things was starting to get behind schedule. All Talbot wanted to do was apply a little pressure on Calder via his wife, so he would see reason, change his mind and sell, but it would seem that the 'hired help' had fucked up big time and now Calder's wife was dead and there was still no guarantee that Calder would sell, but you could bet your life that Talbot's name would now be sitting firmly and squarely in the frame. Jesus, what to do, what to do …

Chapter Eight

Calder had been attending a business meal with a couple of fellow Rotarians and had returned home around eleven. He wasn't unduly concerned that Lizzie wasn't home. She'd been attending a fundraising charity do for the local hospice and he was well aware how some of these events tended to drag on. God knows he'd been to enough in his time, quite often carriages weren't called till one p.m.

After checking his phone for missed calls or texts and walking the dog, Calder retired to bed a little before twelve. Not a particularly deep sleeper, he'd awoken at two-twenty and was a little surprised not to find Lizzie in bed beside him, but then again, he reasoned she may have had a few drinks and decided to take a room in the hotel for the night. Whenever there was a 'do' going on, hotels always offered guests a discount on rooms if they decided to stay over for the night.

Just before ten the next morning Calder rang his wife's mobile whilst he was in his office, and after a number of rings the call went to voicemail. He then looked up the hotel phone number on line and called them and learnt that his wife hadn't actually stayed the night. Calder left his office and rang her mobile again and was surprised to hear her phone start to ring in her handbag which was beside the dresser in the bedroom. He'd noticed the bag there when he'd turned in for the night but thought nothing of it, assuming that she'd changed bags and taken a smaller evening bag with her to match her dress.

A sense of foreboding started to build up inside him and he used her phone to start contacting her friends, it turned out no one had seen or heard from her. Calder sat down and tried to think, knowing Lizzie, there was probably a very simple explanation; the problem was, no matter how hard he tried, he just couldn't think of it.

By lunchtime there still hadn't been any word from her and now Calder was really starting to worry, this was so far out of character for her and the fact she'd left her phone behind, further added to his stress. OK she'd done it a couple of times before, but that was when she'd just popped out to the local shops or something, not when she was going out for a social evening when you didn't know who you were going to meet and who you may need to contact. No something was wrong. Something was very definitely wrong.

Calder phoned round the hospitals checking to see if she'd been admitted during the night but that also proved fruitless. He then called the local newspaper where he had a couple of contacts and asked if there'd been any incidents during the night involving a woman, again the result was negative.

What the hell was going on? What am I missing here, he asked himself. He went back into the bedroom and opened the door to her walk-in wardrobe, but as far as he could tell everything seemed to be in order, nothing seemed to be missing. Not that he knew much about fashion, but at least there were no great gaps in the rails of her hanging clothes and her racks of shoes were still intact. He checked the store cupboard in the hall where they kept amongst other things, their matching suitcases, they were all still there. He breathed a small sigh of relief.

He then went into his office and checked the third drawer down in his desk unit, her passport was still there sitting on top of his own. It was a mystery, what the hell was going on?

Had she been having an affair behind his back and something happened last night that changed everything and she'd run off with him? No that would never happen; he would have noticed the change in her, she was rubbish at keeping secrets at the best of times. OK she had been acting a little strange ever since she'd hit the big 4-0 the year before, but that wasn't unusual, that always seemed to be some kind of landmark age to most women, but damn it all she was still a very sexy and attractive woman despite her own doubts about it.

No, so what did that leave then? Maybe, to satisfy her own self-doubt she'd met someone last night who'd swept her off her feet and to prove to herself that men did still find her attractive she'd gone along with the flattery and had a few drinks too many and they'd ended up in bed somewhere? His stomach dropped at the thought of someone else pawing his woman about and an anger swept through him.

He still couldn't believe that of her, they'd been together for nearly twenty years and she knew what would happen to the pair of them if he ever found out, so it certainly wouldn't have been worth the risk. No something else was going on here and he suddenly had an inkling that it may have something to do with his businesses.

What if some lowlife toe-rag had kidnapped her to make himself a few grand? Oh Jesus, please don't hurt her, he felt his blood run cold at the thought. He didn't know what else to do, he felt totally helpless. He picked up his phone and called a couple of his associates and told them to get their arses over to his place pronto. He never said why but they could tell by his voice that whatever it was it was serious.

All Calder could do now, was wait. And if someone did have her, it wouldn't be a fucking ransom they'd get in return; it would be sheer pain and terror that they'd remember for the rest of their lives!

Chapter Nine

Conner was grinning from ear to ear when he left the side door of the high street jewellers, and why not, he was ten grand richer than when he went in! Thanks a bundle Doyle, nice one son; you can call me anytime you want! He laughed out loud at the thought of the skinny little runt who had even dipped out of the two hundred quid he'd originally offered him. Christ knows where he scored the gilt from but he had been right, it was mint and Bergmann had jumped on it like a starving cat on a mouse. He knew he should have wrangled a bit more out of the old bastard but he was glad to get shot of it, he never held onto anything longer than was necessary. And it now meant that he could give Sonia a ring.

Sonia was a cut above your normal hooker and he'd met her when he drove one of his 'associates' to her flat a few months ago. She charged a grand an hour and from what he'd heard she was worth every penny. When he'd collected his associate later that evening he'd picked up one of her cards from an ornately carved dish by the front door. He'd always thought that a grand for an hour's shag was mental, but then when Reg had batted on and on about what she did and how fantastic she was, and that she did 'girlfriend' for real, he told himself that whenever he had a spare wedge he'd treat himself to an hour's worth, and see if half of what Reg had said was true.

The moment of truth wasn't far away; he'd be giving her a call very soon.

Chapter Ten

Calder like most prominent business men had eyes and ears everywhere; it never hurt to know what was going on around you. Tony Pitman was Calder's right-hand man. His job title was PA but he'd been with Calder for over ten years now and he'd do whatever Mr Calder asked him to do, most of which wouldn't come under the usual requirements for a PA.

Lizzie had been gone for almost a week now and Calder had become a shadow of his former self. His eyes were deep set with dark lines under them and he'd lost a lot of weight, if it wasn't for Pitman, Calder might have starved himself to death by now. Even their beloved dog had been neglected until Pitman made the decision to put the dog in kennels until this was all over one way or the other. Calder was so deeply worried about his wife that he hadn't even noticed that the dog had gone. And for reasons best known to himself, Calder still hadn't involved the police, preferring to sort it out by himself.

One of Tony's contacts was on the phone to him now to say that the police had discovered a body in Asker's pond and had Mrs Calder turned up yet?

Pitman had turned away and cupped his hand over the mouthpiece of the phone and told the caller to hang on. Calder was sat slumped in his chair and Tony pointed to his mobile and said quietly, "Gotta take this boss," and Calder had barely nodded and Pitman had left the room.

"What you got?" Tony asked keeping his voice low and watching the door to Calder's office in case he came out during the call.

"Not a lot. Seems some kids were playing down the pond and they found a woman's body. She'd been in the water for a few days. She was just wearing an evening dress. Her head's been bashed in and someone's cut her fingers off to get at her rings…"

"Fucking hell," Pitman said cutting in and hoping against hope that it wasn't Lizzie. Alright everyone knew Calder was a bit of a bad boy on the quiet, you didn't get to where he was nowadays unless you could stand up to the hard nuts out there, but Lizzie wasn't tainted by any of that, she was a one-off, she was special and she'd never treated him like the hired help. He thought a lot of her as did everyone else that knew her. He also knew that Calder worshipped the woman and if it was her, then the shit would definitely be hitting the fan big time.

"So the cops ain't put a name to her yet then?"

"Not what I've heard of no. She didn't look too pretty and she's got nothing to identify her. They're checking dental records an' all that. Just thought you'd like to know as I heard you'd put a buzz out there for info."

"Yeah thanks, Kenny I owe ya. You get anything else, you call me night or day it doesn't matter, I'll sort you out when I next see you."

"No need Tone, Calder's always done alright by me, this one's on the house, I'm just hoping it ain't his missus, or whoever's done it will wish they'd never been born when Calder gets hold of 'em."

"Yeah you got that right, later mate, cheers." Tony ended the call and leant back against the wall. He was agonising over whether to put Calder in the picture yet or not? If it was Lizzie, then he'd want to know, but if it wasn't, he'd cause him no end of grief for nothing and Calder was already worried out of his head.

Fuck it decisions, decisions …

Chapter Eleven

The next morning two detectives arrived at Calder's house, Pitman had let them in, one, John Toller he vaguely knew. They didn't have to say why they were there, it was written all over their faces.

"Can you just wait in there please gentlemen," Tony said ushering them into the living room and leaving them to it whilst he went to summon Calder from his office. When Pitman left, the two tecs stood around nervously not wanting to sit and waited for the arrival of John Calder, wondering how they'd ended up with this shit detail. This was going to be one of the worst moments of their careers no matter how it turned out. Giving a death notice was one of the hardest things to do in the job and when it involved John Calder's wife who had been murdered and dumped unceremoniously in a pond, it didn't come any worse than that. The two tecs stood in silence and waited.

A few minutes later the door burst open causing both the officers to jump.

"Have you found Lizzie?" Calder asked desperate for some good news but reading their faces he knew it wasn't going to happen.

"Could you sit down please sir," Toller said nervously, "I'm afraid I have some bad news for you." He felt a line of sweat start to dribble down the side of his body and stain his shirt under the armpit.

"Just tell me," Calder said trying to sound calm when his insides were churning over and over. Pitman poured his boss a large shot of whiskey he was going to need it any moment now.

"When did you last see your wife sir?" Toller asked.

"Get to the point," he answered coldly.

The officer was thrown for a moment and then decided to just say what had to be said. "We've found a woman's body sir; it was in Asker's pond. We believe it to be your wife, Elizabeth Calder."

It took Calder a moment to register what had been said, he hadn't heard her called Elizabeth for years.

The officer continued. "We would need you to formally identify the body if and when you can sir, so we're sure …"

"In a pond?" Calder asked distractedly.

"Yes sir, she'd been there for a few days. She was wearing a dark blue evening dress …"

"Lizzie has one," he said quietly, "I'll check …" He turned away and Tony handed him the drink. "I'll do it, you take a seat yeah?" Calder's eyes seemed to have clouded over and he allowed himself to be guided into an armchair. The two officers towered over him feeling awkward and moved back and hovered by the sofa. Tony left the room.

Calder held the glass in both hands and took a long pull on the whiskey and felt the liquid burn down the back of his throat. He waved his hand at the officers inviting them to sit. They did.

Tony returned and bent down and whispered in Calder's ear. "I can't find the dress, it's gone."

Toller stood and produced a photograph he offered it to Tony. "It's a photo of the dress if that helps."

Tony studied the photo and held it for Calder to see. "Looks like hers to me," he said. Calder never replied, he just sat stock still clutching the drink in both hands looking to all the world like a broken man.

Tony handed the photograph back to the officer. "I'll come down and ID the body if that's all right.

I've known Lizzie for over ten years. I don't think Mr Calder's quite up to it yet."

"No that's fine," Toller replied. The other officer stood.

"I'll get someone over to stay with Mr Calder and then I'll be down. You got a card and a number, I'll give you a bell when I'm leaving and I'll meet you there."

Toller reached into his jacket pocket and handed over a card. "Thank you," Pitman said and slipped the card into his pocket.

Toller turned to Calder, "And I'm sorry to be the bearer of such dreadful news sir, may I offer my condolences ..."

Pitman put his hand on Toller's shoulder and moved him away towards the door, "Thanks, I'll be in touch." He escorted the officers to the front door. "You got any leads?" he asked Toller.

Toller looked back towards the sitting room and then answered. "Not a lot, look," he said anxiously, "this is strictly off the record. All I know is that she was found in the pond by a couple of kids who were larking about down there. She'd been in the water for about four days, her skull had been fractured which was the likely cause of death, and..." he hesitated, wondering just how much to tell Pitman, then decided to go ahead and tell him the rest, with someone like Pitman it was better to have him as a 'friend' than as an enemy. "And someone had cut her middle finger off to get her rings."

"Oh Christ," Pitman sighed thinking of the woman who'd only ever been kind to him. Someone would pay for this, and they would pay big time that was a given. "So seeing as Mrs C was dressed up for the evening but never got to where she was supposed to be, that means someone drove her body to the pond, so have you any idea where she was murdered?"

"We're working on it," Toller said guardedly.

"Come on Toller, you can do better than that, this is me you're talking to here not some junior hack from the local rag. What's the general consensus?"

Toller licked his lips nervously and took his time answering. "Look … is there any chance that Calder himself may have had something to do with it …"

Toller never quite finished off his sentence; Pitman grabbed him by his lapels and slammed him back into the wall. The younger police officer started to react and Pitman looked at him and glared. "Don't even think about it sonny!" he said his voice strong and level. The young constable froze and Pitman turned his attention back to Toller. "Calder may not be 'Mr Nice Guy' all the time, but one thing I do know for absolute certain, he worshipped Lizzie as we all did, and I would stake my life on it that he would never hurt her." He applied a bit more pressure to his grip and locked eyes with Toller, "Alright?" he asked.

Toller managed a nod, "Yeah, sorry, but I had to ask."

Pitman released him and flexed his neck, "No you didn't and I'm going to forget you ever did. So is there anyone else in the frame that looks a bit likely cos I ain't got a clue from my side. Calder doesn't always toe the line but I can't see he would ever piss someone off enough for them to take it out on his missus, no way that wouldn't happen. So are we looking for a random burglar, someone she opened the door to, cos there was no sign of a break-in, we checked the whole house out when she went AWOL and nothing showed up. She wasn't carjacked she went out by taxi ..."

Toller interrupted, "D'you know what company she used?" he took out his notebook and pen.

"Yeah Five Star Cabs over on Morley Street, we always use them."

"And are you sure she was actually collected, have you checked?"

Pitman inwardly cursed himself. He should have picked up on that. "I haven't no, but I think Calder did," he said covering his own ineptitude with the lie. Soon as the rozzers had gone he'd be on the phone to Jack and check for himself.

"We have launched a full scale murder enquiry; we will find those responsible ..."

Pitman cut in, "Well let's hope for their sake then that you find them first." His voice was full of menace.

"Now hang on, don't go taking the law into your own hands, that's what we're here for; we'll find them and then they'll be brought to justice."

Pitman sneered. "Just listen to yourself, you sound like a fucking MP touting for votes.

The young constable leant forward and said to Toller, "Don't forget about the jewellery."

"Shit yeah, thank you," Toller said in acknowledgement. He turned back to Pitman, "Look, how much d'you know about Mrs Calder's jewellery?

Obviously, we want to start targeting the local second-hand shops and jewellers, see if anyone's trying to shift the stuff on. Can you get a list, is that possible? I can see Mr Calder's in a bad place at the moment and I don't really want to disturb him again by asking too many questions, it's not the right time. He's got a lot to take on board and I can see how distressed he is."

"Yeah and you can keep that under your hat an' all. That goes for the pair of you," he said locking eyes with the younger officer who baulked at the inflection but immediately got the message.

"I don't know about all of it, but I know she had her favourite bits she always wore on special occasions, one of them was a big gold ruby ring with diamonds set all around it. I know Mr Calder's got photographs of most of the valuable stuff on the computer for insurance purposes; I'll print a copy off and bring it down with me when I come. I shouldn't be too long."

Toller held out his hand to shake and Pitman just nodded and opened the door and let them both out.

Pitman laid back on the closed door his mind racing. Who the hell had a big enough grudge against Calder to kill his wife? And was Calder involved in something that he wasn't aware of and that's why he didn't want to call the police, preferring to handle things himself? But from what Toller had said, even if they had involved the police by the sounds of it they would have been too late to save her anyway.

Pitman had no answers at the moment but one thing was certain; someone would pay and most likely pay with their own life. He took out his mobile and pressed the speed dial to arrange for Steve to come over and sit with Calder whilst he went down the morgue. He put that thought out of his mind for the moment as he went into Calder's office and moved the mouse across the computer screen and clicked onto pictures, he needed to print off the photos of Lizzie's jewellery, and maybe this would give the police the lead they wanted.

Steve reached across the sleeping form of an Asian woman and fumbled for his mobile. "Yeah?"

"It's me," Pitman said, "I need you down the house now."

"Right Roger that." Steve said. He ended the call and was about to swing his legs out of bed and get going but when he looked back at Shawna, she was lying on her side and she looked so bloody sexy, he thought sod it another ten minutes won't hurt, and he gently ran his hand up between her legs and she sighed and rolled over sleepily onto her back. "Oow," she said, "you really are a naughty boy, we can't keep doing this!"

"Yeah we can," Steve replied moving into position.

Shawna smiled and opened her legs and pulled him down on top of her.

Chapter Twelve

Bergmann was shitting bricks; he'd had a visit from the police with a list and photographs of jewellery that had been stolen from a dead woman! In all his years in the business he'd never been involved in anything like this before. Murder! My God no, never!

Yes, OK, he bought the odd piece now and then for which the seller couldn't supply all the details he would have liked, but he was in business and sometimes in business you took a risk, but *this*, this was very serious.

He fussed and fussed over whether or not to call Conner and warn him and finally he had come to the momentous decision that if he wanted to keep his legs that he had to make the call. His hands were visibly shaking as he dialled Conner's number and he heard the phone start to ring.

"Who's this?" Conner asked irritably, pausing the football game he was watching on Sky.

Bergmann had a job to speak he was dreading the outcome of the call. Finally he said, "It's me, Solly."

"Who?" Conner said on the verge of ending the call.

"Solly Bergmann."

"What the fuck are you doing phoning me?" he demanded angrily.

"That jewellery ... the police have been here they've taken some of it ..."

"What!" Conner bellowed. Bergmann almost dropped the phone.

"It's off a dead woman, she was murdered," Solly said, "I had to give details. I know the driver's licence you gave me was false, but they took the details ..."

Conner's mind was racing. That fucking little shit had said the gear wasn't hot now Bergmann was saying it had come from a murdered woman. She wouldn't be the only one he thought when he got hold of Doyle!

"So I'm still in the clear then if you ain't named names? And you ain't named names 'ave ya, Sol?" Conner asked keeping his voice level but the threat was still very evident.

"No names, you know me better than that," Sol replied quickly, "but ..." he hesitated dreading telling Conner the additional news.

"What? Conner asked, "come on, spit it out!"

"The tapes, they took the tapes from my security camera. I said I couldn't remember you, I told them I'd never seen you before, and they took the tapes. You're on there."

"You stupid little prick!" Conner yelled not believing that anyone could be so stupid. "You should have deleted the fucking tapes when I left the shop. Oh Jesus Christ. They'll be coming here then they know me; they'll track me from my motor that's registered to this address. Jesus, you fucking piece of shit you've dropped me right in it!"

"It's not my fault!" Sol said protesting, "you told me they was clean, no worries you said. Now I'm totally out of pocket, they've taken the necklaces and two of the rings with them ..."

But Sol was talking to thin air; Conner had cut the call and was hurriedly shoving some essentials into a holdall, mindful that every second counted. Conner's adrenalin was pumping around his body which is probably why he heard a noise out the front of his house. He quickly stepped up to the side of the window and looked out and saw three policemen creeping up the front path to the house, one of them was holding a door batterer.

"Fuck it!" he said and grabbed the holdall and rushed through the lounge towards the back door. He was hoping that they might not have had the time to identify the back gate to his house yet. He flung open the back door his fist clenched and his body ready to react to anyone who may have been waiting for him. It was clear. He sped down the path and yanked open the rear gate only to be met by a young constable who appeared to be totally shocked by the sudden opening of the gate.

Conner barged past him and started to run full pelt down the lane. Give the young constable his due he recovered quickly and sped after Conner. Keely may have only been in the job for eighteen months but he'd played rugby since he was seven years old and was as fit as a butcher's dog. In no time at all he'd closed the gap between the two of them and then he'd dived at Conner's legs and brought him crashing to the ground.

Conner lost the grip on the holdall as he hit the ground, hard. Part of the air was forced from his lungs and then the young constable grabbed one of his wrists and tried to pull it behind Conner's back and put the handcuffs on him. Keely may have been fit but he was nowhere near as strong as Conner and Conner yanked his wrist back and drove his elbow into Keely's face shattering his nose and sending him unconscious onto his back.

Conner looked both ways down the lane; there was no sign of anyone else so he quickly brushed himself down and placed the constable in the recovery position. He didn't want him choking to death on his own blood; he had enough problems to think about at the moment. Conner checked again and then made his way as fast as he could to the end of the lane where quite by chance a red bus was stood at the bus stop letting an elderly couple off. When they'd got off Conner got on and a few moments later he was hunkered down in the seat with his holdall on his lap, watching as the bus drove past his house. The front door was hanging at a funny angle where they'd smashed the door open to gain entry. He sagged back in the seat. That had been close, much too fucking close. Now as soon as he'd sorted somewhere out to lay low, he'd be paying a visit to Kevin Doyle and Doyle would be wishing in a very short space of time that he'd never made that original phone call!

Chapter Thirteen

Pitman hit the speed dial for the taxi company, after a couple of rings the phone was answered.

"Five Star Cabs."

"Yeah it's Tony Pitman, put Jack on."

There was a slight pause, "He's on his mobile, sorry."

"Tell him it's me." Pitman said.

"Look d'you think you could call back, he doesn't like to be interrupted when he's on the phone?"

"Sonny, if you want to keep your job, you just tell him Tony Pitman's on the phone, he'll want to take this call believe you me."

There was a short pause and Tony could hear some muffled conversation in the background and then Jack came on the line.

"What's up Tone? Sorry 'bout that, I was on me mobile."

"No probs. Jack, last Saturday, you were booked to pick up Lizzie Calder, what happened?"

"Oh yeah, sorry mate, she wasn't there. Phil turned up about twenty past seven, sat outside for a few minutes, you know Mrs Calder, she's always on time. She didn't come out so he rang the bell and waited, nothing. I remember him saying the dog started barking, but that was it, no one came out or answered the door. He called it in and Jess rang the house but there was no reply, so we just thought she'd gone with Mr Calder instead. Why is there a problem?"

"You could say that yeah, Lizzie's dead."

There was a sharp intake of breath from Jack and then he said, "How? I mean what happened, Tone? Christ I'm so sorry she was a lovely lady, one of the best ..."

Pitman cut in, "Someone topped her and dumped her body in Asker's pond."

"Oh sweet Jesus ..." Jack said slumping down in his office chair. After a few moments, he recovered enough to ask, "D'you know who or why?"

"If I knew that, we wouldn't be having this conversation. The feds have just been round and told us. It's all a bit hush-hush cos I'm not sure what's going on meself, Calder's playing it very close to his chest. Lizzie's been missing for nearly a week and he wanted to handle it himself, no cops. He figured it was some youngster trying to make a name for himself, who bagged Lizzie for a ransom and then it looks like it all went tits up. He's in a right old state."

"I can imagine," Jack said. He too thought the world of Lizzie, she was a regular customer who always tipped well and he had known the Calder's for the last eight or nine years. "So what d'you need from me, Tone?"

"I need to speak to the driver, see if he noticed anything unusual or anyone hanging around near the house, that kind of thing. Give him my mobile and get him to give me a call ASAP. You said it was Phil, right?"

"Yeah that's right."

"What d'you know about him?"

"Whoa hold up, Tone!" Jack said, "Phil's a stand up bloke. Been with me for close on three years, he's straight, I never get any truck from him …"

Pitman cut in, "Could someone have got to him, made him an offer or something? Is he the type of person who has something to hide they could blackmail him with? You know, debts, drugs, prossies his wife don't wanna know about, anything?"

"No way, he's probably the best, most reliable driver I've got. He always does the work for the Calder's if it's pre-booked, cos he's the best. If it's an off-the-cuff he can't always do it if he's out on another fare, but I'd vouch for him all the way Tone, straight up."

"OK, I'll take you on your word then Jack. But get him on the phone and I want a call back ASAP, alright?"

"Soon as I hang up I'll give him a bell Tone, promise. And look … I'm really sorry about Mrs Calder, if there's anything …"

Pitman cut in, "Just get him to phone, I'm waiting." He disconnected the call and went back to check on Calder and where the fuck had Steve got to?

Pitman returned to the living room. Calder was still sitting slumped in the armchair. The glass was empty and rested in Calder's lap.

"D'you want a refill boss?" Pitman said scooping up the glass and walking over to the unit to get another drink.

"Give me your thoughts on this." Calder said.

Pitman stopped. A change had come over Calder, it was as if he'd accepted what had happened and now wanted to deal with it, he seemed calm and focused.

"I've had some feelers out, I heard about a body being found in the pond yesterday …"

Calder reared up from his chair, angry, "And you didn't think to tell me! Slipped your mind did it!"

"It wasn't like that boss," Pitman replied calmly, "I didn't want to tell you until I knew for certain it was Mrs C, you had enough on your plate already to worry about."

Calder locked eyes with Pitman whose gaze never faltered. After a moment, Calder nodded and pointed at the glass in Pitman's hand.

"Don't let me stop you," he said, "I could do with another one."

Pitman turned and refilled the glass and handed it to Calder, Calder knocked it back in one long hit and handed the glass back.

"Right then, come on, give me your thoughts," Calder repeated and sat back down in his chair.

Pitman thought about how to phrase the question, Calder had a habit of kicking off if he heard or saw something he didn't like.

"I'm waiting," Calder said, cold and brittle.

Pitman decided to answer a question with a question and take it from there.

"Is there something going on that I don't know about, boss?" he asked keeping his tone even and non-accusing.

Calder eyed him, weighing him up. "Like what?"

"That's what I'm asking," Pitman said perching on the arm of the sofa. "It's just worried me that after Mrs C went missing, OK we checked the house out etc and you made some calls and then ...well you just seemed to have been playing a waiting game as if you knew something or were waiting for something to happen. And the fact you never got the police involved that ..."

Calder interrupted him, "I don't like the police knowing my business you know that. I suspected something but I never thought for one moment it would end up like this."

The door bell sounded.

"That'll be Steve I asked him to come over. Hang on a minute I'll go and let him in."

Pitman left the room and walked down the hall, he checked through the spy hole and then opened the front door, and Steve stepped into the hall.

Pitman closed the door behind him. "You took your fucking time," he reprimanded, "when I tell you to get here, it means *now* not three fucking days later!"

Steve started to grin and then noticed that Pitman wasn't joking and quickly wiped the grin off his face and apologised.

"Sorry Tone, if you'd said it was urgent I would have come straight over. I was in bed, I had a shower …"

Pitman stepped up to him and sniffed. "Had a quickie more like!" Pitman grabbed him by his bollocks and half-lifted him off his feet. Steve squealed and dropped his hands onto Pitman's trying to relieve the pressure. "Don't ever get smart with me, Stevie-boy cos you'll come off worse believe you me, got it?" He gave a little squeeze for emphasis and Steve nodded vigorously, Pitman released him pushing him away at the same time. "Now shape up, we got work to do."

Steve was still smarting and his eyes were watering, he was half bent over.

"Are you with us or not?" Pitman started walking away, "Calder don't like to be kept waiting."

Steve straightened up and wiped his face along his sleeve. "What's the crack then, has Mrs C come home?"

"She's dead," Pitman said and carried on walking towards the sitting room.

Steve hobbled after him awkwardly, still hurting, "Dead, what d'you mean she's dead?"

Pitman stopped and turned and Steve almost collided into him. "What the fuck d'you think I mean? She's *dead*. As in someone smashed her head in and dumped her in a fucking pond and I've got to go and ID the body. So I need you to sit with the old man."

"Jesus … so do we know who killed her?"

"If we *did*, you'd be helping me to dump *their* body. It's being sorted. Now I just need you to sit in with Mr C until I get back. Now d'you think you can do that or shall I get someone else in? Someone I can rely on." He asked sarcastically.

Steve straightened up despite the ache in his groin, "No, I'm cool let's get this done."

Pitman nodded and together they walked back down the hall and into the sitting room.

Chapter Fourteen

Pitman was just leaving the house when his mobile rang. He didn't recognise the number.

"Tony Pitman."

A nervous voice responded. "It's Phil, from Five Star Cabs, Mr Pitman, we have met …"

Pitman cut in, "Yeah I know you Phil, thanks for calling. Now I need to ask you about last Saturday, Mrs Calder's."

"I'm sorry," Phil said interrupting, "if I'd have known I would have waited, honest! Jack's just told me. She was a lovely lady …"

"Yeah, we know that," Pitman said taking back the conversation. "Jack's vouched for you so you've got nothing to worry about. I just need to ask you some questions that's all, it's nothing heavy. So … Jack said you got to the house about seven-twenty, that right?"

"About then, yeah, I always try to be on time, you can't always odds it with the traffic an' that but …"

"Yeah alright I got that. So you waited and Mrs C didn't come out? Was that the usual thing when you went there, she came out without you knocking, yeah?"

"Yeah, she'd always be ready and she'd always come out virtually straight away. I've never had to ring the bell before."

"Right, so this time you waited and she never came out so you rang the doorbell, yeah?"

"I did yeah. And that set the dog off. I didn't even know they had a dog, I've never heard it bark before. It jumped up at the door barking away like mad and frit the life out of me!"

That was interesting Pitman thought, the dog was never usually allowed out into the hall in case it ran out into the road when the front door was opened. They'd lost a dog a few years before from that and Mrs C was very particular about keeping Bonnie back in one of the other rooms when the doorbell went.

"OK so you rang the bell and the dog went mad and then what happened?"

"Nothing, I waited and nothing happened. I rang two more times and the dog just went barmy, so I got back in the cab and called Jess and asked her to call the house to tell them I was outside waiting. Jess called me back and said there was no reply and she gave me another pick-up to go to."

"OK, so did you notice any cars parked close to their driveway that looked out of place? You know something beat up or dodgy? A van delivering to the house or anything or anyone hanging about keeping obs? It could be important. Don't rush it, have a think, go on, take your time."

Pitman waited, his foot started to tap impatiently.

"I remember there was a van, it was white … I think it might have been a Trannie; it was parked a few houses down. I remember it because it was parked at a funny angle, as if it had stopped suddenly and then just been left."

"That's brilliant, Phil, well done. Can you tell me anything else about the van? Was it new, old, clean, dirty? Did it have any writing on it, you know like a company name or logo, anything like that?"

"It wasn't new, new, but it was the new shape. I didn't really notice any writing and it was a bit grubby but I wasn't really looking at it that much. I just drove past it when it was parked up and it was only you saying about it that reminded me. Sorry that's about all I can remember."

"You've done well so far Phil. So, did you notice if there was anyone sat up in it, you know just waiting or watching?"

"I couldn't really say, I only noticed it as it was only a couple of houses away from Mrs Calder's house parked at a funny angle with the back part stuck out in the road, I had to drive out round it. Then I turned into their drive, I'm really sorry Mr Pitman."

"No, you done alright son, thank you and if you remember anything else you give me a bell, yeah?"

"Yeah, yeah course I will! Bye then, bye." The lad disconnected the call and it was only then that he realised his hands were shaking and that his shirt had stuck to his back with sweat. He didn't fancy being in the shoes of the people that had killed Mrs Calder when Tony Pitman got hold of them. He shivered at the thought and shoved his mobile back in his pocket and started up the engine of the taxi and eased out into the traffic.

Chapter Fifteen

Conner had stowed his bag in Larry's flat, although Larry wasn't too happy about the situation. The jungle drums had already been beating and the word on the street was that Conner was wanted by the filth.

Conner had insisted that he would only be staying for a few days and then he was off to Manchester and that Larry had better keep his gob shut and tell no one he was there or he'd fucking pay big time. Larry had agreed, he didn't really have much choice, he'd seen the results of Conner's handiwork before and there was no way he wanted to be on the receiving end of it thank you very much! So he'd given up his bed and he was dossing down on the sofa and that was playing havoc with his back, but he never said anything. It was, after all, only going to be for a few days.

It was dark when Conner left the flat. He was dressed all in black and he carried his favourite little party-piece, a sock filled with two pence pieces and ball bearings. He knew where Doyle lived. It was a small flat above a printer's that had gone out of business about eighteen months ago blaming competition from the Internet. Doyle's landlord was happy for Doyle to stay on, some monthly income was better than none, even if some months it was a little sporadic. At least Doyle could keep an eye on the property and stop squatters from breaking in, so he tolerated the odd lapsed payment and give Doyle his due, he always caught up and paid up.

Doyle's van wasn't there when Conner arrived so he had settled down to wait. The good thing about Doyle's flat, was that there was a small alley to the side of the property that contained a small staircase that led up to his own private entrance, plus Doyle had the use of the back garden such as it was, where he parked his van. From his vantage point, Conner could watch the alleyway and the garden; it was just a case of waiting. Conner constantly fiddled with the weighted sock in his pocket, relishing the moment when that little shit turned up, *not fucking hot he said*! He'd regret saying that line for the rest of his miserably little life and that was a promise!

Conner didn't have long to wait, headlights shone across the scrub grass and Conner pressed himself hard against the side of the building as Doyle's van turned in and parked. Doyle cut the engine and after a few moments got out of the van and locked it behind him and started to make his way across the dead lawn towards the staircase, and as he did, so Conner stepped out in front of him.

Doyle was too preoccupied to notice the man at first, and having drunk a couple of pints that didn't help either, he was only conscious of Conner's presence when he spoke.

"I've been waiting for you, you little fucker!" Conner said blocking Doyle's path.

Doyle's jaw dropped open and for a moment he stood stock-still too shocked to move, and then fear and panic kicked in and he turned and tried to leg it, but Conner swept the sock down in a blinding arc and hit Doyle in the back of his neck sending him sprawling onto the dusty ground.

Conner roughly yanked him up and raced him backwards slamming him into the side of the wall, Doyle went limp and Conner let go of him and watched him slump to the ground, his legs sliding out from under him.

Conner bent down over him and slapped Doyle's face to bring him round. "Oi wake up sleepy head, I need a word with you." Conner slapped him again and Doyle groaned and opened his eyes. He went rigid when he saw who his attacker was.

"We can't keep meeting like this," Conner said in a sickly voice, "we don't want people talking about us, do we?" He manhandled Doyle onto his feet. "Right I'm gonna ask you this once and once only, where d'you get the gear?"

Doyle's head and neck were killing him and his vision wasn't right, Conner looked all blurry and out of focus. He was trapped and he knew he was right in the shit up to his armpits but he just couldn't think straight to even attempt to talk his way out of it, he had no option but to tell Conner the truth.

Conner grabbed Doyle by his collar with both hands, "I ain't got all fucking night, where d'you get the gear from!" he hollered at Doyle and Doyle closed his eyes against the noise, he felt like he was going to be sick at any moment.

"Off a woman, I found her. She was dead …"

Conner interrupted him, "I fucking know that! The cops have been to my gaff and I decked one of 'em to get away! I'm on the fucking news now cos of you!" He never waited to hear anymore he drove his fist into Doyle's face and his head slammed back into the wall and

Doyle tasted blood and felt a tooth drop down onto his tongue. "What woman and where you little prick, or I will break every bone in your body one at a fucking time!" He grabbed Doyle by the collar again but refrained from hitting him until he had some more information. He needed to know just what had happened and just what he was up against first.

"Fishing, I was fishing," Doyle offered weakly, trying to stay focused against the nausea and pain sweeping through his head and body. "I hooked her, she was in the water … she stunk to high heaven and I dint want nothing to do with her, and then I saw the gold …"

Conner yanked him away from the wall. "You told me the gear wasn't hot! That's what you told me!" Doyle tried to clear his head and think of the reason he'd said that to Conner and then he remembered.

"It was like a joke," he muttered, "it wasn't hot cos it had been in the water …" Conner hit him again and Doyle's head rocked back and his eyes rolled up into their sockets and Conner let go of him and he slid down the wall in a heap.

Conner fumbled out a cigarette and lit it and checked around, they couldn't be seen from where they were unless someone deliberately came around the back of the shops and as the printers was the last one in the row, there didn't seem much chance of that happening, so Conner was content to draw on his fag and think until Doyle came to again and he could ask him a few more questions, he was in no rush. Things like this took as long as they took, that was a given in this line of work.

Doyle moaned and put his hand up to his face.

"You're back with us then, are ya?" Conner bent down over him. "D'you know who that was, the woman you found? Have you any idea?"

Doyle shook his head which was a big mistake, the pain was excruciating and he almost blacked out.

"That woman was none other than Lizzie Calder, and there's big money on offer for any information. And I've heard that someone cut her fingers off to get her rings, that better not be you or your life won't be worth living when Calder finds out."

"She was dead … I didn't know it was her, did I? She was all bloated and half-eaten and I just saw the gold …"

"I sure as hell don't want Calder on my case, so I'm putting you in the frame for it to take the pressure off me; But before I do that, I'm putting you in hospital for dropping me in it with the feds." Before Doyle had a chance to say another word, Conner swung the sock and knocked Doyle's head sideways and he hit the ground hard. Conner then laid into him with his boots. Kicking him about the head and body until he lay unmoving and bloodied. Conner thought he might have killed Doyle such was the frenzy he'd unleashed upon him, but as it stood he couldn't give a shit. The score had been settled and now he would contact Calder and grovel and apologise and see what happened next, either way he would be gone in a matter of hours if all went well.

Chapter Sixteen

Pitman's phone rang. "Tony Pitman."

"Look Mr Pitman … you don't actually know me," Conner said, "I've got some info for you, I don't want paying for it, I'm just doing you a favour because there is a connection to me, but I swear to you, I had no part in it."

"No part in what my friend?" Pitman said evenly.

Conner stayed silent for a moment phrasing how he wanted to say things. "Mrs Calder, I just heard, I'm sorry."

"Go on."

"I bought something off someone, some gold, but I didn't know it was from her, Mrs Calder, I swear to God that's true and I never had nothing to do with what happened to her …"

Pitman interrupted, "And what did happen to Mrs Calder?"

Conner wasn't sure how to answer; he knew he was on thin ice. "I heard someone done her in and dumped her body in a pond."

"And did you buy the jewellery from the people that killed Mrs Calder, because if you did you need to tell me their names."

"I dunno, I don't think so. I bought the gear from a geezer I've done bits and pieces of business with before, nothing as grand as this like you know, but he came to me with this big score, seven bits, choice bits they were, but he wouldn't let on where he got them from. I bought it and sold it on, and the next thing I know, I got the rozzers breaking down me front door and I had to put one of 'em down to get away."

"So your fence grassed you up, did he?"

"Not in so many words, no. The feds came into his shop with a list, and they found some of the gear and they took the tapes from the security cameras and I was on it."

"Tsk, tsk, tsk, ain't life a bitch? So we're talking about Solly Bergmann, yes?"

"I ain't a grass."

"You don't have to be, I already know all this, Martin."

Conner's stomach dropped. Pitman was already onto him, oh holy shit and Christ!

"I had nothing to do with it I told you that!" Conner protested.

"So you said," Pitman confirmed. "So who did you buy the gear from and where might we find this person or persons you're referring to?"

Conner had never grassed anyone up before, but as it stood, his name was in the frame with Pitman and Calder and there was no way he wanted them on his case.

"It's a local scroat, Kevin Doyle …"

Pitman cut in, "And where can we find this Doyle character?"

"Ah," Conner said thinking back to the bloodied mess he'd left behind, "well I've just given him a right seeing-to on account of putting my face in the frame with the feds, so if he ain't been found, he'll be round the back of his gaffe."

"Which is where exactly?"

"D'you know the shops in Millham's Road? The last one on the end, it's a printer's, it's closed down now, anyway, he's got the flat above the shop. I left him round the back in the garden, slightly the worst for wear ... if you get my meaning? He's got an old van should be parked round there if he's home."

"We'll be in touch." Pitman said.

"Well what's that mean?" Conner asked fearfully. "I had nothing to do with what happened I told you that and that's the God's honest truth that is!"

"Regardless, you're connected, and as I said, we'll be in touch."

The line went dead and Conner slumped forward and rested his head on the steering wheel of his car. He thought that by giving up Doyle, that would put him in the clear with Pitman and Calder, but he'd badly underestimated their sense of revenge.

He knew he had to come up with something to buy himself back into their favour, because even if he raced up to Manchester, he knew they'd find him, and when they *did*, he would suffer for it all the more, oh fucking hell!

Chapter Seventeen

Sometimes no matter who you are or what you've done, you still somehow find a little bit of luck. Doyle's little bit of luck was in the form of Jack Priest. Jack had been out celebrating a big win on the horses and he'd had much more to drink than he'd planned, so he'd left his car in the pub car park and was making his way to the taxi rank when he realised that he was suddenly desperate for the toilet.

Knowing there was an alleyway at the end of the shops, he thought it might be a likely place to relieve himself, and so he had hurried past the shops and down to the end of the alleyway, made sure he couldn't be seen from the road, and without any further ado, was soon relieving himself against the side of the building. It was then that he heard a strange noise and he swivelled round towards the sound. He thought it may have been a cat although it didn't really sound like one. He finished, shook his penis and tucked it back inside his pants, zipped his trousers up and was just about to leave, when he heard the noise again.

What the hell is that he thought?

Jack took a few tentative steps towards the end of the building and stopped and listened. There it was again. Jack wasn't a brave man but he was a curious man, and he crept to the end of the wall and peered round the side. It took a moment for his eyes to adjust and then he noticed a shape on the ground. At first, he couldn't make out what it was, and then the shape moved and groaned and then it coughed and cried out in pain.

"Christ almighty!" Jack said, realising that it was a person and that they were obviously hurt. He ran over to the body and squatted down alongside the form and his feet slipped on something. It was blood, there was blood pooling out from the body. Jack fumbled out his mobile and switched it on and as he did so it illuminated the body and Jack fell back, shocked at the sight of so much blood and by the state of the person's face. "Oh good God," he mumbled and then set his mind to concentrate on the task at hand. He called the police and after three seconds the call was answered.

"Which emergency service do you require?"

Jack was still a little hazy from the booze and the shock, and it took him a few seconds to focus, "Police and ambulance please, it's an emergency."

"What kind of emergency caller?"

"There's a body, I've found a body. It's a man and he's very, very badly injured, there's blood everywhere. I need the police and an ambulance he's in a very bad way."

"Where is the body please caller?"

"Um, right yes of course," Jack's head was spinning and he had to concentrate very hard to remember exactly where he was, "The shops in Millham's Road, at the end there's an alleyway, round the back of the last shop that's where we are. I don't know what to do he's bleeding badly."

"One moment please caller stay on the line, I'm just alerting the emergency services to you."

There was a change in tone and after a short while the operator returned.

"The emergency services are on their way to you. D'you know the injured person?"

"No I was just," Jack stopped himself explaining, "there's blood everywhere."

"Is the person conscious?"

"Hang on," Jack leant over the body and held his phone close to give him some light. Bubbles of blood were coming from the victim's mouth as he breathed in and out.

"He's breathing, but he's making strange noises and there's bubbles of blood coming from his mouth, he's very poorly."

"Do you have any first aid training sir?"

"Me? Well no, no I'm sorry I don't," Jack could hear a siren, "I can hear a siren I'm going back to the road to direct them in if that's alright?"

"That's fine caller please stay on the line ..." But Jack was already running as best he could and in his haste to help, unbeknown to himself, he had disconnected the call.

Jack waved his hands like a demented windmill and the police car braked hard to a stop just prior to the entrance to the alleyway. Jack could see the policeman inside the car talking into his radio. Jack gestured to the man and the officer raised his hand in acknowledgment, a few seconds later the officer got out of the car and locked it.

"And you are?" the policeman asked Jack.

"Jack Priest, it's this way," and Jack turned and ran as fast as he could down the alleyway with the policeman following closely behind him talking into his radio.

Jack stopped at the end of the alleyway and pointed to the still form lying on the ground. "The body's over there," he said and then felt quite faint with all the alcohol and the shock and the running suddenly catching up with him, and he allowed himself to slowly slide down the wall until he was sitting with his back to the solid feel of bricks behind him, his heart pounding like a train in his chest.

The officer started checking Doyle for signs of life and then very gently moved him into the recovery position. He again spoke into his radio, Jack was too zonked to hear much of the one-way conversation but Jack did hear another siren and pushed himself up and called out to the officer.

"I'll go and direct them," and without waiting for a reply he shuffled as fast as he could back up the alleyway towards the road.

This time it was an ambulance and another police car. Jack greeted the paramedics as they got out of their vehicle.

"You'll need a stretcher he's very badly hurt."

"You found him did you, sir?" The officer asked.

Jack had been so busy directing the paramedics to the scene he hadn't noticed the other officer get out of his car and approach him.

"Yes, yes I did," Jack stammered.

The paramedics ran past them heading down the alley laden down with equipment.

"Would you like to come and sit in the car please if you would, sir? I need to take a few details from you." The policeman reached out put his hand on Jack's shoulder and gently turned him towards his car that was parked behind the other police vehicle. Both the vehicles had their lights flashing, as did the ambulance, and the combination of all the flashing lights made Jack feel a little nauseous.

The policeman noticed the change in the man and supported him, "Come on sir, looks like you've had a bit of a shock you need to have a sit down, come on."

The officer escorted Jack back to his car and opened the back door and helped Jack inside. The officer got in the front seat and picked up a pen and clipboard and turned round to face Jack.

"Now you just take a few moments to settle yourself down and then when you feel well enough, I need to ask you a few questions, if that's alright with you?"

Jack nodded. "Will he be alright d'you think?"

"We'll have to wait and see, he's in a bad way at the moment they're just trying to stabilise him so they can get him to hospital, we'll know more later. Right, so can we start with a few details from you then sir if I may? Your name please?"

And so it went on, name, address, contact numbers, what had he been doing there, had he seen anyone, had he touched the body, from what side had he approached the body etc, etc.

Jack was then taken down to the police station and his clothing and shoes were seized to eliminate any trace fibres and footprints that may have contaminated the crime scene. Jack had to wait for his wife to collect him with a clean set of clothes. She was far from happy, suspecting that Jack had been arrested for being drunk or for doing something stupid, until it was explained that Jack had been instrumental in saving another man's life by his public spirited action and then she was more accommodating towards him.

Chapter Eighteen

Chris Doyle received the phone call from the police regarding his brother at two twenty a.m. He was at the hospital and talking with the staff nurse twenty-three minutes later.

Staff Nurse Linda Collier explained to Chris that his brother was in intensive care and had just undergone surgery to have his spleen and one of his testicles removed, he also had three broken ribs, a broken nose, a fractured jaw and there was a possibility that he may lose the sight in his left eye. There had also been damage to his kidneys and he was currently on a ventilator as he was having difficulty breathing by himself.

Linda said that although he was highly sedated he could visit for a couple of minutes but that Kevin wouldn't be able to respond and she warned him that the next twenty-four hours were crucial. There were a lot of internal injuries that they were monitoring and there was a very real possibility that further surgery might be necessary.

A police officer was sat outside the room reading a magazine and he stood as Chris approached, and asked for details and identification. Chris showed the officer his driving licence and his credit card and the officer made a note on his clipboard. Before Chris was allowed to enter, the officer asked Chris if he had any idea what had happened to his brother and did he have any enemies?

Chris knew his brother wasn't perfect and was obviously fully aware of his past and his criminal record, but he never suspected he was into anything so heavy as to almost get himself killed. So he just shrugged and said no. The officer opened the door and stood aside as Chris entered, closing the door gently behind him.

Nothing had prepared Chris for the sight that greeted him, and he felt the room start to spin and he quickly took some deep breaths and rested one hand against the wall to support himself until the shock passed. Chris looked as white as the sheets on the bed. There was a ventilator tube taped to the side of his mouth and there were drips going into both arms through cannulas attached to the backs of his hands. There were also tubes coming out from under the sheets and draining into plastic bags suspended on metal frames alongside the bed. Connectors were attached to Chris's fingers and chest leading to machines that bleeped and flashed and recorded the pulse and heart rate and God knows what else, Chris wasn't sure what they all did, only that there was a lot of equipment involved in aiding Kevin's recovery.

Kevin was barely recognisable; his face was so bloodied and swollen. One eye was completely closed and there were stitches across the top of his eyebrow and stitches across the bottom of his chin and the bruising had already started to come out, and Kev's face was turning all the colours of the rainbow.

Chris pulled the chair over to the side of the bed and gently rested his hand along his brothers' arm. "What the hell have you got yourself into, you crazy bastard?" Chris said gently as tears welled up in his eyes. He gulped back his feelings and then with more determination he looked down at his brother.

"I swear this to you Bruv, you tell me who did this and they'll be in the room next door. No matter what you've done, you've not done anything to deserve a kicking like this. We'll get this sorted; you just concentrate on getting better. I'll be outside, you take care now …" Chris choked up and stood abruptly and placed the chair back against the wall and left the room, not daring to look back.

The officer rose as Chris came out, "You alright?"

"Not really no. I just can't believe it," he shook his head, "what d'you know about what happened?"

"Not an awful lot I'm afraid. We had a call from a member of the public who'd found your brother round the back of his flat …"

Chris interrupted, "Who was this bloke? What was he doing there? D'you know who he was?" Chris asked agitated.

The officer raised his hand, "Just calm down sir …"

"How the hell can I be calm when someone's almost killed my brother! Could you stay calm?" Chris turned away trying to bring his temper under control, in essence it wasn't so much temper, more shock and frustration.

"We have checked the man out and he's completely innocent, and by all accounts if he hadn't found him when he did, your brother might have choked to death on his own blood. He honestly doesn't know your brother. It turns out he'd had a few drinks too many and had left his car and decided to get a taxi home and he was walking to the taxi rank … when, well he had a call of nature, and he went down the alleyway at the end of the shops to relive himself, and that's when he heard your brother cry out, and he found him and called an ambulance. He's not connected in any way, your brother's lucky he came along when he did."

Chris thought about it, "OK, so he found the body, and I'm grateful to him, but do you know what actually happened?"

"As yet, no sir, he hasn't said a word since he was brought in. He was barely conscious when they found him, and he was in and out of consciousness in the ambulance, and then they took him straight into theatre when he got here and now he's in there." He nodded towards to the Intensive Care room. "I'm sorry; if I get any more information I'll let you know."

"I'm going to wait."

"I don't think he's expected to regain consciousness for quite some time yet sir, probably best to go home and get some sleep. The hospital's got your number, they'll phone you if there's any change."

"No I prefer to wait; I couldn't see me sleeping anyway. I'll just grab one of the seats over there and wait it out. Thanks for your help."

"You're welcome. And look there's a drinks machine down the end there and turn right if you fancy a coffee or a tea, and it does crisps and chocolate bars, all the usual stuff you know."

"Thanks, I'm OK." Chris slumped down on one of the plastic chairs and prepared to wait. The officer returned to his chair and picked up the magazine and started looking at fancy houses out in the country that cost more than he was ever likely to earn in the whole of his lifetime. And now all they could do was wait …

Chapter Nineteen

Kevin Doyle was in intensive care for three days, and Chris remained either outside in the corridor or inside by his bed for almost the whole time. There had been little chance to talk and Kevin found it very difficult to speak when he did, due to the damage to his jaw and the stitches. Chris insisted he was present when the police asked Kevin about what had happened and Kevin had told them, he'd had a few drinks and he'd fallen down the stairs to his flat and couldn't remember anything else and that there was no one else involved so they could all go home now.

The police weren't buying his story but he was sticking to it, so in theory there was nothing else they could do. The detective spoke to Chris and asked him to talk some sense into his brother as he was lucky to be alive, and he said whoever did this might be back to finish the job. Chris thanked the detective for his help and said he would talk to his brother, and the detective handed Chris a card if he needed to contact him. Chris went back into the room, Kevin had been moved into a side room by now and he closed the door behind him.

Kevin was still connected to a drip and he still had the catheter but the ventilator had been removed and some of the machinery.

Chris sat down next to the bed. "They've gone, it's just you and me now, Bro, so what the hell's been going on? And don't give me all that bollocks about falling down the stairs; this is me you're talking to now. You need to level with me, this was a very serious kicking someone gave you, and I'm going to get it sorted so they never lay a finger on you again."

"No," Kev said weakly, "let it go Chris, just let it go."

"Be buggered I will!" Chris replied firmly. "They bloody nigh killed you, just look at the state of you, you're lucky to still be here!"

"I know, I know, but I don't want you getting involved …"

Chris cut in, "I am involved; you're my brother, we're family, end of!" They locked eyes and Kev turned his face away. "I mean it, I'll sort it, now you better tell me what the hell's been going on, and I want the truth, all of it, don't piss me about and tell me bits of it. I want it all, let's get it all out in the open and put this mother to bed."

"You're registered, you can't get involved, you'll likely to go to prison and you'll lose your club and your business and everything …"

"You're assuming I'm going to get caught, I'm not. All the years of training and pain I've put myself through, just be glad of it now. I made you a promise when you were first brought in here that I'd get whoever was responsible for doing this to you, and I intend to keep it. No one does this to my brother, no one."

Kev reached out and gripped Chris's hand and gave a single nod, "OK, better make yourself comfy then, I wanna tell ya a story." He managed a smile and then sank back on the pillow.

"Take it easy, Bro, just take your time, we're in no rush."

But the clock was ticking elsewhere. Conner was sniffing around trying to find out who'd killed Lizzie Calder, he was hoping against hope that he could find the answer and get Calder and Pitman off his back.

Tony Pitman had his people out and about and Kenny had put the word on the street that there was a ten grand reward on offer for info regarding Lizzie, and this news had created a bit of a buzz, so he was fairly confident that some good Intel wouldn't be long in coming through.

Dave Carson had a team trying to track down Kevin Finch and Harry Toke, both of whom had gone to ground big time after they'd done away with Lizzie Calder. Carson and his men were also aware of the money up for grabs should they find them, but if they did they were sworn to get the info back to Talbot so he could decide exactly what to do with them, he didn't want to upset Calder any more than he'd done already, even though it wasn't really down to him, there again, if Calder had just sold him the property in the first place none of this mess would ever have happened.

Reardon on the other hand, was blissfully unaware that it had been two of his men that had killed Lizzie Calder and he carried on, business as usual.

Chapter Twenty

Early on the second morning after the discovery of Lizzie Calder's body in the pond, the divers had found another body, this time of a man. He had been in the water for months as opposed to days, and his body was very badly decomposed and had been partially eaten by crayfish and other amphibians.

The body had been examined and the cause of death, due to the state of the body, hadn't as yet been established. There was no chance the man could be identified by his fingerprints, as both hands had been hacked off at the wrists. The divers were still searching the pond for further evidence, and they'd brought in a large industrial pump to help drain the water from the pond into the field alongside to help speed up the search.

Within an hour of the second body being taken to the morgue, Pitman received a call on his mobile.

"Yeah Kenny, what you got?"

"They've found another body in the pond."

"Christ, anyone we know?"

"Don't have a lot yet. It's a male, been there for quite some time, and guess what?"

"Dunno, humour me."

"Whoever done him, cut both his hands off to avoid fingerprints."

"Shit and we don't have any idea who it is?"

"Naw, sorry Tone, it's still early days yet. They're still trying to work out the cause of death but the body's in a right old state. Sorry, that's all I've got at the mo."

"OK, thanks Kenny, put the word out, see if anyone's gone missing lately. You know anyone not been seen around their old haunts, that kind of thing. It's gotta be someone local. Find out if anyone's pissed someone off or gone back on a deal, you know the score. Have a dig about mate and let me know."

"Sure thing Tone, I'll be in touch. And how's Mr C doing by the way?"

"He's holding it together. Funeral's next Thursday at St Giles, eleven o'clock. Black suit and tie job, you can let people know. I've probably forgotten some; I've got a lot on at the moment."

"If there's anything I can do Tone, just say the word. You've all been sound to me over the years."

"You just keep doing what you're doing, Kenny and keep me up to date, gotta go, later."

"Yeah gotcha."

Pitman tried to think if there was a face that hadn't been seen around for some time but no one came to mind. He'd leave it to Kenny to find out, he had some pretty tight contacts and he'd always come through in the past. Pitman walked back into Calder's office to carry on making the arrangements for the wake, Calder wanted the world to know how much she meant to him so he was pushing the boat out big time.

Carson however was having more luck. One of his guys had discovered Kevin Finch's new shaped Transit van parked in an NCP car park. It had been there for four days, they knew that because of all the parking fines attached to it. Now all they had to do was find Finch. Or Toke, either one would give the other up when the pressure was put on them, and put on them it would be, make no mistake about that!

Both Calder and Pitman knew that Kevin Doyle was still in hospital and Pitman had sent Stevie down to check him out. Stevie had reported back to say that he'd told the staff nurse that he was Doyle's boss, and asked to be brought up to date on when Kevin would be fit enough to return to work. He'd declined to see Doyle claiming that he didn't want to upset him or put any pressure on him, but the nurse could let him know his job would be still be waiting for him when he was well enough to return. The nurse had told him it was likely he'd be off work for a good few months yet. She'd gone into detail about the removal of his spleen and one of his testicles and the fact he was scheduled for an operation to try to save the sight in his eye the following day. She also mentioned his ribs and his jaw and the damage to his kidneys.

Calder and Pitman discussed what they should do about Doyle and Calder must have been in a forgiving mood, most likely brought about by the fact his beloved dog was back home and had made a huge fuss of him, and they'd decided that they'd pay him a visit and give him a gypsy's warning when he left hospital and let it go at that. It looked like he'd suffered enough, and in essence, he'd only found the body by accident and he'd done what the majority of people would do in his position and helped himself to the gold rather than let the fish have it. So nuff said.

Conner though was a different proposition all together, he'd been throwing his weight around a bit lately on their patch and needed to be taught a lesson and brought down a peg or two. He was on the list, but wasn't a priority yet. They still needed to find out who killed Lizzie and why and sort that out first, then they'd deal with the other people involved, every last one of them that had had anything to do with it, they would all suffer. And Calder was just the man to make them suffer!

Chapter Twenty-One

Conner had been going stir-crazy, he'd been keeping a low profile, but Larry was starting to really do his head in. Conner had only been out once since he'd been shacked up with him and the place was a tip. Larry wasn't exactly into cleanliness or personal hygiene. And the money was burning a hole in Conner's pocket, he wanted to see Sonia and he'd made his mind up that tonight was the night.

He'd washed and shaved, he'd have liked to have showered but the shower was broken, well there's a surprise. He'd put on his best threads and when he clocked himself in the mirror he'd grinned at his reflection, "You'll do," Conner said to himself, and then told Larry he was popping out and he'd be back later and no he didn't need to know where he was going.

Conner hadn't dared go back for his motor, fearful that either the police or Calder's men would be watching his gaffe. So he'd walked about half a mile from Larry's flat to the corner of Hendon Road, and then he'd called a taxi and sat right in the corner of the back seat and kept his face turned away to the window. He had the cabbie drop him off two streets away from Sonia's flat and shoved the money through the cabbie's open window. He'd stood on the pavement and turned his back and waited until the taxi had driven away and round the corner before he moved. Calder would have eyes and ears everywhere, he couldn't wait to piss off to Manchester, but he'd been hanging on because one of his contacts said he thought he had a tip about who had been behind the murder of Mrs Calder, and he was waiting to hear back, otherwise to hell with them all, he'd have been long gone.

Ten minutes later as Conner was about to press the entry phone for Sonia's flat, an elderly woman joined him at the main door, she was struggling with some Sainsbury's carrier-bags.

Hoping to surprise Sonia, Conner offered to help the old lady, seizing the opportunity to gain access to the flats without alerting Sonia that he was here.

"D'you want a hand with those love?" Conner asked amiably reaching for the bags.

"Oh would you dear, that's very kind of you," she passed the bags to Conner who let her unlock the door and then he stood aside to let her enter first. "It's nice to know there's still some gentlemen left around here, it certainly makes a change."

"You're very welcome," Conner said walking ahead of her to the lifts. He pressed the button and the lift doors opened. "After you please Ma'am," Conner said gallantly.

The old lady chuckled and almost skipped into the lift.

The doors closed. "I'm going up to three, what floor you want love?" Conner said pressing the buttons.

"Two please," she answered.

A few moments later the lift stopped and the doors opened onto the second floor. The old lady stepped out and held out her hands for the bags.

"No, I'm not doing half a job," Conner said smiling, "we deliver to your door, lead on missus!"

The old lady cackled and made her way down the corridor smiling for all the world to see. She could never understand the kindness of strangers, it was rare nowadays but oh so welcome. She stopped outside number twenty-one and fiddled her key out of her purse and opened the front door and turned on the lights.

"You've been very kind, thank you. Would you like a cup of tea, I can pop the kettle on, it won't take a moment?" She asked hoping that he would keep her company for a little longer, she didn't get to talk to people very much now, a lot of her friends had passed away, three this year already, and she didn't think it would be very much longer until she wouldn't be able to cope by herself anymore, and she'd end up in one of those blessed old people's homes. She shivered at the thought.

Conner handed her back the bags, "Thanks for the offer love, it's a nice thought but I'm meeting someone. Perhaps another time, yeah?"

She brightened at the thought and smiled at the huge frame of a man towering over her. A gentle giant she thought, how charming. "Well any time you're close by, I'm Mrs Thompson, just ring my bell," she giggled, "that sounded rather naughty, didn't it?" They both laughed and then Conner waved goodbye and she regretfully closed the door behind him and returned to the loneliness and quiet of her flat.

Conner got back into the lift and travelled up to the next floor and then made his way down the carpeted corridor until he stood outside Sonia's flat. He flexed his neck and shoulders and tried to hold down his excitement. He'd been with whores before but nothing as posh or classy as Sonia, and he couldn't wait to get his money's worth. Get a good shag under his belt and then he'd leg it up to Manchester in the morning if he hadn't heard anything back from his contact. He breathed out, he was ready, bring it on then bitch he said to himself.

He knocked on the door, after a few moments he heard the lock being drawn back and Sonia opened the door. She almost jerked back in alarm.

"Oh! I wasn't expecting you!" She looked at her watch, "I've got a client due in about twenty minutes. How did you get up here?"

"I helped some old girl in with her shopping on the floor below. Well, ain't you gonna invite me in then?"

Sonia's head was spinning, the word was out about Conner, and she'd lied about having a client, she just didn't want to be alone with the man. She'd heard what he'd done and she didn't want to let him into the flat in case he was one of those punters who liked to be rough with women.

Conner pushed his way into the flat and closed the door. "We can make a start in twenty minutes, but whoever he is he'll have to wait till I'm finished, fuck him!"

Sonia's heart missed a beat. He was a big man and there was no way she could refuse him, and the last thing she wanted was to be beaten up. Apart from the injuries a man like that could inflict on her, it would mean she wouldn't be able to work. Her clients were only used to seeing her looking her best, dazzling, beautifully presented and sexy, not staggering about with black eyes and a broken nose. Time to be Sonia, the perfect host and high-priced escort that she was.

"Well," she said recovering her self-composure. "I certainly didn't expect to see you when I opened the door." She smiled her winning sexy smile. "But you're very welcome. Come and sit down. Would you like something to drink?" She turned and walked towards a unit that had a variety of bottles of drink and glasses displayed.

"If I'd wanted a drink, I'd have gone down the pub. You know why I'm here and I'm as horny as hell!" He laughed and took off his jacket and flung it across the arm of the sofa and then sat down.

Sonia carried on over to the drinks unit. "You don't mind if I do, do you?" She poured herself a whisky and took a sip. She turned and made her way back and sat on the sofa next to him. She noticed his hands. The knuckles were red and grazed.

She put down her drink and gently picked up his hand. "Whatever happened to your hands? They look so sore."

"It's nothing, just part of me job innit."

"But they look so sore."

"Naw they're alright, you think they're bad, you should see the bloke that was on the receiving end of 'em!" He roared with laughter and Sonia reluctantly joined in. She knew the poor man was still in hospital and still wasn't out of the woods yet, and here was this big thug just bragging and laughing about it. Christ, they say it takes all sorts.

Conner was getting a bit pissed off the way she kept staring at his hands, he wanted to get started and he wondered when his time actually begun? An hour didn't seem that long to him, not when it was costing him a grand. "Forget me hands yeah?" He pulled his hand way from her. "I told ya, it's no big deal, someone gets outta line, you have to put 'em back in. That's how it works, it's all sorted now. So how's this work then? Am I on the clock already?"

She smiled at him and ran her long fingers gently down the side of his cheek. "You're not on the clock, darling, not for your first time, you can take as long as you want."

"How about the bloke you've got coming round then?"

She composed herself, "Well, once we sort out the business side of things, I'm going to freshen up whilst you warm up my bed," she gave him one of her sexy looks guaranteed to melt the souls of even the hardest of men, "and then I'll give him a ring and say I'm not feeling too bright. He's a sweetie, he'll understand. And then ... I'm all yours!" She mouthed a kiss at him and stood. "Well when you're ready then, Martin," she said.

He rushed to get up from the deep-seated sofa. "Right yeah course!" He fumbled in his pocket and brought out a large roll of banknotes held together with an elastic band.

"You do know how much I charge, don't you, Martin?" She asked gently, letting her housecoat slip open slightly, giving him a partial view of one of her breasts and her long, slim, tanned legs.

"Yeah, yeah, it's a grand innit?" He counted off the banknotes, they were grubby and crumpled, but money was money and she took it when he handed it to her and leant forward and kissed him very lightly on the mouth.

She tucked the money into the pocket of her housecoat. "The bedroom's through there," she pointed, "unless you need the bathroom first?"

"No I'm good." He started to make his way towards the bedroom.

"Martin?" She called out. He stopped and turned. She slowly undid the belt on her housecoat and shrugged it off and it fell in a heap on the carpet. She was naked underneath.

Conner's jaw literally dropped. "Fucking hell!" he whispered.

She bent down suggestively and picked up the housecoat. "Now you run along and get yourself ready, I'm going to freshen myself up, make that phone call so we won't be disturbed, and then I'm going to give you a night to remember." She blew him a kiss and tucked her free hand under her breast and cupped it for him.

He smiled and licked his lips and then turned and hurried into the bedroom.

Sonia pulled her housecoat back on and took the money out of the pocket and placed it in the drawer in one of the matching side units. She picked up her mobile from the unit and went into the bathroom and shut and locked the door behind her.

She sat on the bathroom stool and flicked through her contacts and pressed the button to make a call.

It was answered after two rings.

"Pitman. Who's this?"

She took a deep breath, "You don't know me Mr Pitman but we have some mutual friends, and I've heard you're looking for Martin Conner."

"You heard right," he said beckoning Stevie over, he cupped his hand over the phone. "Stevie get the car ready and get Johnnie on the phone we may have found Conner." He returned to the caller, "Sorry about that, you were saying you know where Conner is, that right?"

"Yes, he's here in my flat."

"R-i-g-h-t. This ain't a wind up, is it? 'cos if you know me then you'd know I don't respond well to wind-ups."

"It's no wind up Mr Pitman. I'm an escort, and Martin Conner is currently getting himself nice and comfortable in my bed for the shag of his life, only there's no way he's going to get it. I don't know how long it'll take you to get here but please, please, please make it quick. If he kicks off I won't stand a chance."

"Alright, alright, we're on our way. Where'd you live?"

"Courtland's, it's a large block of flats on Avenue Road. I'm in flat thirty-three."

"I know the road, we'll find it. How we gonna get in?"

"I'll leave my door on the latch, if you ring the entry bell for number thirteen, that's my friend Wendy, she's home we spoke earlier, tell her I said to let you in. If she starts to get protective, tell her I'll see her on Tuesday at The Inn-on-the-park for lunch. She'll know you're genuine then we've only just arranged it. And please, please hurry!"

"'bout ten minutes, keep him sweet, we'll do the rest." Pitman cut the call, he shouted to Stevie, "Get Johnnie and Davey-Boy if you can reach him over to Courtland's it's a block of flats over on Avenue Road, Conner's there with some pro. Now move your arse we don't wanna lose him!"

Chapter Twenty-Two

Sonia slipped the phone into her housecoat pocket and then splashed some cold water on her face and dabbed it off with a clean white towel. Her heart was pounding and her hands were trembling. She'd met a few hard men in her time, but she knew Conner was a merciless bastard who thought nothing of giving women a good kicking as well as men. There was a rumour that he'd killed a couple of people over the years but nothing had ever been proved, the police always found it hard to find anyone to testify against him such was his reputation.

And now he was here in her flat and in her bed and it was down to her to keep him occupied until Pitman and his crew turned up. She checked her watch, about five minutes had elapsed since she'd made the call, and she knew any minute now she'd have to make an appearance or he might come looking for her, she exhaled and prepared herself.

She walked back into the lounge and called out to him. "I'll be with you a minute or two, I've just freshened myself up for you and now I'm just going to phone my client up and cancel, and then I'll be in to put a big smile on your face."

"Well get a move on will ya, I'm getting a bit pissed off in here by meself!"

He didn't sound at all happy with the situation.

"Five minutes Martin that's all, and then I'm all yours. So it's fine if you want to get started without me, if you know what I mean?" She laughed her sexiest laugh, "then as soon as I come in there we can get the party started!" She gave him a come-on shriek and he whooped in response.

"Just let me make this phone call and I'll be right with you, sweetie."

Sonia walked over to the front door. She picked up her door keys from the table, thinking that if he came out of the bedroom, then she would make a dash for it locking the door behind her and trapping him inside. At least that way she wouldn't be hurt and he would still be there when Pitman turned up. Her flat was on the third floor so there was no escape from inside her flat, so the worst he could do was wreck it, but she felt under the circumstances that if Conner did that, Pitman would compensate her for any damage he'd caused.

Sonia heard muffled voices outside and she slowly opened her front door. There were three men standing poised ready to strike watching as the door opened. She heaved a sigh of relief and her legs sagged. One of the men stepped forward and gently supported her.

"It's alright, I'm Tony Pitman, these boys are with me." He rested her back against the wall in the corridor. "Is he still in there?"

She nodded, "Yes."

"You OK?"

"Yeah, I'm just really nervous; he's a very big man."

"Well you let us worry about that. So where is he?"

"He's in the main bedroom, that's the one on the left when you go in."

"OK, here's what I want you to do." Tony explained what he wanted from her and Sonia nervously agreed.

"Don't worry; he won't get a chance to hurt you I promise. OK let's go."

All four of them walked back into the flat and quietly positioned themselves outside the bedroom door. The door was pushed to.

Sonia took a deep breath and then spoke to Conner.

"Well I hope you're in the mood for some *hot loving*, big boy. Have I got a surprise for you!"

Conner sounded excited. "Well come on then, I can't wait!"

"OK, well it's a very sexy surprise as a special treat as it's your first visit with me, but you have to close your eyes and no peeking! And I need you to promise me or you'll spoil the surprise. So are you going to close your eyes and pull the sheets back ready for me?"

"Yeah, yeah I'm doing the sheets now and me eyes are closed, they're closed!" He yelled, "just hurry up will ya!"

Sonia walked away and sat down in the armchair nearest the front door to her flat. The three men silently entered the main bedroom. Pitman went to the left hand side of the bed, Stevie to the right hand side and Davey-Boy stood at the bottom of the bed holding the cattle prod. Conner was lying on his back in the king-sized bed, naked; his eyes were closed and his right hand was holding his erect cock.

Pitman nodded and Davey-Boy jabbed Conner under the arse with the prod. Conner screamed and reared up off the bed and as he did so Pitman brought his cosh down hard on top of Conner's head, twice. Whilst Conner groaned and half curled up, Stevie and Davey-Boy yanked his arms behind his back and fastened some large cable-ties around Conner's wrists.

"Give him another one for luck," Pitman said to Davey-Boy, who was very quick to oblige and jabbed Conner right in the crotch where his dead erection now lay. Conner screamed and thrashed about on the bed.

Pitman sat on the side of the bed alongside Conner. "So we meet at last then Conner. Big tough man, ain't cha? Only not quite so tough now, are you?" Pitman flicked the end of Conner's knob and Conner winced and Pitman's crew fell about laughing. "We're going to put your clothes back on you and then there's someone who'd very much like to meet you." He nodded at Stevie and Davey-Boy, "get him dressed."

"I didn't touch her!" Conner said, "You got the wrong man it wasn't me! I swear to you it wasn't me!"

Pitman replied almost casually, "you were part of it though and that's enough for me."

Davey-Boy lifted Conner's legs and Stevie pulled Conner's pants up over his feet and up as far as he could. "D'you wanna lift up fat boy or I'll leave 'em there?"

Conner lifted his bulk up off the bed and Stevie wrestled his pants up his huge, fat body. The trousers followed.

"Just get his shoes on don't piss about with his socks and just get his shirt." Pitman said getting up from the bed.

Pitman's crew pulled Conner's shoes on him and then stood him up. Stevie shoved Conner's socks into his jacket pocket. Pitman went almost head to head with the man but not too close, even though his wrists were bound it wouldn't stop Conner from head-butting him and trying to escape, they weren't in the clear yet.

"Now I'm telling you this for future reference, if you ever think about coming back here and harming that lady out there, it would be more than your life's worth, she's now under my protection, and when I say *my protection*, I mean Mr Calder's. And you do not want to make another mistake. Is that clear?"

Conner looked about him at the three men standing there. He reckoned he could drop Pitman with a good kick to his bollocks but with his wrists tied up he'd be hard-pressed to take the other two so easily and that bastard had that cattle prod and that hurt like a fucking bitch that did. No they had him, but they still had to get him out of the flat and take him somewhere yet, so there might be a better chance to escape later. So he nodded in answer to Pitman's question.

"Grab his coat on the way out." Pitman said and all four left the bedroom. Davey-Boy and Stevie each gripped one of Conner's arms and moved him along. Stevie picked up Conner's coat and tucked it over his arm.

Sonia rose up when they came out of the bedroom and stood against the wall. As they drew almost level Conner hawked and spat a stream of phlegm at her hitting her in the side of her face and hair.

Pitman slowed and then drove his elbow back viciously into Conner's stomach. He doubled over and the men holding him almost lost their grip as he toppled forward. They went down onto their knees with him and as they did so Pitman pulled Conner up by his hair.

"What did I say to you?" Without another word, Pitman slammed his head down into Conner's face and Conner's world exploded and he collapsed face down onto the carpet, blood spewed from his nose and mouth. Pitman turned to Sonia who was crying and wiping at her face and hair with a handful of tissues. "Get the carpet cleaned and let me know how much it's cost and one of my lads will drop an envelope round. Sorry about that, some people are just so thick they don't know when to quit. You gonna be alright?"

Sonia nodded.

"I can send someone round to sit with you if you want some female company, it's no sweat?"

"I'm OK, just a bit shaky, that's all." She perched herself on the arm of the chair to stop her legs from shaking.

"I don't want you to be out of pocket over this, that ain't fair and I don't expect you'll feel like working for a few days, and there's your carpet to get sorted. Check his pockets out Stevie see what he's holding?"

Conner groaned as he was manhandled up onto his feet. Blood was coursing down his face and running down his chest. Stevie dug into Conner's pocket and pulled out the roll of banknotes.

"Result!" Stevie said whipping off the elastic band holding the bounty.

"Count it," Pitman said, "we need to make sure some goes back to Solly, he wasn't to know what he was getting himself into with this shitbag."

Stevie counted the notes into a pile on the floor. "Eight, seven, Tone."

"Right, nice one, OK take a pony each for you two and one for Johnnie, hold a couple of grand back for Solly and give this lovely young lady four grand."

"No that's too much," Sonia protested.

"It ain't our money darling, so look at it like a charity and it's all going to good homes." He grinned and his crew laughed with him.

Stevie divvied up the money, handed Sonia her share and gave the balance to Tony.

Tony looked at Sonia, "You sure you're gonna be alright?"

"Yes and thank you," she said.

"No sweat, you're welcome and thanks for the call." He turned to his crew, "Right then lads, wagons roll, let's get him outside and then I'll get the lift sorted."

They manhandled Conner out of the flat and as they were leaving, Tony bent down to Sonia, "I might pay you a call meself one of these days if that's alright with you, cheap rates for mates, yeah?" He smiled at her and she returned the smile.

"You've got yourself a freebie whenever you want Tony, thank you."

He nodded. "Be lucky," he said and left the flat and closed the door behind him. He heard the lock click into place seconds later.

He grabbed Conner by his hair and helped propel him forward, "Right let's get this prick into the van and then the fun can really begin!"

The crew all laughed and Conner knew then that he should have fucked off to Manchester when he had the chance!

Sonia couldn't believe her luck. She'd made five grand in less than half an hour and she hadn't really had to do anything and she'd get her carpet cleaned as well, *and* she was now under the protection of Mr Calder and Tony Pitman, what is it they say? 'All's well that ends well.' Can't argue with that she thought as she took Conner's grand out of the unit and went back into the bedroom. She opened her wall-to-wall wardrobe and then got down on her knees and moved some shoe boxes to one side to reveal a small metal safe cemented into the floor through the bottom of the wardrobe. She inputted the code and the door sprung open and she placed the money inside along with all the rest. A few more years like this, and she wouldn't have to turn any more tricks, she'd have enough money to buy her own hair salon, and then she could go back to cutting and styling hair again, the job she'd always loved since she was at school.

She stood up and walked across to the bed and started to drag the sheets off, they were going in the wash right now and then she'd take a shower. She wouldn't feel clean again until she had.

Chapter Twenty-Three

Pitman and his crew had managed to get Conner into the back of Johnnie's van and he'd been driven to one of Calder's lock ups. Tony had updated Calder en route and they were presently waiting for him to arrive.

Conner was sitting strapped to a chair with a dark hood still over his head, surrounded by boxes of brand new dishwashers and washing machines, courtesy of a lorry driver who conveniently had his lorry boosted whilst he was having brekkie at a service station on the M1. They were waiting to go into a run-down block of flats that Calder had recently acquired, and when the last few die-hards had 'moved out,' then he would redo the whole block and make a substantial killing on the deal.

Pitman and the lads were laughing and joking and standing or sitting around drinking tea when they heard Calder's motor draw up and park outside. They became alert then and moved further out into the room.

Calder entered via the small tradesmen's entrance.

He nodded at Pitman, "Tone, lads," he said smiling. "Bit of a result I hear. So what have we got so far then?" He walked over and stood in front of Conner. Conner raised his head and Calder whipped off the hood.

Conner groaned, the inside of the mask had been stuck to the dried blood on his face and he blinked rapidly letting his eyes get accustomed to the change of light.

"D'you know who I am?" Calder asked.

"Well I ain't gotta be fucking Mastermind to work it out, have I?" He replied sourly.

The crew exchanged looks, that wasn't what they were expecting, it was a bold move from a man whose wrists were still cable-tied behind his back, and whose arms and legs were firmly strapped to the chair.

"I do so like a challenge," Calder said evenly, unhurried. "So, as you're aware someone murdered my wife, me I'm who I am, but my missus was pure gold, and didn't have an enemy in the world. Everyone loved her and respected her, from the milkman to councillors and all points in-between. So I'm going to ask you once, that's all, just once, and if you know what's good for you you'll tell me the truth. Did you have anything to do with the murder of my lovely wife?"

Conner locked eyes with Calder. "No, and I already told this fucking chicken-shit rabble the same thing an' all. You got the wrong man. I don't know fuck all about what happened to your missus."

Calder pointed at Conner with his index finger, "but you fenced off my wife's jewellery, and I know that for a fact."

Conner pulled a 'so-what' face at him and shrugged. "I didn't know who it belonged to when I *acquired* it, did I? And if you cast your mind back, you'll recall I let your man there know who I got it from *and, and* I paid him a little visit an' all."

"Yes, we heard about that. He's still in hospital, he's had three operations so far and he almost died."

"Well that's what you get when you mess with me; I don't take shit from no one …"

The crew including Calder laughed at that.

"Well you're hardly in the best position to bargain now, are you? You've been making waves on my patch for a few months now. We've had more police mooching about lately than we've had for years, and I believe that's all down to you. And I don't like it."

"I just got a job to do an' I do it, you gotta understand that."

Calder's tone was hard, "I understand you're making waves and rocking my fucking boat and I don't take too kindly to that. Dave Palmer ring any bells to you?"

Conner knew the name but didn't answer straight away. He waited to hear what was coming next.

"You broke both his legs. That was four months ago and he hasn't worked since, he's still on crutches. He used to work for me sometimes, did you know that?"

"No, I didn't. He owed money on a motor and he was behind with his payments, that's all I needed to know."

"And now he can't work because you smashed both his legs and the car's been repossessed. No one wins that way. That's not the way to do business."

"It is in my book! You fuck with me you get what's coming."

"And Doyle deserved to almost die, did he?"

"Fucking A yeah! He sold me stuff that was so hot there must have been steam coming off it and he told me it was fine. That little prick lied to me. And I've got a surprise coming for that little Jew boy an' all. He dobbed me in it with the filth, and now because of him I ended up decking one of 'em and there's a warrant out for me. So join the club, you want your pound of flesh, you fucking take it!"

"You do not go anywhere near Solly Bergmann, do I make myself clear?"

Conner looked at him and said nothing.

"That is not a request. Am I making myself clear?" Calder nodded to Pitman who walked up behind Conner and swiped him hard with his cosh. It caught Conner on the side of his head so unexpectedly he almost toppled the chair over and he cried out with pain and shock.

"I *said*, am I making myself clear?"

Conner tried to turn his head to see where Pitman was, but Pitman was standing directly behind him out of his eye line.

"Alright," Conner replied reluctantly.

"So, what d'you know about a new shape white Ford Transit then?" Calder asked pacing up and down in front of Conner.

"Is that what they brought me here in? If that ain't it, then I don't know fuck all 'bout no van."

"I'm not talking about our van; it's not the new shape. I'm talking about a grubby new shaped Ford Transit that was parked near my house when my wife went missing. What can you tell me about *that* van?"

"It was white and grubby ..." He laughed and Pitman slammed the cosh down on the back of his neck without being asked. He almost pitched forward onto the floor but Pitman was quick to grab him and haul him upright, Stevie moved in from the side and helped settle him back in the chair.

"This is your last chance to save yourself a whole mess of pain. Do you know who abducted my wife and do you know anyone that owns a Transit, apart from us? And if I were you, I'd quit trying to show how tough you are, because it won't mean a thing when they bring the welding gear over here in a minute, and we take your kecks off and start work."

Conner's stomach dropped and his balls constricted. It was time to back down, he'd shown face, he hadn't crumbled and bottled it in front of them all, but you have to know when to draw the line and quit.

Conner considered for a moment, "if I tell you what I know, what happens to me?"

"Depends on what you tell me. If you had a hand in killing my wife, then I shall take great pleasure in killing you ..."

Conner interrupted, "No, no I had nothing to do with that I swear to God I keep telling you that! That's straight up, that is honest!" Conner showed real fear for the first time and he struggled to hold back his bladder which suddenly felt like it was about to burst.

"What have you got to tell me then?"

Conner looked at the men standing in front and to the side of him, not to mention fucking Pitman stationed out of sight with that bleedin' cosh, and he knew he was in the worst trouble he'd ever been in and he suddenly feared for his life.

"Doyle phoned me about the jewellery and I bought it off him, and I told your man there that," he nodded his head slightly backwards to indicate Tony. "I sold it on to Bergmann, and you got my word I won't touch him. He dropped me in it with the FEDs 'cos he still had the security tapes, and then I done Doyle for ..."

Calder interrupted him, "We already know all this, you're just trying to buy yourself some time ..."

"No, no I'm not, I'm just working me way through the story. My fucking head's killing me, so I'm making sure I get it all right for ya. I heard about a van, a white Trannie. One of Carson's boys found it in the NCP car park on Howden Road. It's been there for a few days and had a load of penalty tickets all over it."

"Where does Carson fit into all this? Did he have something to do with it?"

"Dunno, he might have," he shrugged, grateful that he was taking some of the pressure off himself and moving it onto someone else.

"I think his boys are joining in trying to get their hands on the reward. I did hear a whisper about a certain person though, that's why I ain't legged it. I was waiting to get confirmation, then I was gonna give him up to you to get you off my back. I thought we could do a swap like. You know, I give him to you and you let me walk?"

"What name did you hear?"

Conner looked at all the faces crowded in all around him. He had no choice, there was no escape but he might not get as badly hurt as he suspected he was going to, if he coughed.

"Finch, Kevin Finch. It's his van they found."

"Get on it," Calder said to Pitman. "Get Carson on the blower and find out just what the fuck he knows."

Tone whipped out his mobile and started pressing buttons; he walked away to the other side of the lock up for a bit more privacy.

"What about me then?" Conner asked expectantly.

"You know what?" Calder asked. Conner shook his head, worried sick about what was going to happen next. "There's two things in life I can't hack, *bullies*, which you clearly are, and grasses." He turned to Stevie, "Get the welding kit set up, let's give this monkey something to remember us by."

Conner screamed in protest and Davey-Boy jabbed him with the cattle prod and Conner jerked so hard he fell forward onto the floor with the chair hanging onto his back. All the men laughed as Stevie wheeled the welding unit over and started to connect it up.

Chapter Twenty-Four

Pitman called the police an hour later telling them that if they were still looking for Martin Conner, they'd find him at Redlands Industrial Estate in a commercial skip at the back of P & P Plastics, and they'd best bring an ambulance along as well as he didn't look too healthy when they'd last seen him.

Pitman had cut the call and opened up the back of the pay as you go phone and dropped the SIM card down a drain and inserted a new one. He'd bought a job-lot of SIM cards off eBay and they came in handy when he needed to make a phone call and didn't want it traced.

The word was now out on the street big-time, that Calder was looking for Finch and they'd already had three calls from 'public-spirited' people quick to gain favour with Calder informing of previous sightings. One of the callers had given an address for Finch, but he couldn't say for certain that he was actually there at the moment.

It was a start. Pitman had sent Stevie and Johnnie on ahead as he was en route to a hairdresser's where he'd been reliably informed Finch's girlfriend worked. He pulled up a couple of spaces away from the salon and watched the comings and goings for a few minutes, and then he got out of his car, locked it and entered the salon.

A young girl was sat behind the reception desk and she greeted him warmly.

"Can I help you? Unfortunately, we only do ladies hair, we're not a unisex salon," she explained politely.

"I don't want me hair doing thanks love. I'm looking for Jade?"

"You're not the only one," a stylist said stopping work and turning towards him. "I'm Jenny, this is my salon and I've not clapped eyes on her for almost a week. No word, no show, no nothing."

"I take it you've tried phoning her?"

"Loads of times yeah," said the receptionist, "it just goes straight to voicemail."

"I dropped round her flat as well after work, what night was that Kim? Was it Wednesday or Thursday?"

"I think it was Thursday, no tell a lie, it might have been Wed …"

Pitman cut them off. "I need her address, it's important."

"We can't just give out staff addresses," the receptionist started to say and then she stopped mid-sentence when she saw the look Pitman gave her as he started to advance towards her. "Jenny, can you say something please!" she said alarmed.

Jenny moved forward and confronted the man. "Can you tell me who you are and why you need Jade's address please?"

"No to all those questions." Pitman replied coldly.

"Well I'm sorry but I don't know who you are, and I'm not prepared to give out addresses for members of my staff," she said determinedly.

Pitman slowly slid his hand along the top of the reception desk shoving all the shampoos and gels onto the floor.

"I'm calling the police!" the receptionist said reaching for the phone. Pitman grabbed the phone and yanked it, and the wires pulled out of the wall. The woman who was in the middle of having her hair styled got up quickly still with the gown over her shoulders, grabbed her coat off the peg and walked out.

"Carole!" Jenny shouted after her, "It's alright!" She turned to Pitman. "Well thanks very much for that." she said flatly, and then after a moment's thought she said to Pitman. "Look ... is Jade in trouble?"

"Not from me she's not. But she could be from her boyfriend, Kevin Finch? That's why I need her address to check up on her."

"Well that's different then, you should have said. I've warned her about him time and time again. Kim, write down Jade's address and her mobile number please and give it to the gentleman. Maybe she'll answer the phone to you as she wouldn't recognise your number. I just hope she's alright."

Kim wrote down the details and handed the slip of paper to Pitman. He checked the details. "Thanks. Can you give me a bit of a description; I haven't got a clue what she looks like?"

"Oh right, yes OK," Jenny said. "Well she's twenty-three, about five-two, quite slim, dresses in ridiculously short skirts, and the last time she was here, the ends of her hair were bright pink. You'd know her if you saw her."

"OK, thanks for that."

Jenny grabbed a business card and handed it to Pitman. "Can you do me a favour; just let me know if she's alright if you speak to her? I'd appreciate it."

Pitman nodded and took the card, and then looked in turn at the two ladies and reached into his pocket and flipped out a fifty-pound note and laid it on the reception desk.

"Sorry about the mess ladies, slight misunderstanding I think."

He turned and left the ladies standing speechless behind him, as he gently closed the door and returned to his motor.

Stevie called Pitman as he was driving away and he hit the hands free. "What you got?" Pitman asked.

"He's not here, Tone. It don't look like he's been here for a few days. The place was all shut up and it stinks. You know old takeaways and shit like that. It's a right old dump. Johnnie spoke to one of his neighbours in the flat next door, and he said he had to bang on the wall a few days ago as Finch and some bird were going at it hammer and tongs. But he's heard nothing since. He said he was surprised we didn't find a dead body in there going on the row they were having."

"OK I'm on my way over to fourteen Cavendish Place, its block of flats on Fisher's Road; it's where Finch's girlfriend lives. I've been down to where she works and had a little chat, and they've given me her address. Same thing really, they said she hadn't been in for nearly a week. Looks like he dumped his wheels and they're shacked up somewhere, could be they're at her flat. I'll meet you there; you never know we might get lucky. I've just got to pay a little visit to someone en route, shouldn't take too long."

"Righto, number fourteen yeah?"

"That's the one, see you in a bit. You'll probably be there before me so wait out and just keep eyes on it, and we'll all go in together. I want the front and back covered, alright?"

"Yep no sweat, Tone, later." Stevie cut the call and said to Johnnie. "Right we need to get over to fourteen Cavendish Place; it's on Fisher's Road. It's where Finch's bird lives. Tone's on his way over but he's just gotta see someone first, but he's hoping the pair of 'em might be there. If it was me though with all this heat coming down on me, I'd be long fucking gone, that's for sure."

Johnnie nodded in agreement and started the van.

Chapter Twenty-Five

Pitman drove into Top Class Cars and parked up to one side where he was virtually hidden behind a row of stationary vehicles up for sale. This was Dave Carson's pitch, his pride and joy; it was time to have a word.

Pitman got out of his car, locked it and made his way over to the office, which was really just a glorified caravan reached by a set of wooden stairs. Tony entered without knocking and Carson and his 'assistant,' a black guy called Marvin Reid, jumped back in alarm, neither of them had noticed Pitman drive in or mount the stairs, and he'd caught them completely by surprise. Marvin recovered and fronted up to Pitman.

Pitman sneered, "Behave yourself son, it ain't worth it," Pitman said easily, putting his weight on his back foot just in case the black man decided to ignore his advice and tried to make a name for himself.

"It's OK, Marv, this is Tony Pitman."

The black man took a couple of steps forward and then stopped. "I've heard of you Pitman," he said suitably unimpressed and pulled a face. "So?"

"So remember what you've heard, and multiply it tenfold if your little brain will let you," Pitman said coolly.

The black man stiffened. He was a new addition to Carson's team and he hadn't had a real chance to prove himself yet, this could be the time and place to make his mark.

Carson got up, "Marv, just take it easy, Tony's just popped in for a word, it's OK."

"Some other time then maybe?" Marv said, and walked back and stood alongside Carson's desk in the traditional 'bouncer's stance.' Pitman grinned at the man.

"So," Carson said affably, "what can I do for you then, Tone? New motor, is it? I've got some good cars out there ..."

Pitman cut him off. "Cut the crap, save that for your punters; you know why I'm here, now sit down and let's talk!" Pitman gripped Carson by his shoulder and shoved him back down in his chair. Marv took a step forward, his fists clenched ready.

"Just tell this gorilla to take a hike, will ya? Otherwise he'll be sipping liquid through a fucking straw for months." Pitman locked eyes with Marv.

"It's OK, Marv," Carson said.

The black man returned to his previous position alongside the desk and adopted his bouncer's stance once again.

Pitman looked at the man. "Yeah you look great, *well hard*," Pitman allowed himself a little grin, "now *fuck off* we need to talk business, *private business*, so do one."

Pitman watched the man's eyes as he weighed him up. He could see he was thinking, should I or shouldn't I? Marvin looked to Carson, who nodded towards the door.

Pitman suddenly moved forward swiftly stopping only inches from the black man and said "Boo!" Marvin almost lost his footing and struggled to recover his composure.

"Where the fuck d'you get these losers from?" Pitman asked Carson, as the black man made his way towards the door casting anxious looks back over his shoulder. Marvin exited and slammed the door behind him, it made the whole of the caravan shake and some paperwork fell down from one of the shelves.

"Seems like a nice boy," Pitman remarked, "right let's get down to business then," Pitman said pulling out the other chair and sitting across from Carson. "So further to our earlier little chat, what can you tell me now then?" Pitman asked, making himself more comfortable.

Carson rubbed the back of his hand across his mouth; he had become visibly very nervous. "Not a lot really, Tone, sorry. You know like I told you, I don't really know much."

"I ain't got time to piss about, you know what happened to Lizzie and I will find the people responsible, and a dicky-bird told me you have some information that might help me, so 'sing away' when you're ready then," Pitman said coldly.

Carson stammered, "Tone, I ... look I don't really know anything ..."

Pitman picked up the overflowing heavy glass ashtray in one smooth movement and slammed it down hard on Carson's hand. Carson screamed in agony and Pitman grabbed Carson's fingers and bent them up. Carson reared up from his chair on tiptoe trying to relieve the pressure.

"Tone Christ stop!" he yelled.

The door burst open and Marvin came charging towards Pitman. Pitman let go of Carson's fingers and kicked his chair at the fast-approaching black man. The chair sped forward on its castors and hit Reid just below the knees and he careered over the top of it. And as he did, so Pitman whipped out his cosh and brought it down heavily across the black man's head and he hit the floor and half-bounced up again and then lay still.

"Now, where were we?" Pitman asked retrieving his chair and calmly sitting back down. Carson stood nursing his damaged fingers and looked down at the still form on the floor on the other side of his desk. "Sit down!" Pitman ordered and Carson almost stumbled over in his haste to comply.

Pitman waited whilst Carson settled himself down still clutching his damaged fingers. "Right, so you were just about to tell me all you know about Lizzie Calder. Thing is see *Dave*, I've been given your name and that fits in with what I already know, so unless you tell me something I *don't know*, then that just puts you in the frame for smashing Lizzie Calder's head in and dumping her in a pond. And you know what will happen to you then, don't you?" Pitman said evenly and unhurried. Carson stood horrified. "Tone you gotta believe me, I had nothing to do with that!"

"Sit," Pitman said "you're making the room look untidy." Carson sat and as he did, so Pitman heard a scraping sound behind him, and spun to see the black man starting to recover. "Oh hello," Pitman said kindly, then rose out of his chair in one fluid movement and rapped the cosh down on Marvin's head sending him crashing back down onto the floor.

Pitman sat down and turned his attention back to Carson. "Facts, I know you supplied the muscle that was or wasn't involved in Lizzie's death. Namely two dickheads called Kevin Finch and Harry Toke. Finch's white Trannie was seen parked outside Lizzie's the day she went missing, and it's been clocked sitting in the NCP car park in Howden Road. Finch has now gone to ground somewhere with Jade, his hairdressing bird, who hasn't been seen for almost a week. Finch isn't at his gaffe, we've already been there, and we've got his bird's place staked out. So I need to talk to these boys. Now I know they don't work for Talbot, so where'd you get 'em from and where can I find 'em. And bear in mind, the clock is *ticking*." Pitman sat back relaxed, and waited.

Carson kept fidgeting and licking his lips. Pitman could almost see the cogs turning as he was trying to work out just what to say that would allow the least amount of blame to be attributed to him.

Finally, Carson started to speak. "It wasn't meant to be like that you know. It's a God Almighty fuck up. Look, far as I know, there's some property that Calder owns ..."

"Mr Calder to you," Pitman said interrupting.

"Yeah, yeah, sorry, Tone," Carson gushed apologetically, "anyway, Talbot's got a big building project going on, and I mean *big*, it's worth millions, and slap-bang in the middle of all this, is this block of six shops with flats over 'em that Mr Calder owns. Talbot's tried to buy the block off him but Cald ... sorry! Mr Calder's not selling. So he wanted to put a bit of pressure on him to make him change his mind. The idea was to put the frighteners on Mrs Calder." Carson threw his hands up in the air, "I had no one available! We'd had some problems with shipments and one of the clubs; so anyway, I used a couple of Reardon's boys ..."

Pitman interrupted, "Tommy Reardon's involved in this, is he?" he asked interested.

"Not really no," Carson said shaking his head to emphasise the point. "I know Tommy, and I know a few of his lads so I phoned Finch and kind of borrowed him and Toke."

"What and Reardon don't know?"

"Not yet, no. He ain't got a clue."

"Then you are right up shit creek from two fucking directions at once my ole son! Tommy's good friends with Calder and the fact you've implicated him in this, that means that you can kiss goodbye to any thoughts you got of ever drawing your pension. He'll do you sure as eggs is eggs!" Pitman let out a long sigh. "Jesus, I wouldn't want to be in your shoes for love nor money when this goes public."

Carson stood, the fear showing on his face and sweat marks soaking through his shirt under his armpits. "It wasn't my fault! I only hired them in to do a simple job. It was just a snatch and hold for a couple of days, that's all. So Cal, Mr Calder, would see sense and sell the block. Then her dog attacked Toke and she laid into Finch with a poker and then all hell broke loose. It was an accident, Tone you gotta believe me, it wasn't planned, I swear to God that was never meant to happen! Talbot's already gone mental at me and told me to sort it out, but I'm like you and I can't fucking find 'em either! Just the van, we found that, but that's all I've managed to find so far. I'm shelling out banknotes like sweets to try and find out where they are but nothing's coming in. You'd have thought with the reward you've put up as well, that we'd have had something by now. There's nothing mate, really, if I knew I'd tell you, you know that Tone ... Christ we go back years ..."

"Yeah and if you think that's gonna save you now, forget it. Lizzie was special to me, to all of us, and everyone that had a hand in her death is going to get what's coming to them. You ask Conner. We set to work on him with a portable welding unit, Jesus what a fucking stink." Pitman laughed and Carson felt his legs start to buckle and he reached out with his hand on the desk to steady himself and Pitman grabbed his damaged fingers and bent them back on themselves savagely snapping two of them. Carson cried out and Tony smashed the cosh down across his check and Carson bounced off the desk and hit the floor.

Pitman moved around the other side of the desk. Carson had wet himself and urine was pooling out around him. Pitman reached down and dragged Carson up and slammed him back in his chair.

"I need Toke's address and phone number, and if he drives a motor I want to know what it is and where he parks it." Pitman tore a page out of the desk diary and picked up a biro and rammed it into Carson's hand. Carson cried out in pain. "Write it all down and you may save yourself some grief. Your choice. But don't make me wait or have to ask you again, because my patience is starting to wear a little thin and I need to be somewhere."

Carson struggled to get his mobile out of his trouser pocket, Pitman just watched him. Carson succeeded and scrolled down the list of contacts and wrote down Toke's number. Carson was gritting his teeth against the pain in his hand as he wrote.

"I'm not sure of Toke's address, that's straight up that is, honest. I think he lives on Greenslades Estate somewhere, more than that I can't tell you. He's got a Focus, blue it is; it's had a bit of a bash on the nearside. I suppose he parks it on the estate, but I don't know for sure. But I know he's got a brother. I don't know where he lives but I know where he works. Temple & Moore's on Queens Road. They make furnishings for boats and things, he works in there. His name's Jeff."

"Is that it?" Pitman asked.

Carson started to shake his head. "I don't know anymore, Tone, believe you me if I did I'd tell you, you know I would!"

Pitman scooped up the page from the diary with Toke's number on and shoved it into his pocket and then reached out and grabbed Carson by his hair and slammed his face down onto the desk. Pitman lifted him up again and slammed his face back down again three times in quick succession then shoved him hard away. Carson fell backwards unconscious onto the floor, his face a bloodied pulp. Satisfied, Pitman made his way towards the door and as he passed Marvin, Pitman kicked him hard in the ribs partially lifting his body off the floor. There was no response from the black man he was still out for the count.

"Fucking lightweight," Pitman said in passing, "Wouldn't make it onto my team." He opened the door and as he started to make his way down the stairs so someone was making their way up. Pitman stopped and checked to see if the person was a threat.

The man was middle-aged and wearing corduroy trousers and an old zip up jacket and a cap.

"They're shut mate, they've just gone out to pick up a motor that's broken down, I wouldn't waste your money if I were you. I've just come back to complain about the clutch going on me wife's motor we bought from here last week. He's a right dodgy character I can tell you that."

"Oh right, well thanks very much for that. I did think the car I looked at seemed a bit overpriced, I definitely won't bother now. Thanks again, you've probably saved me a lot of money." The man turned and made his way back down the stairs and got into an old Volvo estate and drove away. Pitman allowed himself a wry smile. No doubt Carson had had better days than this Pitman thought as he unlocked his car and started heading for Cavendish Place and his crew. Toke would have to wait; one bad guy at a time, easy does it, tiger.

Chapter Twenty-Six

The incident room was in full swing. They were now investigating two murders. Elizabeth Calder and a male they now knew to be Clive Russell. Although the male had been in the water for quite some time and the perpetrators had gone to the trouble of removing his hands to make identification more difficult, they had somehow managed to overlook the fact that in the inside pocket of his jacket, had been his wallet, complete with credit cards and driving licence. Sometimes it wasn't the criminals that had all the luck.

Detective Inspector Chris White had just given his pep talk to the team to keep up their motivation and had dished out specific tasks to specific officers. Motive was the key question. Who or why did someone want Elizabeth Calder murdered? And was there a connection to Clive Russell and if so, what?

Russell was known to the police. He'd run a small building company that employed seven men plus some sub-contractors, and Russell mixed with some rather unsavoury characters as he was known to like a flutter on the horses and would often play poker into the early hours of the morning. When he went missing his son had reported it and all the usual misper investigations had been done with a negative result. Russell's son Jack had taken over the business and it was still operating.

It had been established due to the decomposition of Russell's body that he had been in the water for at least four months. The divers had continued the search for another two days after the second body had been found. The industrial pump had virtually drained the pond, and the fish had been collected by the owner of another private lake nearby, who had arranged for holding tanks to be brought in to house the fish until the search had been completed.

The officers had then sifted through the mud and found both of Mrs Calder's shoes, plus a machete, although that had been in the pond for a considerable amount of time as it was rusted right through in places and they were confident it had no connection with either of the current murders, but it was still being examined by the forensics team with the possibility that it may be connected to something else.

Clearly there were other 'illegal' forces trying to find the person or persons responsible for the murder of Elizabeth Calder. Kevin Doyle had been severely beaten, and almost killed, they believe by Martin Conner, although Doyle was still insisting he'd fallen down his stairs having drunk too much. But it was known that Conner had bought Mrs Calder's jewellery, probably from Kevin Doyle and had sold it to Solly Bergmann. The police in a routine check had recovered certain items matching the list that Tony Pitman had given them. And Conner had been identified as the seller in footage from the security tape seized from the jeweller's shop.

Conner had injured a police officer following his attempted arrest, and he'd escaped from his home address, but following a tip-off, he'd recently been found in a commercial skip around the back of an industrial estate. The word *grass* had been branded onto his back and his hands had been welded together. He was currently under arrest and waiting for a skin-grafting operation.

Doyle was still too weak to be officially interviewed, although as yet they had no actual evidence against him, but he was suspected of originally selling the jewellery to Conner. The question was, did he take the jewellery from her dead body or was Doyle involved in the actual killing and disposal of the body?

There was also the fact that although Mrs Calder had apparently been missing for almost a week, her disappearance hadn't been reported, and John Calder had subsequently been brought in for questioning, although nothing had been forthcoming from the interview. It was clear however, to all and sundry, that he had been deeply fond of his wife and although he claimed to have had his own reasons which were 'personal' as to why he hadn't involved the police, no evidence had been found that could implicate him in anyway, and his solicitor had had him released very swiftly after the interview.

Members of staff from Calder's clubs and businesses had also been interviewed including Tony Pitman, but as it stood, there was nothing to implicate any of the staff in any way, and again it was blatantly clear that they had all been very fond of Mrs Calder. Seemingly on paper she didn't appear to have an enemy in the world. So why was she kidnapped and murdered then and by whom? It didn't seem likely that it would have been just for her jewellery.

Detective Inspector Chris White stared at the listings and the photographs on the whiteboards, willing himself to find a connection that would drive the case forward, but as yet there were no significant leads for them to follow.

They suspected that Pitman, or members of Calder's 'staff,' had been responsible for the injuries to Conner but Conner wasn't saying a word, and nothing had been gained from the interviews with those they suspected of being involved. Conveniently, they'd all been playing cards around Calder's house in an attempt to cheer themselves up following the loss of their boss's wife and her rather grand funeral, and in essence, each had given the other an alibi.

They were currently looking into Calder's business affairs and checking bank details, phone records and holding companies to see if there was a link that would provide them with answers. They also had uniform currently making a round of all the local bookies to see if Clive Russell owed money and had also taken away his home computer to see if he was into online gambling and also checking his bank accounts.

It was a slow, time consuming procedure, but as yet they had very little to go on, so they had to check out every angle they could think of and it all took time.

Chapter Twenty-Seven

Pitman rendezvoused with his crew nine minutes later; he parked up behind Johnnie's van which was about twenty metres away from the front entrance to the flats, and walked up to the driver's window to speak to him. Johnnie wound down his window and explained that Stevie was round the back of the property keeping obs from there.

"OK, good work. Right well I've got a description of Finch's girlfriend. She's twenty-three, about five-two, slim and wears very short skirts …"

"Yeah bring it on!" Johnnie said brightly.

"*And*," Pitman continued, "parts of her hair are pink."

"Pink?" Johnnie asked pulling a face. "Oh well, she should be easy to spot then. So are we going in now then to check?"

"In a bit yeah, I just want to update Stevie." Pitman took out his mobile and called Steve.

Stevie answered almost as the phone rang. "Yeah boss, what's happening?"

"Johnnie and me are going in in a minute. You alright there?"

"Yeah sweet, there's only the one door out the back and I've got that covered."

"I'll prank you when we're outside his flat. And keep your eye out for Finch's bird. She's early twenties, 'bout five-two, wears short skirts and parts of her hair are pink."

Stevie grinned, "Can't wait. Speak to you soon." He disconnected the call and started to limber up and flex his muscles.

"You know you said his bird had pink hair, well don't turn round, but she's just getting out of a cab with bags of shopping. It's gotta be her."

"OK, well let me know when the cab's gone and we'll follow her into the block and take it from there."

"Cab's just leaving now; she's walking up the driveway to the entrance."

Pitman turned and started to follow. "OK, let Stevie know and then catch me up." Pitman hurried after the girl who was indeed wearing a very short skirt and who had bright pink ends to her hair.

She struggled to open the door laden down with her shopping. Pitman opened the door and held it for her.

"Thanks," she said nodding and walked away towards the lift.

"D'you want a hand?" Pitman asked following her towards the lift.

"No I'm alright now," she said as she noticed Johnnie enter the front door. She turned away and walked quickly towards the lifts and hit the button, the doors opened and she stepped inside, so did Pitman, who held the door open for Johnnie. Johnnie stood in the entrance to the lift stopping the doors from closing.

"Hello Jade," Pitman said and smiled at her.

Jade tilted her head back and sighed. "Oh fuck it," she said. "I told him we should have had stuff delivered, but oh no he wouldn't listen." She shook her head. "I ain't part of it. Look," she said, and dumped the bags on the floor. She pulled her hair back from her face and there was a nasty bruise on her cheek spreading right back to her ear. Then she rolled up her sleeve and revealed some angry bruises and then pulled up her top. There were some bright red welts across her flat stomach and across her ribs. "He did that to me. We had a God Almighty row about all this." She let go of her top and pulled her sleeve back down. "It freaked me out big time when he told me and I told him to turn himself into the police or tell whoever he needed to tell. I had nothing to do with it honest. First I knew about it was when he came back to his flat, and he was in a right old state. Said a job had gone tits up big time and they'd killed some woman. I couldn't believe what he was saying to me! Jesus I didn't want any part of something like that, and I told him I couldn't stay and that I wanted nothing more to do with him and he just laid into me. Then he threatened me with all sorts, and threatened to hurt my mum and my sister if I didn't stay or if I told anyone. So what could I do? He's got a right old temper on him when he wants, and he really scared me. I'm sorry if you knew the woman. I'm trapped in the middle of it all and I'm really frightened." She stopped talking and then looked back at Pitman. "Are *you* going to hurt me?" She asked, and then lowered her head and her whole body sagged and Pitman noticed a tear start to roll down her face.

Pitman put his hand on her shoulder and she stiffened, fearing the worst. "No, you're alright love; we're not going to hurt you." She sniffed back her tears and turned into Pitman and hugged him seeking comfort from her ordeal. "It's OK, come on, it's over, we'll deal with him, he won't hurt you anymore. Is he in there?" Pitman asked holding her at arm's length.

Jade nodded, "He was when I left yeah. D'you want the keys to me flat?"

"Be handy if we could." Pitman replied. "Is there just him in there, no one else?"

"Should be, there was another bloke came round the other night, but he didn't stay long. I don't know what happened or what they talked about, he shoved me in the bedroom and locked the door and didn't let me out till he'd gone. He was quite a big bloke though. Had lots of tats and a ring through his eyebrow." She handed over a set of keys. "It's the silver one you have to turn it twice when you put it in."

"You better wait down here then love." Pitman said handing her her shopping.

"I don't want to wait here. I don't want to see him ever again I told you that and I meant it. Look when you've finished, could you drop the keys in me letter box on the wall just over there, number fourteen, and I'll come back later. I want to go and see me mum and me sister and make sure they're alright."

"Yeah will do, and thanks for the keys and you take care, and don't worry about you or your family, nothing's going to happen to them, you got my word on it. And I'll pop the keys in your letter box when we've finished. And here are," Pitman fished out a twenty pond note and handed it to her. "Get yourself a cab, go on, scoot." He nodded that the conversation was over and Jade thanked him and then he turned to Johnnie. "Let Stevie know we're on our way up."

Jade held the door back with her foot and struggled out of the entrance and made her way back down the path towards the kerb. She stopped and put some of the shopping down and took out her mobile and called a cab. Johnnie updated Steve that they had the keys and that Jade was on her way out, and she wasn't anything to do with it. Johnnie yelled out that that was a shame as she had fucking gorgeous legs, then Pitman pressed the button and the doors to the lift closed and the lift started to move upwards.

The lift had only just started when Pitman's phone rang. It was Stevie.

"Tone!" He yelled, "He's come out the back and he's cut me, he's gone over a fence into someone's garden!"

"Shit! How bad you hurt, Stevie?" Pitman demanded punching the button for the ground floor.

"It's a slash more than anything. He just came out the door full pelt swinging this bloody great kitchen knife at me. I want expecting that Tone, sorry."

"Can you see him?" The lift stopped at the next floor and Pitman jabbed at the button again and the doors closed and the lift started to make its way back down to the ground floor.

There was a pause, then Stevie said, "I've just climbed over the fence, and I've just seen him go over the back one, it looks like it's a service road that runs alongside the back of the flats. It probably comes out near Baker's Road I think."

The lift doors opened and Pitman and Johnnie barged out into the entrance. "Johnnie'll pick you up in the van; I'll try and cut him off down the end of Baker's Road. You sure you're alright?" He asked fishing his car keys out of his pocket and slamming out of the doors to the flats and running back to his car.

"Yeah I'm alright, stings like a bastard though. He'll fucking pay for that when we catch up with him!"

"Amen to that," Pitman said flinging his mobile onto the passenger seat and settling himself behind the wheel. He slammed the car door, fired up the engine, rammed it into reverse and then sped forward down the road leaving tyre marks on the road behind him.

He watched Johnnie through his rear-view mirror jump into the van, spin it round and take off in the opposite direction to pick up Stevie. Pitman went back to concentrating, it was never a good idea to speed like a lunatic in a built-up area, there were too many things to look out for and his senses were on full alert.

Pitman was watching for movement in the service road running opposite to where he was driving, and trying to watch the road ahead, when a red car indicated and without checking that the road was clear, moved out in front of him.

"Fucking hell!" he yelled and swerved and slammed on his brakes. He missed the car by a matter of inches and the driver whoever he or she was, had the audacity to beep their horn at him! He hit the accelerator again and powered off in search of Toke, who by now had probably been alerted by the squealing of tyres and the beeping horn, and had more than likely gone to ground to wait it out. *That's what I would have done* Pitman thought.

Pitman slowed down as he reached the end of the road and then stopped and waited at the junction looking left and right. No sign of Finch. Pitman turned left and turned down the service road, he was pleased to see right at the other end of it, a white Transit slowly moving towards him, which he suspected was Johnnie.

Knowing his boys had the top end covered, Pitman turned off the engine and got out of his car and locked it. He began trying garage doors and garden gates, trying to flush Finch out. If he was here they needed to find him or where he went next would be anyone's guess.

Twenty minutes later they'd called it a day and abandoned the search. Finch had got lucky this time but his luck was running out and sooner or later they'd find him and the longer it took; the worse it would be for him.

Pitman had given Stevie an address of a practice nurse called Sue who always seemed to have enough bits and pieces at home to help a wounded army, and he'd called Sue up and told her to expect Stevie. He'd bunged Stevie a fifty to give to her and then they'd parted company and Pitman had returned to Calder's to make sure he was OK. Calder still had a long way to go to come to terms with his loss and he was having some very bad depressions lately where his temper was quick to fire up and no one, not even Pitman was exempt from Calder's wrath.

They still had Toke's address and they would hit his pad in the early hours of the morning, and if that didn't work, they now knew where his brother worked. And if enough pressure was brought to bear, Pitman was confident his brother would talk. Either that or he'd have to develop a taste for hospital food, because that's where he'd end up if he didn't.

Pitman had sworn to get revenge on everyone involved in Lizzie's murder and he wasn't the sort of man who gave up easily, especially when it involved someone he had thought such a lot of. It didn't matter how big the world was, he'd find them and they'd regret the day they were born, and that was a given!

Chapter Twenty-Eight

When Marvin had come to, he'd taken one look at Dave Carson and gone into panic mode. Although he was hurting himself, his injuries were nothing compared to Carson's. Carson's face was wrecked and he was still bleeding, but the worrying thing was, he was having difficulty breathing.

Marvin picked up Carson's mobile and scrolled down until he found Talbot's number; he hesitated for a moment and then came to a decision, and pressed the call button.

Talbot was sat in his office working when the phone rang. "How's it going, I was rather hoping you'd have phoned me before this with some news?" Talbot said irritably.

"It's Marv, Mr Talbot, not Dave."

"What *you* phoning me for? You put that lazy bastard on the phone I wanna speak to him right now!" Talbot bellowed, pissed off that Carson had had his lackey phone him instead of himself.

"I, I can't," Marvin stammered, "he's hurt, *we're* hurt," he added quickly.

"What you talking about, you're hurt? If this is some kind of joke …"

Marvin interrupted him, "It's not, it's not, no! Pitman was here asking questions, and he's beat the shit out of

Carson, he really needs an ambulance. He can hardly breathe. There's blood everywhere …"

"Alright, alright," Talbot said cutting in, "Let me think about this for a minute. What was Pitman asking questions about?"

"He beat me up a bit and I pretended to be out so I could listen, he asked about Finch and Toke …"

"Oh Holy Christ," Talbot groaned and he stood. "What did Carson tell him?"

Marvin had nothing to lose now, he was tied into Talbot like it or not. "He told him about borrowing them two off Tommy Reardon. He told him Tommy didn't know nothing about it, and he gave him Toke's address and told him where his brother worked. Pitman already knew Finch and Toke did it; he just hadn't been able to find 'em."

Talbot was fuming he started to pace up and down. "I warned him! I fucking knew this would happen and it would all come back to bite me on the fucking arse!"

"Carson's real bad Mr Talbot, he's still bleeding."

"Serves him fucking right!" Talbot replied. There was a pause as Talbot stopped to think. "OK, OK, here's what you do. Trash the place up a bit, and then call the police and an ambulance. Say you'd both been out testing a motor, say it looked like it had something wrong with it and when you came back, there was a gang of hoodies in the office knocking the place over and they attacked you. Make sure Carson sticks to the same story, I don't want the filth coming in my direction, I've got too much at stake to have them making fucking waves on my patch. So you got that straight then, have you? Gang of hoodies trashing the place? Now call an ambulance and get yourself checked over an' all. But do not mention

Pitman's name to anyone about this. He was never there. You got that?"

"Yes," Marvin replied, "I got that." He hung up and made a promise to himself that he would meet up again with Pitman and then he'd show him that he was definitely up to the job.

Marvin went over to the shelves and reached up to pull the box files down from the shelf and the pain in his ribs hit him hard and took his breath away. "Damn you Pitman you motherfucker!" He groaned holding his side. "I am gonna have your white arse you better believe it!" He tucked his elbow into his side and reached up with his other hand and pulled the files down off the shelf and scattered the contents around on the floor, then he picked up Carson's phone and called for an ambulance and the police. He then sat down and started to go over his story one more time to make sure he'd got it right. Now was not the time to piss Talbot off, and with Carson going to be out of play for some time, you never know, he might step up a peg or two, he'd have to wait and see how it all panned out.

Chapter Twenty-Nine

Jade had brooded and brooded over what to do. She knew it was Carson that Kev had done the job for and where was he when they'd needed him? Nowhere that's where. He'd dropped them like a hot coal when the job had gone wrong. She knew Kevin had phoned him time and time again and he'd never once answered his phone. That wasn't right, that wasn't fair.

OK Kevin hadn't been the best of boyfriends, especially when he didn't get his own way, but when he was sober, he was always up for a laugh and he could be great company, and there was a time when she began to think he might be The One. But then he had taken up with that lowlife waster Harry Toke, and within a few short weeks he'd changed big time.

Kevin started going out more and more with Toke, leaving her at home and he'd come back late at night, more often than not, the worse for wear and then he'd want sex. If it was late and she'd already gone to bed, he'd wake her up, usually by opening her mouth and sticking his cock in it. Mr Finch was not the most romantic of lovers she'd ever had. But when he was flush, he always liked to treat her and they'd had some great days away and some great meals out.

If only Harry bloody Toke hadn't come along and introduced him to Carson, and if only they hadn't gone on that last job together, if, if, bloody if! It perhaps wouldn't have been so bad if Carson had stuck by them and tried to help them and sort things out, then maybe it would all have been different? But she'd never know now. Kevin had been involved in something that had led to a woman's death and she could never forgive him for that, nor could she forgive him for attacking her when she'd argued the toss with him about what he should do, no he was history now, you make your bed and you lie in it, but she still wanted to get her own back on Carson.

Then the idea came to her as she was washing up the dishes, and when she'd finished the chore, she'd dried her hands, then taken the top off the bottle of washing-up liquid and drained it into a jug and put the jug back on the draining board. Then she'd opened the storage cupboard in the hall, and having rooted about moving various tins of paint and oil and anti-freeze for the car, she found what she'd been looking for. A tin of paint remover. She closed the cupboard and went back into the kitchen and opened the can and carefully poured the contents into the washing-up bottle. She put the squeezy top back on and then went and changed into some dark clothes.

She left the flat and went downstairs with the bottle in the jacket pocket of her hoodie. She unlocked the bike store and wheeled her bike out. She made sure her lights were working properly and then she cycled away.

Fourteen minutes later she stopped and dragged her bike behind a large van that was parked in front of a small row of garages. She pulled her hoodie up and pulled her scarf across the lower part of her face and checked that there was no one about, and then she bent over slightly and adopted a limp, all the time making sure she was never facing the CCTV cameras that were strategically placed around the site of Top Class Cars.

When she was certain there was no one around, she took the container from her pocket and began making her way around the lot, squirting the paint remover over all the bonnets and boots of the cars. She'd targeted twenty-five cars before the container had run out. She looked back at her handiwork; the paint on some of the cars was already starting to react. The paint was scrunching up and bubbling, serves you bloody right she thought. I can't hurt you physically but I can still hurt you financially and cause you an awful lot of grief and inconvenience. Yeah well, serves you right.

Satisfied she shoved the empty container back in her pocket, and still bent over and limping, she left the lot and returned to her bike. She kept her hood up and cycled home, feeling strangely buoyant and happy, knowing she'd at least achieved some small victory for both herself and Kev.

She locked her bike back in the store and went back upstairs to her flat. It would seem strange not having Kevin around anymore; they'd been going out for almost a year. But that's life, as one door closes and all that. She hung her hoodie on the coat pegs by the door, feeling a small twinge of regret when she remembered Kevin putting them up for her all those months ago. They'd had such a job to keep the pegs all in a line, which wasn't helped by the fact they kept falling about laughing when their neighbour had banged on the wall complaining about the noise of all the drilling, and that had caused a big lump of plaster to fall off the wall. She could still see where Kev had filled in the hole and painted over it, the colour never did quite match the original, but usually his coat covered the mark but not anymore.

Just something else for her to get used to. She took the top off the container and rinsed it thoroughly and then poured the washing-up liquid back into the bottle and replaced it back on the window sill. It was if nothing at all had happened, but you could bet your life Carson would notice the difference when he turned up for work the next day.

Although unbeknown to Jade, he wouldn't return to work for close on two months, having had to have extensive and very costly dental treatment to replace and repair his broken teeth and repairs made to correct and straighten his broken nose and jaw. His business also collapsed due to the majority of cars not being insured whilst they were on the lot waiting to be sold. What goes around comes around; maybe he should have thought of that ...

Chapter Thirty

Pitman was on his mobile to Kenny.

"I've got a name for you. Clive Russell. His was the other body in the pond. Been there about four months or so. Right bodge job from what I've heard. They cut his hands off so there wouldn't be any fingerprints, and then left his wallet with all his credit cards and driver's licence in his jacket pocket. What a bunch of fucking muppets!" He grinned at the thought.

"I know the name. Bit of a gambler. Does building work, that right?"

"Used to yeah, his boy reported him missing and took the business over."

"You don't think the boy was involved in some way, do you?"

"That's not what I've heard. Russell was a betting man like you said, and he was always getting in deeper than he could afford. You know the type, one more hand, one more throw of the dice whatever, and then suddenly you're collecting markers from all and sundry. I heard a buzz someone called one in for a fair old wedge."

"Whose name was on it?"

"It's not verified, but I heard it was Reardon."

"Reardon? No that don't sit right. He's usually much too clever to show out like that. There's got to be more to it than that. We all know Reardon ain't the Pope, and yeah he's had some people sorted over the years, but I've never heard of him having someone taken out, especially not for a gambling debt.

"As I said, it's not official, that came from another source."

"You think it could have been Finch and Toke that done him?"

"No names have been put to it yet, but it's possible. You know what a couple of fucking clowns them two are. I mean just look at the cock-up with Mrs C. Christ sorry Tone, that sounded a bit off, I didn't mean anything ..."

Pitman cut in, "It's alright, don't sweat it. Still no word about Finch or Toke?"

"I'm still on it. I heard you nearly had Finch at his bird's place and that Stevie got sliced. He alright?"

"Yeah, his pride was hurt more than the cut. He feels bad that he let me down. We came that fucking close to bagging him. We had a good old search about but he got lucky and went to ground and we couldn't flush him out. Toke ain't answering his phone but we knew he had a place on Greenslades Estate, and Davie-Boy went down for a sniff about and little Cindy, Craig's eldest daughter came through with Toke's address, so we'll be paying him a little visit about three o'clock in the morning."

"Good luck with that, and I'll keep me ear to the ground about Finch. He's bound to surface sooner or later and someone will tip us the wink."

"Right well thanks again, Kenny, keep on it, talk to you later."

"Yeah be lucky, Tone." Kenny disconnected the call and went back inside the pub.

Chapter Thirty-One

Finch had been in touch with Toke and told him Pitman was onto them and how close he'd been to getting caught by Pitman. It was only the fact that Finch had been looking out for Jade to come back from shopping, that he'd seen the taxi pull away and then he'd recognised Pitman coming up behind her and then another bloke had got out of a van that was parked there. He'd only had a few minutes to shove some stuff into a backpack and make a run for it and he'd slashed another one of Pitman's boys who'd been waiting for him at the rear entrance to the flats.

This had freaked Toke out. He knew what a mad bastard Pitman could be and it was now common knowledge what had happened to Conner and both Finch and Toke were shitting themselves. Toke had put on a beanie hat and glasses to help disguise himself and had gone to a pub to meet a man he'd heard about who he hoped would be able to help him.

The man's name was Agile and it was rumoured he used to be some kind of acrobat and he could backflip and spin and Christ knows what else, but his greatest claim to fame was that he could supply you with whatever you wanted, whenever you wanted it, if you had the bread up front. He was a fixer and one of the best in the business.

The man nodded once at Toke and left the bar. Toke didn't rush out after him; instead he calmly finished his drink and then strolled out of the pub in an easy carefree manner, as if he had all the time in the world and not a care in the world.

Yeah right.

Toke left the pub and turned left and entered the car park. He spotted Agile leaning against the wall of the landlord's garage and walked across to meet him, all the time looking around anxiously.

Toke stopped a few feet away from the man, "Are you …"

Agile interrupted him before he'd finished, "No fucking names man!"

"Sorry," Toke offered.

The man moved in close. "Turn and face the wall and hold your arms out straight and spread your legs." It was not a request.

"What?" Toke began to say but Agile grabbed him and spun him round and shoved him hard against the wall, pressing Toke's face against the brickwork."

"Just do as your fucking told man!" He pulled Toke's right arm out straight and Toke volunteered his left arm and dutifully spread his legs. This was no time to argue. The man hopefully had something he was after.

Agile ran his hands expertly along both of Toke's arms and then up and down his legs and patted him all over his body. Agile then grabbed Toke's hat and pulled it off and looked inside. Satisfied he shoved the hat back into Toke's hand.

"Undo your coat and pull up your shirt." Agile said.

"What?" Toke asked confused.

Agile braced himself for action locking eyes with Toke almost daring him to challenge him. "Just do it," he said.

Toke undid his coat and untucked his shirt and pulled it up.

"And the back," Agile ordered.

Toke did as he was asked and then suddenly cottoned on. "Fuck me you think I'm wired, don't ya! You've gotta be fucking mental, why would I do that!" Toke tucked his shirt back in after Agile had finished checking him over.

"I don't know you personally. We have a mutual friend and that's the only reason I'm even speaking to you. And I ain't stayed out of the slammer by taking chances.

"Yeah I got that, no sweat. Sorry," he offered as an afterthought.

Agile nodded and then cast a brief look around the car park. "Our mutual friend said you had some heavy people leaning on you, that right?"

"Something like that yeah," Toke answered grudgingly.

"Anything or anyone I should know about? Cos I don't want no one knocking on my door in the early hours, you dig?"

"No you're OK. It's an old score between me and this geezer, and I just want to level up the odds a bit, that's all."

Agile studied the man for almost thirty seconds and then he nodded and walked away.

Toke stood there uncertain as to whether he should follow or not.

Agile arrived at the rear of a large dark Audi and popped the boot. He turned and inclined his head for Toke to join him. Toke looked around and then hurried over and joined Agile at the opened boot. He looked inside and let out a gasp. The inside of the boot contained foam lined cases all complete with different types of guns.

"Fucking hell!" Toke said reaching inside the boot.

Agile grabbed his hand and twisted it.

"Aw shit!" Toke cried out. Agile still held Toke's hand in a weird grip that had Toke up on his toes fearful that his wrist would be snapped if he dared to move.

"*You* never touch the merchandise. *I* show you. You dig?"

"Yeah, yeah!" Toke said nodding his head furiously up and down. Agile released his grip and Toke stood back and massaged his sore wrist.

"What type of thing you looking for?" Agile asked.

Toke shook his head, he was nervous. He looked back in the boot at the merchandise. "I dunno, I don't know much about guns."

"You ever fired a gun before?"

"Me? Christ no! Only a pellet rifle when I was about twelve years old and that's it." Toke ran the back of his hand across his lips. His mouth had gone dry.

"Are you looking to waste someone or fuck 'em up for a bit or just scare 'em? You need to give me some idea of what you wanna do. Especially as you don't know your way around guns. So what d'you wanna do man?"

Toke thought for a moment. Agile kept one hand on the lid of the boot ready to slam it down if someone came along, and waited for Toke to reply.

"It might be all three. I just dunno see. I'm in a dodgy situation and I don't know what the outcome's gonna be. Just give me something that's easy to use that I ain't gonna shoot meself with, that can keep the other fuckers away. You got anything like that?"

Agile pulled a face. He didn't like supplying guns to amateurs and he was rather reluctant to get involved, this fucker better have the cash on him or I might be using one of the guns on him myself he thought.

The whole thing was freaking Toke out. He thought the guy might have a couple of guns in a holdall or a carrier bag or something, not loads of 'em all laid out in special foam-lined cases. This was serious shit and he knew he was way out of his depth. But he knew Pitman would keep searching and sooner or later he'd find Finch or himself and he knew that day wasn't too far off and he wanted to be ready and have half a chance when the time came. It was up to Finch what he did. He knew that once Pitman nabbed Finch, he would give him up; Finch had a very low threshold for pain which wasn't much use against a man like Pitman. They'd shown photos in the press of what had happened to Conner although as yet the cops hadn't arrested anyone over it, but the word on the street, was that it was the work of Pitman and his crew, and Conner didn't even have anything to do with killing the woman. So what the hell did Calder and Pitman have in mind for him and Finch he wondered, but whatever it was, it would be painful and more than likely end in disablement or death. He had to make a decision and fast to even things up before it was too late.

"Have you got something that can fire single shots and then like fire automatically?" Toke asked, feeling that he hadn't made a particularly good job of trying to explain himself.

Agile looked at Toke weighing him up, sod it, we're here now he thought let's get it done, get my money and get out of here.

Agile reached inside the boot and took out a black pistol. "Beretta 9 mm, made in Italy and used by the American Military." He racked the slide forwards. "When you rack the slide like that, you put a round into the chamber so it's ready to fire. Single shot or semi-automatic. Holds fifteen in a clip, double stacked, direct feed, less chance of jamming. There's a bit of a kick on it so you need to hold the gun with both hands. Otherwise you won't hit a damn thing unless it's two feet in front of you. You hold it like this to control the recoil." Agile took a quick look around and then demonstrated holding the gun with one hand and the other hand supporting the hand underneath. He stood with his legs slightly apart and braced his legs. He turned back to Toke. "This is the safety lever. When it's pointing down like that the gun won't fire. When you turn the lever up into this position, you'll see a red dot displayed just there. Can you see that?" He turned the gun on its side to show Toke.

Toke nodded, desperately trying to remember everything that Agile was telling him. It could be the difference between life and death if he got it wrong.

Agile continued. "The gun's empty at the moment, I've got fully loaded clips for it so it's not a problem. Now the trigger has a second pull on it. You squeeze it once, and it's quite hard and then as you keep the pressure on it goes into its second phase and continues through to actually fire. First phase, second phase." Agile pulled the trigger and there was a metallic click. "Had the gun been loaded a single bullet would have fired then." Agile held the gun on its side. "See there," he indicated where he meant, "those marks are where the serial number's been ground off, and it's never been fired, so it's clean and untraceable. And that means, should the shit hit the fan, you didn't get the piece from me. Is that clear?" He asked strongly.

Toke nodded enthusiastically. "Yeah, yeah, I wouldn't …"

Agile grabbed Toke behind the head and raised the gun and held it inches from Toke's face. "That's right my friend, you wouldn't fucking dare because you'd be dead!" He released Toke, "Just so long as you're clear on that point. Right anything else you wanna know?"

"No," Toke said totally overwhelmed by events, "price," he mumbled. "How much is it?"

Agile reached down inside the boot and replaced the gun in its case and as he started to straighten up, Toke grabbed the boot lid and slammed it down hard on his head. Toke raised the lid and brought it crashing down again on Agile who was laid across the open boot. Toke smashed the lid down a third time and Agile slipped backwards down onto the ground. Toke reached inside and lifted up the case containing the Beretta. Nestled inside the case alongside the gun, were three clips of bullets.

"Fucking result," Toke said grinning for the first time. He looked around and checked it was clear. He then helped himself to two more guns, bigger guns in cases, he didn't have a clue what they were called or how they worked but there was always a market for guns and maybe he could buy some protection and arm them up himself. He was just about to leave when Agile groaned and started to come round. Toke lifted the gun case and smashed it down on Agile's head and he collapsed unconscious in a heap. Toke then went through the man's pockets; fuck it, in for a penny! Agile had close to three grand in his wallet. Toke helped himself to the money and then grabbed Agile under his arms and rested him on the edge of the boot. He then bent down and grabbed Agile's legs and shoved him into the boot and slammed the lid closed.

Job done.

Now I need to get out of here and sort out what to do next Toke thought to himself. He knew a few hard cases but whether or not they wanted to go up against Calder and Pitman, well, that was a different story, but it was worth a few phone calls to find out, especially as he could now equip them with firepower. Toke had a final look around and then walked over to the far side of the car park where he'd parked his old Focus behind a plumber's van. He unlocked it and shoved the other two guns in the boot and then pulled out an old raincoat he kept in there for emergencies, and put the Beretta on the passenger seat of the car and covered it with the coat. He thought about stopping to load the gun there and then, whilst he hopefully could still remember what he'd been told, but then decided the risk was too great and he started the car and drove slowly out of car park, now seemingly armed to the teeth and ready to do battle. Bring it on then, I'll be fucking waiting for you Pitman!

Chapter Thirty-Two

At ten to three, Johnnie's van and Pitman's Beemer set off for Greenslades Estate. At seven minutes past three Pitman parked on the corner of Toke's road and Johnnie parked six houses down from Toke's house. They sat and kept obs for ten minutes. No lights came on, and they saw no one. The estate was sleeping.

Pitman phoned Johnnie. It was answered immediately. "Yes boss."

"Right, Stevie and me will take the front of the house, you and Davey-Boy take the back. On my go you put the door in and we'll all come in at the same time. You take the ground floor, we'll take the stairs. Is everybody set?" Pitman asked, the familiar adrenalin rush starting to build before the action commenced.

There were various assents and yeses from the crew and then Pitman pulled on his balaclava. Stevie followed suit. "You ready?" Pitman asked checking his cosh and pulling on a pair of thin leather gloves.

Stevie nodded and picked up the heavy metal battering ram. He left it on the seat, opened the door, climbed out and then retrieved the ram, nudging the door closed with his elbow. Pitman got out the car and secured it. They stayed still for a moment checking there was no one out walking a dog or late night revellers staggering home, and satisfied it was all clear; they made their way towards Toke's house.

Two minutes later the four of them had assembled outside the front hedge of the house next door.

"We'll give you thirty seconds to get round the back and then I'll prank you and then let's hit it and get it done. Any questions guys?"

There were none.

"Just don't kill him, we want him still breathing when we take him back. Right get going." He nodded towards Johnnie and Davey-Boy and they crept quietly down the shared driveway and disappeared around the back of the house.

Pitman and Steve made their way up to the front door. As luck would have it, the house had a small open porch at the front of the house. That would shield them a bit from the neighbours and the nearest street lamp was about thirty yards away, so it was fairly dark where they were. Pitman took out his mobile ready to prank Johnnie and get things started when his phone started to ring.

"Fucking hell!" Pitman said almost dropping the phone he'd been so surprised at receiving a call. He beckoned to Steve to join him at the side of the porch and answered the phone when he noticed it was from Kenny. "You don't half choose your fucking moments Kenny my old lad," Pitman said, and then there was a series of loud bangs followed by parts of the front door disintegrating and flying off in all directions.

"Jesus Christ!" Pitman yelled, "Leg it, leg it!" And he and Stevie broke into a run.

Stevie somehow managed to hang onto the battering ram and wrangle his mobile out of his pocket. He hit the speed dial and Johnnie's phone started to vibrate. Stevie and Pitman continued running back towards their car.

"Johnnie, Johnnie!" Stevie yelled, "get outta there! Toke's tooled up and he's just blasted fucking great holes in the front door! Meet you back at the bosses, go, go, go!" Stevie cut the call and shoved the phone back in his pocket.

Pitman and Stevie arrived at the car at the same time as lights started going on in houses close by. Pitman pressed the fob and the car unlocked and Stevie opened the rear door and shoved the ram on the back seat and jumped in. Pitman slide in and fired up the engine and keeping the lights turned off, gunned the motor down the street and away. Both of them ripped their balaclavas off and stowed them under the seats.

Pitman slowed as he came to the next junction and then dropped his speed right down as he turned right. He pressed the button for hands free and called Kenny back.

Kenny answered straight away. "You alright, Tone? What the fuck was that?"

"Toke was tooled up. He blew the fucking front door away."

"Jesus, you alright?" Kenny asked concerned.

"Apart from the buzzing in me ears, yeah. Wait out." He turned to Stevie, "Get Johnnie on the blower make sure they're alright."

Stevie pulled out his phone and hit the speed dial again. Pitman resumed his call with Kenny.

"So it's a bit late for social chit-chat, so I assume you've got some good news for me?"

There was a slight pause. "Well yes and no really," he replied.

Pitman heard sirens and pulled into the kerb between two cars and turned off the engine. He turned and gestured to Stevie to drop down out of sight and he too slid down on his seat until neither of them could be seen by any passing vehicles. The sirens grew louder and then two police vehicles, with their lights flashing and sirens wailing went flying past. When they were out of sight, Pitman started the car and eased out and began driving again, this time he switched his lights on.

"You were saying?" he said to Kenny.

Kenny sighed. "Yeah, well it's not a lot of use to you now. I was ringing to let you know that Toke had got hold of some guns …"

"Definitely a bit fucking late then!" he said lightly.

"Sorry, Tone I'd only just got word."

"So where'd he get 'em from then?"

"Oh mate you are not going to believe this …"

"Try me," Pitman said interrupting.

"He blagged them off Agile."

"You're kidding me!" Pitman replied taken aback. He never would have thought that Agile would have sold guns to a lowlife like Toke to use against him.

"Hold your horses, Tone, it wasn't like that. Age's been on holiday for nearly three weeks, how the other half live, that's what I say; anyway he had no knowledge of what's been going on. So cut a long story short. Turns out, Toke's uncle knows him, seems their dads used to work together years ago, and Toke got in touch with him. Now this is the best bit. Agey shows him a nine mill, and when he's reaching into the boot to put the gun back, Toke only slams the boot lid down on him. Oh not once, but three or four times, then nicks some guns, robs his wallet and dumps poor old Agey in the boot and pisses off!

Unbelievable. He'd still be in there now if he hadn't had his phone with him. Luckily, he called Marley up and he came and got him out. 'Cos then he had to take him up the hospital to get some stitches put in his head. And he is fuming and when I say *fuming*, I mean fucking look out, the man is on fire!"

"Right well we know for certain Tokey-Boy's got some shooters now, so if he wants a fucking war, we'll give him one."

Stevie tapped Pitman on the arm.

"Hang on Kenny." He turned to Stevie.

"They're alright they're going the long way back, cos the feds are all over the place."

Pitman nodded. "OK, good." He then resumed his conversation with Kenny. "I'm just thinking, seems Toke's place is crawling with cops so he may well be getting nicked even as we speak. Put the word out I want to know what's happening, just keep me up to date."

"Yeah will do Tone, and I'm sorry I couldn't have got to you sooner. And it goes without saying that Agey said he wouldn't have sold the gun if he knew it was someone going up against you and he wants you to know that."

"I already do Kenny, tell him not to sweat it and if there's anything I can do, just let me know. Right I'm signing off I'm almost back at the ranch now, later."

"Yeah thanks, Tone."

Pitman cut the call and a few seconds later he pulled up onto Calder's driveway and turned off the engine. "Put the ram back in the garage in the pit and get yourself back home. You alright?"

"Yeah, yeah, bit of a strange one really, not exactly what we had in mind was it?" He smiled and Pitman joined in.

161

"You can fucking say that again," he said and patted Stevie on the shoulder as he made his way past with the ram heading for the garage. Pitman sighed and made his way to the front door wondering what Calder would make of the balls-up when he gave him a breakdown of the evening's events? The upside was, none of Pitman's crew had been injured and they now knew that Toke had some serious fire power so they wouldn't be caught on the hop next time.

Chapter Thirty-Three

The next evening the local papers were full of the news of the shooting. A police spokesman said they were interested in speaking to Harry Toke whose house had been at the centre of the shooting which had taken place in the early hours of the morning. They didn't believe that Mr Toke had been injured, but they were anxious to speak with him. If anyone had any information regarding last night's incident or the actual whereabouts of Mr Toke, they were advised to call the following numbers. They also warned the public not to approach the man if they saw him, as they believed he could be armed and dangerous but to contact the police immediately.

Meanwhile Stevie had gone down to do a recce on Temple & Moore's in Queens Street. It was a small road off one of the main drags, and it was one of two small businesses that were located about thirty yards apart. Both had large fenced in areas where large lorries could load and unload and access to Temple's yard was easy. The gates were wide open.

Stevie noted that security was basically nonexistent; the business didn't even have security cameras. Stevie watched a van drive into the rear car park and the driver got out and just walked in through a side door of the building. The van belonged to a stationary supplies company and the driver had been holding a few items when he entered. He returned a few minutes later empty-handed, got back into his van and drove out of the yard.

Every now and then employees would come out the back and light up a ciggie, lean against the wall to smoke it and then return to work. Stevie fired up the engine and returned to Calder's to make his report.

Pitman listened to Stevie's report and then phoned Temple & Moore's and asked what time they closed as he wanted to come down and discuss some business regarding new upholstery for the seating on his yacht. He was told they closed at five. Pitman was told to ask for David Reynolds when he came down, who would be only too pleased to assist him with his enquiry. Pitman told the receptionist that he had been recommended by an associate of one of their employees, Jeff Toke and was he working today? The girl, Rita, who wasn't the brightest star in the sky and had always had a soft spot for 'handsome' Jeff, replied that he was. Pitman picked up on her reaction and slipped into social mood and asked if he still had that beat up old VW Beetle he used to drive years ago? Rita replied no he drove a Nissan now. Pitman laughed and asked if it was red, stating that people that drove red cars considered themselves sexy. She laughed along with him and said no it was black and it was always immaculate as it was his pride and joy. Pitman said he probably wouldn't be able to make it down until tomorrow as he still had business to attend to, and then remarked that he was looking forward to meeting her and hung up.

Rita held the phone a moment longer reflecting to herself what a nice man he was, and she wondered what he looked like? Whenever she enjoyed a phone call with a prospective new client, she always tried to imagine what they looked like, to date she had always been wrong but this time she felt she knew that the gentleman would be tall, dark and handsome. She then chastised herself; she'd forgotten to ask his name! Oh well, they didn't get many ad hoc visitors so she would know him the minute he walked into reception and introduced himself she was sure of it.

Fifteen minutes before Temple's were due to close, Pitman, Stevie and Johnnie were parked up in the Transit. It was now sporting magnetic signs proclaiming it to belong to Warner & Sons, builders and decorators. There were some used folded dust sheets stored in the area above the cab and tins of paint and brushes in a plastic container bungee strapped to the side of the van, and a tool box with some basic tools. It didn't hurt to try and look the part. The van was also sporting false number plates. Pitman had quite a few sets courtesy of a scrap metal merchant who owed Pitman a favour. They had been taken from old cars that had long ago been scrapped. They came in handy from time to time, especially when jobs were done in daylight.

Further up the road, Davey-Boy was sitting astride his motor bike having a fag, his helmet rested on the fuel tank of his bike. He finished his ciggie and checked his watch, it was five to. He put his helmet back on.

A few minutes after five, a steady procession of cars, cycles, motorcycles and people began to emerge from the rear car park. At four minutes past five a black Nissan that looked in showroom condition inched its way out into the road and turned right passing in front of their van.

"That's gotta be it," Pitman said hitting the speed dial for Davey-Boy. Davey-Boy answered via his Bluetooth headset. "Our man's just left," Pitman said, "Black Nissan, you can't miss it the shine'll blind ya!" Pitman disconnected and told Stevie to follow but to keep his distance he didn't want to spook the man, not just yet anyway.

Davey-Boy kept a discreet distance, he knew what he was doing, he'd done this countless times before.

After a relatively short journey the Nissan turned into a small estate that ended in a T-junction, the Nissan turned right and drove up the last driveway on the left. The driver never left the car but operated the garage door by remote and the door slid up revealing a neat and tidy interior.

Davey-Boy had stopped and to any idol watcher he was just answering a call on his headset.

"He's home. We're in Tremont Drive. It's a little housing estate off Condor Road. I can't see the number from here, but it's the last house on the left turning right off the T-junction. There's no other car on the driveway. Hang on; he's just come out of the garage going up to the front door. No one's dashed out to meet him with open arms," Davey-Boy grinned, "he's putting his key in and he's in the house and the door's closed. He doesn't seem very bothered by what his brother's been up to. He never looked round once or checked before he went in. Unless he's fucking good at it cos I never clocked him sussing anything out. You don't reckon our boy's in there with him, do ya?"

"Don't think so," Pitman replied, "but you never know. OK, if you can find a quiet corner to keep obs just in case he goes out, fine, if not we're parked up in Regent Street come and r.v. with us."

Davey-Boy affirmed and then cut the call.

Not long to wait now and then the fun would begin all over again Davey-Boy thought.

God he loved his job!

Chapter Thirty-Four

Conner was out on bail and had returned to his home. He'd had some basic surgery done on his hands and they seemed to be healing well, the surgeon had said they would try and arrange for the skin grafting to be done after the trial, which would also give his hands more time to heal and the skin to replenish.

Conner had had his front door repaired and now spent a lot of his time just slobbing around and watching Sky and drinking. His trial was in two months' time, and Conner had considered taking off. He knew a couple of bods out in Spain that ran a bar and a few old muckers of his had done a runner and ended up out there, but he thought the law had changed and you could now be extradited from Spain and brought back to England to stand trial. He'd gone on the Net to the Government website to try and suss it out but it had proved to be so complicated he decided you had to be a lawyer to make any sense of it, so he had given up and was now just biding his time and trying to think of a way out of the situation.

Unbeknown to Conner a solution was coming his way in the shape of Chris Doyle who at that very moment was walking up the path to his front door. It was mid-morning and most of the cars in the road had disappeared, their owners having gone to work hours ago, the area was fairly quiet and the beauty of Conner's flat was, that Conner basically being a lazy individual, had neglected the Leylandii hedge in the front garden that grew at an alarming rate and it now offered quite a nice screen from the road.

Doyle rang Conner's door bell and he heard the chimes sound inside the house. A few moments later he detected a slight movement from behind the curtains, no doubt Conner checking out who was at the door. Chris looked down at his clipboard as if he was checking the name and address and then rang the bell again. He transferred the clipboard to his left hand and waited.

A few more seconds passed and then Conner opened the door.

"Whatever it is you're trying to flog I ain't interested, alright!" he said gruffly and started to close the door.

Chris looked up and said reassuringly, "Mr Conner we have a mutual acquaintance and he's asked me to pass on a message to you."

Conner stopped. What was this all about then he thought? Was this puny little guy going to offer him a job of some sort then? He could do with the money, but there again he always could but if it was heavy stuff he'd have to take it easy, his hands were still a bit sore. But if it was to put the frighteners on someone or recover some money, his sheer size would usually be enough to convince people to pay up, so he was definitely interested. Conner looked both ways down the road and then fully opened the door.

"Better come in then, excuse the mess I've been away. I had a bit of an accident." He stepped back to let the stranger in, "First door on the right."

Doyle walked past him and entered the lounge and Conner closed the front door.

The room was fairly small and stunk of smoke. There was a beat-up old sofa that wouldn't look out of place down the tip and an armchair whose springs were so low the bottom of the chair rested on the floor. The carpet was threadbare in places and the coffee table was cluttered with several old pizza boxes, an overflowing ashtray and lots of empty beer cans. The only possession of any note was the huge flat screen TV that dominated the room and almost covered one whole wall.

Conner moved forward quickly and grabbed some old newspapers off the sofa. "D'you wanna sit?" Doyle shook his head. "No I'm fine this won't take long," he said calmly.

Conner watched as Doyle put his clipboard face down on the table, mainly to disguise the fact that the paperwork on there was a spread sheet from a client he had printed off to make it look a little more authentic to anyone catching a quick glance.

"What's this message you got then?" Conner asked.

"It's from my brother actually." Doyle replied evenly.

"And who's he then when he's at home?" Conner asked.

"His name's Kevin. Kevin Doyle."

It took a few seconds for the name to register with Conner and then he was suddenly aware that the man in front of him was moving and turning. Before Conner had time to react Doyle's perfectly executed spinning back kick slammed into Conner's head and sent him reeling backwards. Doyle came forward and used a front snap kick to connect with Conner right between his legs. Conner fell back against the lounge door clutching his testicles. Doyle was relentless, he attacked Conner with a three punch combination to the face and ended with an inverted punch into Conner's solar plexus, his knuckles went in deep and Conner sank to the floor fighting for breath.

Doyle looked down at the slab of lard bleeding and wheezing beneath him.

"This is what we call, 'a taste of your own medicine.' My brother's lost the sight in his right eye and I won't bore you with all the other injuries you inflicted on him. Hard man that you think you are. Hard man, my arse, you're just a big lump of shit. Come on then, big tough man, one-handed. I'll put one hand behind my back, come on let's see how tough you really are then." Doyle put his left hand behind his back and waited. Blood ran from Connor's nose and mouth and his left eye had started to swell.

Conner looked at the thin man not believing the pain the skinny little runt had inflicted on him and so quickly, and he supported himself on his hands and managed to stand. Christ, his face, head, chest and testicles all hurt and his eye was watering so much he had to blink rapidly to try and keep it clear, but there was no way this little shit was going to hammer him anymore. He was ready now and Conner would end it, one hand behind his back, the cocky little fucker, well he'd soon learn that cocky made you dead.

Conner snatched his jacket off the hook on the back of the door and fumbled the large flick-knife out of the pocket. He saw the man move and he flung his jacket at the man and stepped to the side swinging the knife down in a murderous arch. It hit thin air the man wasn't there. The coffee table reared up and struck Conner knocking him backwards. He fought to keep his balance and clung onto the knife. Conner grinned at the man.

"One-handed you said! Ain't so fucking clever now are ya!" Conner wiped at his eye and watched the man.

With the coffee table out of the way, Doyle now had a clear space in which to fight. Conner constantly flicked the knife around in front of him daring the man to come forward and play. If he tried, it would be the last thing he ever did. Doyle wouldn't be the first man Conner had knifed to death and he probably wouldn't be the last given the nature of his job and the risks it involved.

Doyle set his balance and breathed, preparing himself. He suddenly yelled out a Kiai tightening every muscle in his body and leapt towards Conner. Conner was momentarily thrown by the movement and the shrill noise and slashed out on instinct rather than judgement or defence. Doyle's arm struck the inside of Conner's arm that was holding the knife and directed it away from his body and then Doyle hit Conner with another inverted punch straight into his solar plexus again. As Conner started to crumble from the blow, the arm that had blocked the knife hand was suddenly gripped at the wrist in a ridiculously powerful grip and Conner's wrist bent at an incredible angle and the pain was intense Conner let go of the knife in an instant and then he heard a loud snap and he knew his wrist was broken.

The pain hit Conner and he cried out just as Doyle's elbow came whizzing round in a vicious sweep and smashed into the side of his face shattering his jaw and knocking him out.

Doyle flicked the knife out of harm's way with his foot and calmed his breathing and slowed his adrenalin.

Job done, a promise kept he thought.

Doyle picked up the knife. It was razor sharp and deadly. He looked at the floorboards visible through the hole in the carpet and knelt down on the floor holding the knife. He wriggled the blade inbetween two floor boards and pushed the blade down about four inches and then drove his palm hard against the handle snapping the blade in two.

Doyle picked up an old sweater from the side of the sofa and wiped his prints off the handle of the knife. He stood and looked around remembering if there was anything else in the room he'd touched that he needed to clean. He looked at the huge TV showing someone skiing down a hill in the snow and he walked across to Conner who was lying spark out on the floor blocking the door. Doyle reached down and dragged Conner to one side and went out into the hall. He located the kitchen and grabbed the kettle and filled it with water and returned to the lounge. Conner was still out of it. Doyle went over to the TV and poured some of the contents of the kettle into the back of the TV. The TV sizzled and then went phut and whoosh and the picture and sound went off. Just for good measure, Doyle landed a side-thrust kick into the screen and the TV rocked back into the wall and came off its stand as the screen disintegrated into thousands of small pieces and the TV crashed onto the floor.

Doyle nodded, satisfied.

He walked across to Conner and poured the remainder of the water on his head. Conner spluttered and stirred and then gave out a groan as he tried to focus and move.

Doyle knelt down beside him and lifted his face upwards with his fingers under his chin. Conner cried out in pain. "You ever go anywhere near my brother again and I'll kill you, and you know I can do it.

Sleep tight." Doyle let go of Conner's chin and drove the palm heel of his hand into the side of his face. Conner fell sideways, sparko.

Doyle opened the front door and cleaned his prints off the bell and the door and then flung the sweater back into the hall and pushed the door shut with his foot. Just in case any nosey neighbours were watching, Doyle stood at the front gate and looked at his clipboard, and then at his watch. Decisions, decisions, he ticked a box on the clipboard and then walked back down the road towards where his car was parked three streets away.

That was for you bruv. I've always got your back he mumbled to himself.

Chapter Thirty-Five

Calder was just getting ready to step into the shower when his mobile rang; he cursed and wrapped a towel around himself. It was probably Pitman, he knew he was paying Toke's brother a little visit and the call was more than likely to give him an update.

He picked up his phone and didn't recognise the number, it wasn't Pitman.

"Yeah?" he answered, annoyed now that whoever it was they'd disturbed him.

"Word is you're hunting two of my boys," Reardon said coldly. "I've had the cops round here looking for Toke. So what the fuck's going on? I don't need this shit from you."

"And you can wind your neck back in an' all!" Calder said irritably, "You ain't got a fucking clue what your boys have been up to otherwise you'd have had a visit from me weeks ago!"

"What you on about?" Reardon said smarting from the lecture.

"Two of your muppets, Finch and Toke, kidnapped my missus and then beat her head in, cut her fingers off to get her rings and then dumped her body in Askers pond! So yes you can bet your fucking life I'm looking for 'em!"

Reardon was taken aback. He'd heard about Calder's wife, fortunately he'd been out of the country at the time negotiating for a night club in Ibiza, and he'd only been fed snippets, although he did send a very large bouquet. But he'd never had a clue that any of his team were involved. This changed everything big time. He needed to climb down and eat humble pie or he was in the shit big time and he didn't want the grief of Calder's crew coming down on him, they'd lived in almost perfect harmony for nearly ten years and he didn't want to spoil their working relationship.

"You sure it's them?" Reardon asked.

"Positive," Calder replied. "So you better sit down and I'll bring you up to speed and if I was you, I'd pour myself a stiff one cos I think you're gonna need it."

Reardon did just that. He poured himself a large whisky and dropped into a chair, the phone clasped to his ear. "Let's have it then John," he asked almost politely and then took a large swig at the whisky.

"Right," Calder replied. "What I know so far is this: Carson supplied both of 'em, whether or not it was anything to do with Talbot I ain't made me mind up yet. I don't wanna rock the boat till I'm sure that's why I want to find your boys and have a little talk with 'em. Finch's van was seen parked outside my gaffe the evening she went missing. Lizzie's body was found in the pond and obviously the police are involved now big time. Oh and while we're at it, it looks like those two dickheads were also responsible for the other body the police found in the pond, a Mr Clive Russell."

Reardon felt his stomach drop. He knew about Russell but he never thought that that would be coming back to haunt him as well. This little scenario was getting bigger by the minute and his mind was racing as to how he could convince Calder that he had nothing to do with it.

"Anyway," Calder continued, "Finch dumped his van in a NCP car park and went to ground. We found him shacked up with his hairdresser girlfriend and he cut one of my crew and got away. We sussed out Toke's place on the Greenslades Estate and we came down in the early hours to take him out and he started blasting away with a fucking nine mill! Turns out he'd try to *buy* a gun and then robbed the bloke instead, took 3 guns and word is, he's getting ready to go to war with me and you can bet your bottom dollar that he'll lose. The police are hot on his trail; his face has been on the news and splashed all over the local rags, he'll surface sooner or later and we'll bag him. There's a price on him and someone will grass him up especially as they know it's me that's looking for him. But we ain't seen hide nor hair of Finch since, fuck knows where he's got to. We've got an address for Toke's brother and Tony and the boys are just about to pay him a little visit and if he knows where his brother is, I promise you he'll end up telling us, that is a given."

"Jesus H Christ," Reardon said. His head was spinning trying to take everything in that Calder had told him. "Carson's in hospital I heard that was down to you, that right?"

"Yeah, he supplied the muscle that did away with Lizzie so he's as much to blame as they are. If you ask me I'd say I let him off lightly. Ask Conner he didn't fare so well."

"Conner?" Reardon asked confused, "where does he fit in with all of this then?"

"He fenced off Lizzie's jewellery and he damn nigh killed the person who sold it to him. Some small time no-count called Kevin Doyle. He's still in hospital now.

Reardon let out a long sigh. "Fucking hell, bring back the old days that's what I say, you knew who was who then, I can't keep up with all this shit." He thought for a moment. "Look John, if there's anything I can do you've only got to say the word and it's done. Anything at all, I want this over with just as much as you do. And I swear to God I had nothing to do with it, I mean there's never been any truck between us and I want to keep it that way."

"You got any idea where either of them might be? You know someplace they could hole up that I don't know about? I don't think they've done a runner, I think they're still around we just can't find 'em. Not yet anyway and the longer it takes the more pain it's gonna cost 'em.

"You tried Finch's flat?"

"Yeah he hadn't been there for days.

"You got his mobile number?"

"Yeah he's not answering I think he's ditched it."

"John I'm sorry, I've got no more suggestions. If I think of anything I'll give you a ring and don't forget if there's anything I can do …"

Calder cut in, "Yeah I know, I'll be in touch." He cut the call.

Reardon slammed the phone down on his desk. What a fucking mess. He'd not only lost two men, no matter what happened there was no way he could ever use them again, but Carson was going to be out of action for weeks if not months and he still had a business to run. He'd already been casting Carson some slack to spend time selling his cars as his manager was off sick recovering from a double hernia op and now this lot. He'd have to see who else was out there. He didn't think he could rely on this new black guy that Carson had been raving about; obviously he was no match for Pitman that was for sure. Reardon sat back in his chair and started to rack his brains to think if there was somewhere else that he could think of that Toke or Finch could be. It would gain favour back with Calder if he could find them; the last thing he wanted was to fall foul of Calder. He needed him as an ally not as an enemy.

Chapter Thirty-Six

"OK boys let's go pay Mr Toke a visit," Pitman said smiling.

Stevie turned the engine on and they drove up and parked outside Toke's house. Both Stevie and Johnnie were wearing painters' overalls and they got out of the van and opened the back doors and pulled out the dust sheets.

Pitman climbed out and glanced around, it seemed quiet enough. "OK let's go," he said and all three walked up the drive to Toke's front door. Both Stevie and Johnnie had guns concealed under the dust sheets, you could never be too careful.

They arrived at the front door and all stood to the side of the door, not in front of it. They didn't want to tempt fate, they'd been lucky before and no one had been hurt but it didn't pay to push your luck you were only given so much.

Pitman rang the bell and after a few moments they could make out someone through the glass of the door walking towards it. They were all tense and wound up, the adrenalin working overtime.

Jeff Toke opened the door and didn't seem particularly surprised that there were three men stood on his doorstep pretending to be painters and decorators.

Toke nodded. "I've been expecting you," he said calmly and stood back and held the door open for them to enter.

"No, after you," Pitman said, "You walk in front of us and we'll shut the door."

Toke never argued or questioned he just did as he was asked. Stevie and Johnnie exchanged glances and then followed Pitman and Toke into the house. Johnnie closed the door behind them. Toke walked into the lounge and stood watching and waiting from the doorway. Pitman turned to Stevie and Johnnie.

"Check upstairs and keep your wits about you, this all seems too easy to me."

"Gotcha," Stevie said and flung the dust sheet on the floor and slid the safety catch off on his gun. Johnnie followed suit and together they slowly climbed the stairs.

"There's no one else here," Toke said as he watched the two men making their way cautiously up the stairs.

"So you say," Pitman said.

"I know who you are and why you're here. Your name's Tony Pitman and you're looking for my brother. He's allegedly involved in a murder. That's right, isn't it?" Toke said as he sat down in one of the armchairs and crossed his legs casually. He seemed very relaxed and not at all fazed that men with guns were parading around freely inside his house.

"So if he's not here, where is he?" Pitman asked.

"What will you do to him when you find him?" Toke asked steepling his fingers.

"You don't need to trouble yourself over that."

"You'll kill him, won't you?"

"My boss wants to speak to him, beyond that I can't say for sure what'll happen to him. I will say this: I wouldn't want to be in his shoes when we do find him. He killed my boss's wife, cut off her fingers to steal her rings and then dumped her body in a pond."

Toke sat upright clearly shocked by the revelation. "Christ! Is that true? I mean really true?"

"You read the local papers, don't you? Elizabeth Calder, wife of John Calder the property developer, check it out."

Toke stood abruptly and Pitman's hand dropped to his cosh, ready to fight.

Toke held his hands up in front of him. "Sorry, sorry, I'm not going to do anything, I'm just shocked at what you've just told me. I can't believe it. He told me he'd had a run-in with you over an old grudge and some of your men had attacked him and he'd killed one of them in self-defence. He came to me for help and money."

"Did you give him any?"

Toke shook his head. "No ... I gave up helping him out a very long time ago. He maybe my brother but we're not close, and haven't been since we were kids. That's the first time I've seen him for about three or four years. He's been trouble ever since he was old enough to walk. We first had the police round knocking on the door when he was eight years old, and they've been coming round knocking ever since. My father walked out on us because of him. He was always getting into trouble with the police and dad found it very difficult to cope with the shame. He was Mason, d'you know what that is? A Freemason?"

"Course I do," Pitman replied sarcastically.

"Well then you'll understand the shame and humiliation it put my father through and he couldn't stand it anymore and just walked out. That in turn caused my mother to have a breakdown and she's never fully recovered from it and that's all thanks to my *wonderful* brother. So you do what you have to do, he means nothing to me at all ... nothing. Good bloody riddance if you ask me." He slumped back down in the armchair and covered his face with his hands.

Stevie and Johnnie entered the lounge; they were still holding their firearms.

"All clear boss we've checked all round, there's no one else here." They both made their weapons safe and Stevie unzipped his overalls and tucked his gun into the belt of his trousers and Johnnie slid his into one of the long pocket of his overalls.

"OK, thanks," Pitman said a little distractedly.

"What's the story here then boss?" Johnnie asked.

"He's not here," Pitman said.

"But you can bet your life he knows where he is though. We gonna find out boss?" Johnnie asked looking forward to making the man sing his socks off.

Pitman shook his head. "No, we're done here, let's go."

Stevie couldn't believe his ears. "What we're going, just like that? His brother tried shooting us, Finch slashed me with a fucking great carving knife and we've bagged his brother and you're just letting him go? What the fuck's that all about then?"

Toke looked around the room at the three men, knowing that a single word from Pitman could get him a right battering or worse. "There is somewhere you could try," Toke offered. "It's a long shot but I know he's kipped there before when he was on the run. My dad's got an allotment, tail-end of Regal Road, far as I know he still pays the annual rent on it although he hasn't been near the place for years, but there's a fair-sized shed on his plot.

As you come in the main gate, its right down the bottom on the left, its painted green, you can't miss it. He sometimes dosses down in there."

Stevie bent down close to Toke's chair. "If you're setting us up, I'll set fire to your house when you're still in it." He pulled the gun out and aimed it at Toke's face. "You listening?"

"I heard you," Toke said remaining calm, "And I'm not setting you up. I'm merely giving you a possible hiding place but going on what you've just told me, if he is there, then I would advise extreme caution, especially if he is as you say, armed. He won't think twice about using it against you."

"And neither will I!" Stevie said straightening up and putting his gun back.

Pitman inclined his head towards the door signalling for his men to leave, they filed out into the hall and waited. Pitman held his hand out towards Toke, and Toke shook it.

"I know you're only doing as you're told, I get that, and I understand what the outcome's likely to be it's just not something I want to be associated with. If you could make it quick, then I would be grateful." He nodded at Pitman and Pitman nodded once in reply and then left the room.

"Get the sheets and let's go," Pitman said and opened the front door and let himself out.

Steve and Johnnie exchanged looks and then dutifully picked up the dust sheets and left the house closing the door behind them, neither of them spoke, both lost in their own thoughts as to what had gone on between their boss and Toke. It was unlike Tony not to get stuck in to gather all the info he could, perhaps he was getting soft in his old age? This might be a good time to step up to the mark and let young blood show the way Stevie thought.

It didn't pay to be complacent in this game; people had to know that if they crossed you they suffered for it, and that's all there was to it. It was as simple as that.

Fifteen minutes later they drove past the allotment and sussed out the shed that Toke had mentioned. It was big and it was green and it was down the bottom of the allotment on the left, just like Toke had said. There were too many people in there at the moment working on their own little plots; they'd have to wait until it was dark to pay brother Toke a visit.

Pitman called up Davey-Boy and updated him and told him to get his arse down to the allotments and keep a discreet watch on the place. They'd be coming back later when it was dark and deserted.

Chapter Thirty-Seven

Detective Inspector White was studying the white boards in the incident room. As it stood they were making very slow progress on both the murders of Elizabeth Calder and Clive Russell. They knew Russell had bad debts and that he had been involved in some heavy poker nights trying to change his luck but he'd only ended up owing more money. One name had come into the frame, Tommy Reardon. It was known that Russell was into Reardon for quite a sizeable sum and pressure had been brought to bear to make Russell settle his bill.

Russell's bank statements didn't show that there had been any large cash withdrawals or large cheques paid out and he was maxed right up to the hilt on his home mortgage and his business premises, plus some of the local tradesmen had put his company on stop as their accounts hadn't been settled.

Reardon was known to have held some large poker nights and a grass had reported that Russell had been at two that he knew of, at both of which he'd lost heavily and had been given markers.

Now Martin Conway had been hospitalised again and he was keeping very tight-lipped about what had happened but obviously, someone had it in for him. Then there was the shooting at Harry Toke's house and Toke had fled the scene and nothing had been seen or heard of him since, despite extensive coverage in the press and throughout the media. So who was Toke shooting at and who was it that was trying to break into his house?

Then there was Dave Carson. He'd had a right seeing-to and so had his so-called bodyguard. And then to cap it all someone had poured paint remover over three-quarters of the cars in his lot and caused thousands of pound's worth of damage.

Just what the hell was going on? Pitman couldn't be involved in all of this lot surely? It just didn't add up. The house to house was still going on at Toke's Estate but so far it had all proved negative.

The Inspector couldn't recall another case that had featured so heavily in the press and media that had resulted in so little information coming back. Either the public just didn't know anything or people were too frightened to come forward. The Inspector suspected it was the latter.

Chapter Thirty-Eight

At just gone eleven o'clock Pitman and his crew arrived. They parked in the street just up from the allotment and having conferred with Davey-Boy, Pitman sent him home for some rest although he had protested that he wanted to stay. Stevie climbed over the rear fence and winced as he dropped silently to the ground. The slash to his chest was still sore but the stitches had held and the wound was healing nicely which was all that mattered.

Pitman and Johnnie made their way through the main gate of the allotment. There were street lights in the road running alongside so that gave them enough light to see their way. There was also a well-worn path that ran through the allotment and then branched off to the individual plots so progress was easy.

Stevie had made a silent recce around the large shed and he was certain Toke was inside. A dim light filtered through the gap down the sides of the door and Stevie thought he had heard someone inside. He'd given the thumbs up to Pitman when he and Johnnie were close enough to see the gesture.

Pitman nodded to Johnnie and he dropped to one knee and unscrewed the cap on the petrol can. He crept forward and quickly started to shake the contents out onto the ground around the shed. He worked quickly knowing that the smell would alert Toke and then he would most likely start blasting away.

Finished, Johnnie looked to Pitman for approval and Pitman gave the thumbs up to Stevie who nodded in reply and drew and cocked his weapon. Johnnie lit the petrol-soaked rag and threw it towards the shed and suddenly there was a swoosh and the petrol ignited.

Johnnie racked the slide on his gun and crouched down to wait. Within a few moments, the sides of the shed were ablaze sending flames into the air and lighting up the sky.

Toke had been asleep, zipped into an old sleeping bag when suddenly he had smelt both smoke and petrol fumes. Waking from a deep sleep fuelled by excess alcohol, he had started to panic not realising at first where he was and finding himself constrained inside the sleeping bag. He had struggled out of the bag and whilst still on all fours he had grabbed the 9 mill.

He had started to cough as the flames had taken hold on the dry timber and then in a desperate bid to escape he had fumbled with the gun and slipped the safety off and just held down the trigger and sprayed from side to side not knowing where his attackers were but knowing the door was the only way out.

Pitman had been lying prone on the ground and although he had instructed Johnnie to do the same, once the fire had started, he had been amazed at how quickly it had spread engulfing the shed in a matter of minutes and Johnnie had stood up to watch.

They heard the gun start up and then bullets ripped through the flimsy sides of the shed into the night in all directions. Johnnie clutched at his chest and spun sideways and fell, hitting the ground hard. Pitman yelled out for Stevie to stay down and then the shed door burst open and Toke came out at a run blasting the gun from side to side.

Pitman pressed himself down into the dirt. Stevie was better placed being totally out of the line of fire and fired twice hitting Toke in the side and upper chest. Toke fell backwards and almost landed back inside the entrance to the shed.

Pitman yelled out. "Stevie, Johnnie's hit, you alright?" It was getting harder to see with the flames and smoke blowing about but Pitman was crouching and moving forwards towards Johnnie as he spoke.

"Yeah I'm alright! I got him; I got Toke he's down!" Stevie replied as he too started to move across to join the others.

Pitman reached Johnnie, he was still conscious but bleeding badly.

"Just breathe easy Johnnie boy we'll get you out of here." Johnnie managed to nod weakly. Stevie joined Pitman.

"Fucking hell," Stevie said crouching down alongside Pitman and seeing the blood. "How bad is he?"

"Dunno, he's hit in the chest. Get him in the motor I'm going to check on Toke and then we better get the hell out of here. You can bet your arse people'll be phoning the cops and fire brigade any minute now."

Pitman helped Stevie pull Johnnie to his feet and then Stevie flung him over his shoulder and started making his way back to the car.

Pitman picked up Johnnie's gun and approached the still form of Toke. He held the gun out in front of him. Although Toke wasn't moving it could be a trap and one man down was more than enough. Pitman reached Toke, the heat coming off the burning shed was quite intense and Pitman had to scrunch up his shoulder to give his face some protection from the flames. He kicked the gun away towards the blazing shed and then dropped down to examine Toke. Toke's eyes were open and his face was screwed up in a painful expression. Pitman checked for a pulse and couldn't find one. He looked along the line of Toke's chest and it was still: the man was dead. Good fucking riddance his brother had said and now it was done.

Pitman got his hands under Toke's arms and half sat him up and then braced himself and lifted Toke to his feet so his back was resting against him. Then with a supreme effort he charged the body forwards and flung it into the blazing shed. It erupted in a shower of flames as it hit the burning floor and the flames seemed to take on an even fiercer roar as they started to consume the body.

Pitman had a further check of the area to make sure there was nothing that could incriminate him or his crew. He saw Toke's gun near the entrance to the shed and managed to kick it inside and then he noticed the petrol can. It had caught fire at some point and had melted into a smouldering misshapen object that would be too hot and sticky to pick up. He had no choice; he'd have to leave it behind, although he was certain it would be of no use to the cops. You certainly couldn't get any fingerprints off it and it was just a bog standard Jerry-can you could buy in any garage or supermarket, so half-crouching, he jogged away from the inferno after Stevie.

As Pitman reached the main entrance a man wearing a dressing gown and pyjamas was crossing the road towards him waving a torch.

Fuck it Pitman thought as he pulled his jacket collar up to help hide more of his face. "I've just seen two kids climbing over the back fence I'm just going to see if I can cut them off. I've phoned the police and the fire brigade." And without waiting for a reply Pitman took off at a run away from the man down the side of the allotment in the direction Stevie had taken.

By the time Pitman got back to the car, Stevie was already waiting. Stevie held Johnnie upright against the side of the car. Pitman pressed the key fob as he approached and the cars lights blinked off and on.

Pitman yanked open the back door and helped Stevie gently lay Johnnie across on the rear seats. Pitman and Stevie jumped in the car and Pitman started the engine and they sped away from the scene, the flames still visible in the rear-view mirror as they tried to put some distance between them and the burning shed.

They got to Sue's address in record time, the house was in darkness. Pitman jumped out and ran up the path and rang the doorbell several times then returned to help Stevie haul Johnnie out of the car. The upstairs light went on and the side of the curtain was pulled back as they struggled up the path with Johnnie. As they reached the front door Sue opened it. She was wearing a dressing gown and slippers and her hair was tangled. She rubbed at her eyes.

"Sorry Sue," Pitman said as she stepped aside to let them in. "Got a bit of an emergency."

Sue closed the door behind them. "Take him in the kitchen and put him on the table." She opened the hall cupboard and pulled out her case and quickly followed them down the hall.

Sue scrambled the pot plant and the placemats off the table to make way as they gently laid the man's body on the table. He was bleeding quite badly but appeared to still be conscious.

"What happened?" she asked as she started to push his jumper up his chest.

"Gunshot," Tony answered almost matter-of-factly."

"Christ Tony," Sue replied stopping what she was doing, "I'm not a bloody surgeon I'm a practice nurse."

"I'm not expecting miracles just do what you can please." She held his look and then sighed.

"Get his jacket and top off," she ordered and then went over to the sink and filled the kettle with water and switched it on. She returned to the table and opened her case and pulled on a pair of thin latex gloves.

Tony and Steve had managed to get Johnnie's jacket off and were struggling to get Johnnie's jumper off over his head.

"Leave it," Sue said reaching into her case and pulling out a pair of scissors. She deftly cut the jumper straight up the middle and pulled the clothing apart.

"Oh Christ," Stevie said seeing the hole in Johnnie's chest, it was still bleeding.

Sue tried to feel around Johnnie's back. "You'll need to lift him up but do it gently he's lost quite a bit of blood."

Pitman and Stevie gently raised Johnnie up into the sitting position. Sue looked. "There's no exit wound; the bullet's still inside him and it's got to come out."

"Can you do it?" Pitman asked.

"No I can't!" Sue replied firmly. "It's way out of my league. He needs to go to hospital, Tone. I'm sorry."

"But could you try?" Pitman asked kindly his eyes pleading with her. Sue sighed and ran her hand up through her hair.

"I could go to prison for this you know," she said in reply.

Tony laid his hand on her arm. "Do what you can Sue, yeah? Please?"

She looked at him and then back at the man bleeding onto her kitchen table and sighed and shook her head. "Tony Pitman you owe me big bloody time after this I can tell you!" She reached back into her case and brought out a syringe and a small vial of liquid and set to work.

"Thanks love, I won't forget this," Pitman said gratefully.

"I won't bloody let you!" Sue replied and found a suitable vein in Johnnie's arm and pushed the needle in.

Twenty minutes later the bullet had been found and extracted, the wound cleaned, sterilised and stitched and Sue was now busily taping gauze and an antiseptic cream over the wound. "He'll need to rest he's lost a fair amount of blood and to be honest I'm not sure whether what I've done is enough. He may have other injuries, his body will have gone into shock, then there's …"

Tony interrupted, "Sue, Sue, you've been bloody brilliant, straight up you have. I can't thank you enough. Now drink your tea we've got some thinking to do." He pushed a mug across to her.

Sue looked at the mug and then stood, "I need something stronger than that!" She left the room and returned moments later with a bottle of whisky.

"That's more like it!" Stevie said grabbing some glasses from the cupboard. He passed one to her and Sue poured herself a generous helping and then knocked it back in one long hard swallow. She gasped for breath and banged the glass down. "Shit!" she said, "What a bloody night! Tony Pitman I will never forgive you for this, you've put years on me!"

"Come here you," he said lightly and scooped her in his arms and hugged her tightly. Her arms snaked round his back and she held him tightly in return, the tension easing away.

Johnnie was still unconscious but for now he was fast asleep in the spare room and that's where he'd stay for the next few days. It was decided that Sue would throw a 'sickie' and stay off work to look after him and if there were any complications she would phone Tony immediately and they'd have to take him to the hospital and leave him in the car park and call it in, but for now it looked like he would be OK, the next twenty-four hours would be the telling point. All they could do now was wait.

Tony promised to send someone round in the morning to clean Sue's kitchen from top to bottom and to bring her a special envelope. Sue hugged them both in turn and quietly closed the door behind them and then slowly climbed the stairs to her bedroom knowing that there was no way she'd get back to sleep tonight.

Tony dropped Stevie off at his flat and ordered him to shower and then bag up everything he'd worn tonight and dump it in one of the municipal bins down on the industrial estate ASAP. Pitman also took the gun off him. That would be broken down into pieces and the parts disposed of down various drains around the town in the early hours of the morning when he took Bonnie, Calder's dog out for a very late night walk.

Well it was a result in part. Toke was out of the frame and had paid the ultimate price for his crime. And Pitman reckoned that when Finch got to hear about it he would panic and stick his head above the parapet and someone would see him and phone it in. The net was closing.

Chapter Thirty-Nine

To the men of blue watch, it was just a typical act of wanton vandalism, they'd already attended a blazing wheelie bin earlier that evening and now here they were at a shed fire on an allotment. By the time they'd arrived the shed had almost burnt itself out and they had been able to douse the flames using the stored water from the engine.

One of the fire fighters jogged up to the Fire Chief.

"We've got a body in the shed."

"You sure?" The Fire Chief asked, knowing before he even replied that it was no doubt true. Ken Collins had been on the team for eight years and was a good solid fire fighter and not used to making wild accusations. If he said there was a body, then there was a body.

"Yeah definitely."

"OK, if the fire's dead, pull everyone back and contain the area. Don't touch a thing and stop the other guys from moving about, we don't want to destroy any evidence that might still be there. I'll call it in."

"There's something else as well," Collins added.

The Fire Chief sighed, "I can't wait, go on, what is it?"

"It looks like there's a gun just inside the door. It's burnt but it's still pretty clear from the shape what it is."

"Oh Christ, it just gets better and better. Right well just leave it where it is and we'll wait for the police. They can sort it out."

Collins nodded and jogged back to the remains of the shed. The fire was out, there were just a few coils of smoke rising from the burnt embers.

The Fire Chief grasped his radio and called up the control room to break the news and start the ball rolling. It was going to be a long night.

Chapter Forty

The next morning Kenny was on the phone to Pitman.

"You wouldn't happen to know anything about a burnt up body on an allotment, would you?" Kenny asked lightly, already knowing the answer.

"What's the buzz?" Pitman answered.

"Turns out Toke was shot and burned to a crisp last night in a shed down on Regal Road allotments."

"How d'you know it's Toke if you say he was burnt?"

"Well Toke was well-known for wearing a ring on every finger of his right hand and it turns out that when they moved the body his right arm had been trapped underneath him and there were the rings, burnt up, but one on every finger. Bingo!"

"Anything else I should know about?" Pitman asked as he noticed another call was waiting.

"Yeah they found a gun as well, beyond that I don't know very much. The place is swarming with feds I can tell you that for nothing though."

"OK thanks Kenny."

"No sweat. Any news on Finch yet?"

"No not a dicky-bird. I'm hoping this will flush him out. He's gotta show up sooner or later. Anyone pointing fingers in our direction yet?"

"You're up on the board and no doubt you'll get another visit pretty soon."

"Yeah I kinda figured that. Thanks for the heads up Kenny, speak to you soon, cheers."

"Any time, Tone." Pitman cut the call and connected the other call. It was Sue.

"Tone?" She sounded anxious.

"Yeah go ahead Sue, what's up?"

"It's Johnnie; he's in a pretty bad way. He's burning up and the wound looks like it's become infected. It's very red and angry."

This is all I fucking need Pitman thought. "What d'you suggest Sue?" Pitman asked making sure he kept his voice level and calm.

"He's got to go to hospital Tony I'm sorry. I can't even get him to take any fluids, his body's on fire, it's raging. His temperature's 40.5 …"

Tony interrupted, "What should it be then?"

"Normal temperature for a healthy adult is 37c. If it gets any higher he could start convulsing and it could damage his brain …"

Tony cut in again, "OK, OK just give me a second to think." The police would be putting two and two together and it wouldn't take them long to include Tony and the boys in their equation, he had to act fast. "OK Sue, try and bring his temperature down and get some liquid inside him, we'll be there in about twenty minutes."

"What you going to do?"

"Take your advice and get him to hospital. See you in a bit." Tony cut off the call and phoned Stevie.

"Yes boss," Stevie said.

"My place as quick as you can, Johnnie's rough as hell, just mind the speed camera on Morgan Road."

"What's happened?" Stevie asked but he was talking to thin air, Pitman had already disconnected the call.

Pitman grabbed a hat and a dark coat and virtually ran out of the front door and up his drive. He unlocked the garage and entered pulling the door down behind him. He walked across to a large sturdy unit on the far wall and pressed a switch hidden under the workbench. The unit moved aside revealing a neat alcove cut out into the brickwork. There were some handguns wrapped in oiled-paper and a small safe cemented into the floor. Hanging on the wall were three sets of car number plates. He selected a set and knelt down behind the old Astra and deftly changed the plates putting the real ones back into the alcove and then he clicked the switch and the unit glided back into place. He opened the garage door and drove the car out onto the driveway and as he did he saw the front of Stevie's car nose up to the driveway entrance and then heard a car door slam and Stevie jogged into view.

Tony closed and locked the garage. "Jump in," he said and they both climbed into the Astra and Tony spun the car round in a tight curve and then headed out into the road en route to Sue's.

"So how bad is he?" Stevie asked.

"Very, we've got to get him to hospital and dump him off. He's burning up and his temperature's gone through the roof, Sue's shitting bricks and if she's worried I'm worried."

"Christ," Stevie said in reply. "So how we gonna do it then?"

"There's going to be no finesse about it, we've just got to get him in the car and get him to the hospital and then dump him off and leave."

"Christ that don't seem right," Stevie said almost in protest.

"So what do you suggest we do with someone who's been shot then, eh? March into A & E and try to explain that we burnt down a shed with a nutter in it and then my mate here shot and killed *him* and I chucked the dead body back into the flames to get rid of it and in between our mate here got blasted with a stolen illegal firearm? Well that would make a cracking story that would," Pitman replied sarcastically. "No we leave him as close to the entrance as we can, bearing in mind they have CCTV cameras all over the sodding place, then we get the fuck out of there and phone it in and get him the help he needs. That's all we *can* do, we sure as hell can't wait around."

"Yeah sorry Tone I want thinking."

"It's alright; we're all a bit tense at the moment. The cops have already identified Toke and we're liable to get a visit later, so the shit just goes on and on. You're going have to say you were with Shanie or whatever her bloody name is last night watching a DVD or something."

"It's Shawna, and it's no sweat, she'll cover for me if they need to speak to her she's a good girl."

"She better fucking be we can't afford to have anyone looking too closely at us at the moment. Let's just hope that Johnnie can keep his gob shut and he's not too far out of it to drop himself in it. There's not a lot we can do about that, we've just got to trust to luck and keep our fingers crossed."

Tony braked to a halt outside Sue's house and then reversed the car up her drive. No sooner were they out of the car than Sue had the front door open.

"How is he?" Tony asked stepping inside.

"He's bad, Tone," Sue replied. "I still can't get him to drink anything."

"OK, come on Stevie." They walked past Sue and went upstairs. Stevie gave her a little wave and a smile as he walked past.

Tony had to admit that Johnnie looked as rough as hell. He was bright red and very hot to the touch.

"Christ he's baking," Stevie said helping Tony sit Johnnie up. Pitman's phoned started to ring. Tony checked the number, it was Calder. Well sod it he'd have to wait, there were more important things to get sorted first. No doubt the police were there or on their way, Calder would have to deal with it himself, right now Johnnie was the priority and that's all there was to it.

Between them Pitman and Stevie carried Johnnie downstairs. Sue opened the rear door to the car and they gently sat Johnnie in the back seat, Steve got in with him and put a seatbelt on Johnnie.

Pitman leant down and gave Sue a peck on the cheek. "Thanks for all you've done love, I'll be in touch."

She touched him gently on the arm. "You take care of yourself; I don't want you joining him in hospital."

Pitman smiled and hugged her and then climbed into the car and drove out the drive.

They arrived at the hospital fourteen minutes later. Tony did a quick drive past and selected a spot almost opposite the entrance that had a couple of wooden benches for the benefit of the patients. He'd instructed Steve to look up the number of the hospital en route and Stevie had programmed it into the pay as you go phone. He handed it back to Pitman.

Tony took the phone. He looked around it seemed fairly quiet. There was an elderly woman on a walking frame close to the entrance and two men stood outside smoking despite the signs forbidden them to do so. It was time to get it done. Both men got out the car and as gently as they could they manhandled Johnnie out of the car and propped him up on the bench. Tony checked around again, nothing had changed and he and Stevie got back into the car and slowly drove out of the hospital grounds. They stopped just beyond the entrance where they could still see Johnnie on the bench and then Tony called the hospital.

When they answered, he said, "There's a man's body on one of the benches at the entrance to the hospital, he looks pretty rough you need to get a doctor out to him straight away." He cut the call and took the SIM card out of the phone and replaced it with an identical one.

Twenty seconds later a security man came out of the entrance, looked around and then made his way over to the bench. They watched as he bent down and gave Johnnie the once over, then he stood up and spoke into his radio and moments later a doctor and a nurse came running out of the hospital. A porter followed closely behind pushing a wheelchair, all three quickly made their way over to the bench. Tony had seen enough, he slipped the car into gear and drove slowly away, one problem down, now he had to get the car back and see what Calder wanted. Welcome to another day in fucking Paradise!

Chapter Forty-One

Tony let himself into Calder's house; Bonnie came up to meet him wagging her tail, pleased to see him. Pitman bent down and stroked her neck and she nuzzled into him. "How you doing beautiful?" he said.

Calder stepped out of his office. "I phoned you twice, where the hell you been?"

Tony stood up and Bonnie trotted back to the kitchen. "Yeah I know sorry, I was a bit tied up."

"Doing what?" Calder asked coldly.

"We had a problem."

"Like what?" Calder said.

"It was Johnnie, he was burning up and his temperature was going through the roof …"

Calder interrupted. "I thought you dealt with that?"

"So did I," Pitman replied, not really in the mood to be cross-examined.

"So what does that mean then?" Calder pressed.

"It means I got him patched up and we thought he was doing OK, unfortunately it looks like he's picked up an infection …"

"Which means what?" Calder said butting in again.

"It means I've sorted it."

"How?"

"I dropped him off down the hospital. I had no choice."

Calder whinged, "Oh for fuck's sake that's all we need! I thought you already had some nurse sorting him out?"

"I did, she took the bullet out and stitched him and patched him up, but he's developed an infection and he was just burning up. And I mean burning up; you only had to be near him to feel the heat coming off him. I had to get him to the hospital he was in a really bad way. I put a set of false plates on the Astra and me and Stevie placed him on a seat in the grounds of the hospital and our backs were always facing away from the cameras. I phoned it in and the staff came out with a wheelchair and we drove away. It's sorted, it's OK."

"Says you," Calder said sarcastically. "I've had the rozzers on the phone they've asked me to come in, *voluntarily*. They want to speak to me about Toke and now one of your boys is in hospital with a fucking gunshot wound. This is all going to come back on me big time, you know that don't you? No matter what it's going to come back to me. Jesus wept!" He slapped his hand against the wall and Bonnie barked and came running back into the hall. "It's alright girl, good girl," Calder said and patted her head. Bonnie stretched and trotted back to her bed.

"So what time you got to go in then?" Pitman asked.

"Two, some Detective Sergeant wants to speak to me. He said it might be better if I brought my brief in with me. How fucking serious does that sound to you?"

"They're bluffing. Even if they tie Toke in with you somehow, you were with a whole bunch of highly respected local business men all night. Christ you've got loads of witnesses so that puts you in the clear, and how would a respectable business man like you know that Toke had something to do with Lizzie's murder? They're just clutching at straws."

"Let's just hope you're right. It might step up a bit when they find out that one of the men that works for me is in hospital with a gunshot wound though, wouldn't you say?" he added a little sarcastically.

"You can't be expected to know what your staff get up to when they're not at work, it's not down to you what they do in their own time, is it? And he's only one of dozens of people that work for you and in theory you don't have anything to do with the actual staff."

"Christ you've really got it all off Pat, haven't you? They'll have you in as well though, that goes without saying."

"No sweat, I was in the Tavern till half ten with Chrissie and then we left. She pretended to be a bit more boozed up than she really was and we showed out a bit. So anyone would assume that we were leaving before closing to have a right old session and just to make it look good, she stayed at mine last night and Patsy next door saw her leave as she was parked part-way across her drive. It's covered boss; give me credit for something, will you?"

"Alright if you say so," Calder said a little reluctantly.

"Straight up, they've got nothing on you boss, really, it's going to be fine."

"I'll remind you you said that when they've slapped the cuffs on me and they're taking me down," he said lightly.

"It will be alright. Finch'll show up soon and we'll get him sorted and then it'll all be over. The feds will have to work bloody hard to gather enough evidence on us to do anything about it. Give it a few months and it'll all have blown over. You'll see."

"OK, well … I'd better get ready, Morgan's picking me up in twenty minutes. I'll let you know what happens, and try and keep a low profile if you can unless of course our *friend* shows up. Anyway, I'll leave it to you. See you later."

"Yeah, good luck boss." *I think you're gonna need it* Pitman muttered to himself as he opened the front door and let himself out of the house.

Chapter Forty-Two

Calder along with his solicitor Jeffrey Morgan, were sitting in the interview room, together with Detective Constable Pardy and heading the interview, Detective Sergeant Willis. Willis had told the tape the names of those present, declared the time and date and then looked down at his notes and addressed John Calder.

"Thank you for coming in Mr Calder, I'd just like to make it clear that you're not under arrest, and that you've attended this interview voluntarily, and that you're free to go at any time, but I must remind you that you are under oath and that anything you do say may be given in evidence. Do you understand that?"

Calder looked at Morgan who nodded at Calder.

"Yes," Calder replied.

The Sergeant made a note and continued. "Can you tell me where you were last evening between the hours of 23:00 and 23:30."

"Why?" Calder asked locking eyes with Willis.

There was a slight hesitation from Willis; he wasn't expecting Calder to answer with a question of his own. He realised he would have to choose his words carefully if he wanted to glean anything of note from this interview. "Because an incident occurred a little after 23:00 last evening that we believe may or may not be connected to the murder of your wife."

Calder never blinked, he continued to maintain eye contact with Willis. "Well which is it Sergeant, connected or not connected, because if it's *not* connected then we shouldn't really be wasting each other's time should we? We've both probably got other things we'd rather be doing."

Christ Willis thought, this is going to be hard going and that's without his solicitor poking his nose in. "I believe the incident *is* related but our enquiries are still ongoing at this time as I'm sure you'll appreciate."

"Would it not have been more prudent then to have waited until you were sure of your facts before you asked me to come down to the station?"

"I understand what you're saying sir, but I'm just trying to establish some background at this point in time."

Calder leant back towards his solicitor and Morgan whispered something to him. Calder sat back up as he replied. "I was at a meeting of the Chamber of Trade, and in case you're not aware, I'm the current Chairman."

"And this meeting was held where sir?"

"The Cumberland Hotel. I was there from about 7:30 and left, by taxi, at around 12:30. Would you like the name of the taxi company I used and a list of fellow members who could vouch for my presence? My credit card can certainly bear witness to the fact I was there!" He gave the Sergeant a grin and settled back to wait for a response.

Willis made another note. "That's fine sir, thank you. Does the name Harry Toke mean anything to you?"

"Toke?" Calder paused for a moment to think. "No I can't say that it does. In what pretext?"

"We found Toke's body last night in a burnt out shed on an allotment in Regal Road. An accelerant had been used to set fire to the shed."

"And why would you think that this would have anything to do with me?" Calder asked keeping his voice light but with a slightly irritated edge to it, mainly to suggest that the Sergeant was wasting his valuable time.

The Sergeant paused for a moment. "We are of the opinion that Toke, along with others, was connected to the disappearance and subsequent murder of Elizabeth Calder."

There was a distinctive edge now to Calder's voice and he leant forward towards Willis. "Are you telling me you had a suspect and you failed to arrest him and that he somehow ended up burnt to death in a bloody *shed*!"

Willis went on the defensive. "There's a lot more to it than that sir, I'm just not obliged to tell you any more than that at this time…"

Calder interrupted, "Well I think you should! My wife was abducted and murdered and you had a suspect or *suspects* yet you failed to apprehend them and now one of them is dead! What type of half-arsed investigation are you running here Sergeant!"

Morgan tapped lightly on Calder's arm and Calder pulled his arm away and sat back in his seat and folded his arms. Make of that what you will he thought to himself, over to you then, Sarge.

Morgan addressed the Sergeant. "My client has given you his whereabouts for last evening, which of course can be verified and he's also made it clear that he has no knowledge of Mr Toke who has tragically died, so I fail to see that we can be of any further use to you regarding this matter. So unless there's something else you wished to put to Mr Calder, we'll be on our way." Morgan gathered his notebook and pen and placed them back into his briefcase.

Willis watched with interest, he had one parting shot yet to try. "Does the name Kevin Finch mean anything to you Mr Calder?" He watched Calder closely as he replied.

"Is this another random name out of a hat, or is this another suspect you're keeping us in the dark about?"

"Could you just answer the question please sir?"

"No, I've never heard of Kevin Finch or Mr Toke and now I think I've heard enough." Calder stood. "And I would appreciate it if you would be kind enough to keep me in the loop in future, after all it was *my wife* that was murdered and I'm far from happy with the progress you've made so far to bring the perpetrators to justice. I won't hold my breath for a quick result." Calder added sarcastically as he followed Morgan out of the door leaving it wide open behind them.

"Christ on a crutch!" Willis said slinging his pen across the table. "Well that went fucking well then!" He remembered the tape and jabbed it viciously with his finger to stop it. He shook his head and gathered up the paperwork and put it back into the file. He turned to the young Constable, "Well I hope you picked up some good interview tips there then!" He said flatly and left the room slamming the door shut behind him leaving the Constable to sort out the tapes.

Chapter Forty-Three

The following afternoon two detectives arrived at Calder's house and rang the doorbell. Calder had been sat watching the racing, he'd put quite a hefty bet on and two horses had come through and he was waiting on the last race of the day at Salisbury to get underway to see if he'd make a bob or two.

"Oh shit," he groaned as he got up and went to answer the door. Bonnie joined him from the kitchen and stood alongside him as he peered through the spy hole and recognised one of the police officers from when he had come to the house before to break the news about his wife. What the fuck did they want now?

Calder opened the door. "Yes?" he asked abruptly.

Toller flashed his warrant card "We're sorry to trouble you sir, I'm ..."

"Yeah, I know who you are," Calder interrupted wondering if the race had started yet and how long this conversation was going take.

Toller replaced his warrant card back in his pocket. "May we have a word?" Toller asked a little nervously.

"Well in case you're not aware I was down the station yesterday ..."

It was Toller's turn now to interrupt, "It's nothing to do with that sir."

"Well what is it about then?" Calder asked knowing for certain now that he was going to miss the race.

"It's about a member of your staff."

"A member of my staff? I've only got the one, Tony Pitman; you met him when you were here before."

"It's not about Mr Pitman sir."

"Well I don't have any more staff that I deal with directly!" Calder replied irritably. Bonnie noticed the change in tone of her master's voice and she stiffened and growled at the detectives. "Easy girl," Calder said stroking her neck, "these are supposed to be the *good guys*."

Toller shifted nervously, "Would you mind if we came in sir, it might be easier to talk?"

"I would mind, yeah. I was watching the racing and you've just interrupted what could have been a winning streak."

Toller pressed on relentless. "It is important sir."

Calder sighed, "Oh God, alright come in, it'll probably be all over now anyway so this better be good." Calder stood aside and ushered them in. He directed them into the lounge and closed the door behind them. Calder followed them in and looked at the screen, the race was over and the adverts were on.

Brilliant. He'd have to phone up now to find out whether or not his horse had won. He turned back to Toller. "Well? What's it all about then?"

"It's about Johnnie Polden sir?"

"Johnnie Polden? Who the hell is Johnnie Polden?" he asked irritably.

The two detectives exchanged looks. "We understand he works for you sir?"

"Possibly he does if you say he does, but I wouldn't know. Like I already told you, Pitman is the only member of staff that I deal with directly. He's my PA and helps with the day to day running of things and he's been a rock during these very distressing times."

"Yes sir, I appreciate that. Well Mr Polden has been in hospital and he gave your name as his employer, he has no next of kin."

"Right," Calder replied, "But as I said the name means nothing to me, you'd be better off speaking to my accountant. That's what I have one for. He deals with staff etc, not me."

"Mr Polden works for Guardian Securities if that helps sir?" Toller added hopefully.

"It's a company I use in connection with my clubs, they supply the doormen. Beyond that I can't really tell you very much." Calder shrugged.

Toller charged ahead. "He's dead."

"Who is?"

"Johnnie Polden sir."

Calder was thrown and needed to control himself. "Dead how? You mean in a car crash or something? It certainly won't be in connection to any of my clubs or else I would have already been informed. And if it's drugs-related, then that certainly isn't anything to do with any of my businesses. You can check your records; there's never been any trouble with drugs at any of my clubs. I won't tolerate anything to do with drugs."

"He was shot."

"Shot? Jesus! By who? Have you arrested someone?"

"Not yet sir, no."

"Well when did all this happen?"

"It's all a little vague at the moment we're still making enquiries. He died at-" Toller checked his pocket notebook, "-sixteen forty this afternoon at St. Mary's Hospital. Now this is where it all gets a little strange. Seems someone had patched him up and taken the bullet out but it looks like his condition worsened overnight and he was dumped off in the hospital grounds before lunch and someone phoned the hospital reception and told them about the body. We're looking at the tapes from the CCTV but we're not getting a lot from it. The plates on the car they used were false and the two men that dumped him were very conscious of the cameras and kept their backs to them all the time. Seems his wound had become infected, largely because a small fragment of the bullet had sheared off and damaged the left ventricle of his heart. He died of a massive stroke about an hour ago."

"Well I'm sorry," Calder said, "I can't really think of anything I can say to help you. As I said, I don't have any dealing with other members of my staff, it's all done through an employment agency my accountant uses. Hang on." Calder walked across to a bureau and pulled down the front and fiddled in a slim folder and came out clutching a card. He handed it across to the detective. "That's my accountant, all his details are on there, I suggest you make an appointment to see him, hopefully he may be able to furnish you with more information. Now if there's nothing else, I need to phone my bookies, I could be sitting on a nice little packet." Calder held his arm out and directed the officers towards the lounge door.

Toller looked at the card and put it in his pocket and then followed his fellow detective out of the room. Calder let them out.

"If anything comes to mind I'll give you a ring, sorry I couldn't be any more helpful." He closed the door and hurried back into the lounge and picked up his mobile from the arm of his chair. What the hell was Pitman playing at; he hit the speed dial for Tony's number, the horse racing suddenly forgotten as he listened to the phone start to ring.

Chapter Forty-Four

Detective Inspector Chris White watched as Sergeant Willis wrote on the whiteboard. When he'd finished he nodded at the Inspector. "Over to you sir," the Sergeant said and sat down. The room was full of detectives sitting or standing, some were holding pens and notebooks ready to write down anything of significance and their conversation petered out as they waited eagerly for the Inspector to begin.

The Detective Inspector addressed his team. "So good morning everyone, now, as you can all see," he said and pointed at the whiteboards, "we've had some new developments. The body found in the burnt-out shed on the allotment on Regal Road has now been positively identified as one Harry Toke; no doubt quite a few of you are familiar with that name."

There was a general hum of agreement from the assembled detectives.

The Inspector resumed. "Now Toke was shot twice with a .357 Magnum, as yet we've had no match but our enquiries are still continuing. We do know however from the angle of the body, that after he was shot, Toke's body was picked up and thrown into the burning shed, forensics haven't been able to establish yet whether or not he was dead at that time. A gun, not the one that shot him, was found inside the shed. This weapon has been identified as a 9mm, possibly a Beretta, but that's not been confirmed yet either as it was quite badly burnt and distorted in the blaze. Again, enquiries are continuing. Now as you know, there was a shooting at Toke's home address on the Greenslades Estate and two bullets recovered at the scene were in fact 9 millimetres. So we think it's fairly safe to assume that the gun discovered in the shed alongside Toke was in fact his. There was also a melted plastic can found at the scene that had contained petrol, which was the accelerant used to set fire to the shed. Now I think it's fairly safe to say that Toke had probably been hiding out in the shed for a few days. Uniform conducted house-to-house in the immediate area following the fire and a Mr Richmond from 17 Regal Road went to investigate the fire at approximately half past eleven and he met a male leaving the allotment. This male was described as white, about five feet ten to six foot, about thirty to forty-five years of age, English speaking and wearing dark clothing. So he should be very easy to find."

He waited for the laughter and comments to die down and then he resumed. "And a Mrs Jarvis who lives at number 22 Regal Road phoned the fire brigade at 23:18 There are still a few houses that uniform have to go back to but I think it's safe to say that the man in black was definitely involved. No one reported seeing or hearing anything unusual until the fire engine turned up, so I don't think they'll be anything else of much use coming back from the house-to-house. Now, this is where it all starts gathering speed as it were." He pointed back to the board. "Johnnie Polden died yesterday in St Mary's from a gunshot wound. Now Mr Polden is known to us, not because he has a criminal record but because he works for

Guardian Securities that supply bouncers cum doormen for the local clubs and pubs in the area. He has, until now, been of previous good behaviour. Now it's too much of a coincidence to me that there is firstly a shooting involving Toke at his home address and then Toke is shot down whilst hiding in an allotment. Toke, we believe together with Kevin Finch, were involved in the abduction and killing of Elizabeth Calder. Polden works for Calder. Connection, connection, connection!" He punched his fist into his other palm.

"John Calder has been in on a voluntary basis and interviewed, and has a cast iron alibi for the evening of the fire and claims not to actually know Polden, Polden being one of a large number of people that are employed via an employment agency used by his accountant. This has been verified by both his accountant and the employment agency. Tony Pitman however, whom some of you may also know, has yet to be interviewed, DS Toller is in the throes of bringing Pitman in now. Pitman for those of you that don't know is Calder's right-hand man. He's a bit of a bad lad, but he's very canny and although we suspect he's behind some beatings etc, we've never been able to prove anything. Martin Conner recently is a good case in point. We're checking CCTV cameras in the area to see if Pitman's car can be identified as being anywhere near the vicinity of the fire. Now going back to Polden, prior to being dropped off at the hospital, Polden had been treated by someone that had some nursing skills. The bullet had been removed and the wound had been cleaned and stitched, unfortunately for the person treating him, they didn't realise that a small part of the bullet had sheared off on impact and had travelled upwards and damaged Polden's left ventricle.

Polden then developed an infection that triggered a massive stroke that led to his death. So did Polden shoot and kill Toke and did Toke shoot and kill Polden? SOCO are still at the scene and as yet, apart from some blood close to the shed that has been identified as belonging to Toke, there doesn't seem to be any more blood. Which makes me think that more than one person was involved and that they carried the wounded Polden away from the scene. There are quite a lot of footprints in and around the shed that SOCO have made casts of, but as yet we haven't had a chance to check on either Toke's or Polden's shoes. But it does suggest there were more people involved than just the two of them."

Detective Inspector White paused to let them take in what he's told them so far.

"So, we need to interview Pitman and any other of his close associates. We had them in before when Mrs Calder's body was first discovered, so bring them in again. Uniform have been issued with a search warrant and are currently going through Polden's flat with a fine-toothed comb, I'm doubtful they'll turn anything up but it's worth a try. I need someone to go back to the hospital and speak to the security guard who was first on the scene. Get a statement from him and from the doctor and nurse that treated Polden. I also want the tape from the CCTV and I want the clothes Polden was wearing when he was brought into hospital seized and passed to forensics. There may be some cross-evidence, we may be lucky you never know. OK people, Sergeant Willis has some other specific tasks for some of you, so let's get to it and sew this bloody case up. I think four bodies is enough, don't you?"

It was a rhetorical question and he wasn't waiting for any answers. The detectives broke up, some forming into groups to discuss what their next tasks were and some were heading for the door and exiting when Detective Constable Frears came hurrying into the room.

"Sir! Sir!" he said waving his notes in the air excitedly and catching the Detective Inspector's notice.

"Hold up everyone please wait," the Detective Inspector said and waited until Frears reached him. "What have you got for us then, Tim?" he asked hopefully, gesturing Tim forward. "The floor is yours," he announced and stepped to the side.

Frears wasn't used to being centre stage and he felt his stomach drop at the thought of addressing the room full of detectives but it was too late to back down now and he was confident that he'd unearthed some important information that was very relevant to the case. He fussed with his notes bringing them into order and then looked out at the assembled, expectant faces. Oh God, here we go then.

"Hi everybody ... right, well I've been doing some background work into the businesses belonging to John Calder and I think I've come up with something. You're all probably aware of the large building project that's currently under way slightly to the West of the main town centre." There was a ready chorus of assent from the detectives. "Well as you may or not know, it will contain a major supermarket, a five screen cinema complex, a night-club and bars, more shops with flats above and a large car park. This project is set to cost millions. The money is being funded from a conglomerate of companies channelling money into a single company that seems to be the main beneficiary as it were, called Global Holdings.

This is an offshore company but more about that in a moment." Frears was into it now, his nerves gone as his confident built as he recited what he had learnt out loud.

"Now as you've already seen, a number of houses and shops in that area have already been razed to the ground and in time that whole area must be cleared for the project to be fully realised and to make way for all the proposed redevelopment. Now almost slap bang in the middle of it all is a small block of six shops with accommodation above. Four of the shops are still trading and all of the flats are still occupied; now this is where it gets really interesting." He took a breath and carried on. "The block of flats are owned by John Calder." There were murmurs and brief snatches of conversation from the assembled throng. "And the director of Global Holdings is none other than Steven Talbot! And Talbot as we already know has strong links to Tommy Reardon for whom both Harry Toke and Kevin Finch work for. I think that Talbot together with Tommy Reardon sent Toke and Finch to put pressure on Calder to sell his property because without those properties, it places the whole project in jeopardy, and delays to a project of that size could cost the companies involved a small fortune. I think Reardon and Talbot have some explaining to do!"

The Detective Inspector started to applaud and this was taken up by the assembled detectives in the room.

"Tim, well done indeed. That's the breakthrough we've been looking for, brilliant. Right type up everything you've got and I want copies on my desk ASAP." He turned to Sergeant Willis. "David, I want you to pick up Talbot and Reardon and bring them in for questioning. Usual spiel, helping with enquiries etc, etc, if they don't want to come in voluntarily arrest them on suspicion of accessory to murder, that should shake them up a bit. Right get a couple of teams together and bring them in, the rest of you carry on with your allotted tasks and let's go get 'em!" He applauded again and then clapped Tim on the shoulder and shook his hand. "A great job Tim, well done. I think you deserve a coffee!"

Tim felt his face flush with embarrassment and pride as the room quickly cleared and Tim followed Detective Inspector White out of the incident room heading for the coffee machine and a well-earned cuppa.

Chapter Forty-Five

Upon hearing of the death of Johnnie Polden, Pitman had presented himself straightaway at the police station, together with Jeffrey Morgan, Calder's solicitor, hoping to gain a few brownie points. They were now sitting in the interview room with detectives Toller and Moore. The preliminaries over, Toller commenced the interview.

"Thank you for coming in Mr Pitman. Now as you've already been informed, Mr Polden who I believe you know, died earlier today from a gunshot wound. What can you tell me about that?"

"Nothing really. Mr Calder told me what had happened and said you lot had been round to his place and that you'd want to interview me as I knew Johnnie, so here I am. But with regards to the shooting, what makes you think that I would know anything other than what Mr Calder had told me?"

The ball was definitely back in Toller's court and he knew it, he would have to be careful how he played it.

"There's a lot of rumours and speculation flying about out there and I was wondering what you'd heard?"

"I've heard only what Mr Calder told me. That Johnnie had been shot and that he'd died from a stroke and that no arrests had been made … again," he added for effect.

"So where were you yesterday evening, say from twenty hundred until midnight?"

"I was down The Tavern, drinking. I was with a girlfriend of mine, Chrissie. I picked her up just before eight and we left there about half ten. And before you ask, yes, a lot of people can verify the fact I was in the pub and *again,* before you ask, Chrissie stayed all night. My next door neighbour can also confirm that as Chrissie had left her car partially across her driveway. With regards as to how we spent the rest of the evening, would you like a detailed blow by blow account? Although I can't guarantee my timing would be spot on, you might be better off asking Chrissie." He smiled and sat back and relaxed in his chair.

"And this would be Chrissie who?" Toller asked.

"Dixon."

"She's not a nurse is she?" Toller asked.

"No she's not. But she's game. If you've got a nurse's outfit, she'd probably wear it if that's what turns you on."

"What does she do?"

Pitman smiled. "Just about everything."

"Look Pitman," Toller responded irritably, "this is not the time for jokes. Two men are dead and one of them is connected to you."

"And that's why I'm here … to help you with your enquiries. I think that's the technical term, isn't it?"

"So what can you tell me about Mr Polden?"

"Not a lot really. We've met a few times and we've had a few beers together and that's about it really. I don't tend to socialise much with Mr Calder's employees."

"So how come you've been out drinking with Mr Polden then? Why him?"

"I didn't say I'd been out drinking with him. I said we'd had a few beers together. Mr Calder has three night clubs and two casinos and quite a number of other businesses which you're no doubt aware of, and I've met Johnnie, Mr Polden on several different occasions in the clubs and we've had a drink together when we've been discussing business."

"What type of business?"

"Club business. To do with *the club*." Pitman raised an eyebrow at Toller and relaxed back into his chair.

"So do you know any of Mr Polden's associates?"

"I'm on nodding terms with quite a few yes. Again, we meet in the clubs to do with business. As I said, I don't generally socialise with them outside of the clubs and businesses."

Toller looked at his notes. "Do you know David Raine?"

"I know a Davey-Boy, what his surname is I wouldn't have a clue."

"And how about Steven Morgan. Do you know him?"

"Again, I know a Stevie from the clubs but I'm not familiar with any of their surnames. It might be the Steve you're referring to, it might not be. You'd be better off speaking to Mr Calder's accountant he deals with all the staff through Pentangle Employment Agency. Neither Mr Calder nor myself have very much to do with staff only when a problem of some sort arises. I do know that all three have been interviewed before when Mrs Calder's body was found.'"

"So would you know if Steve Morgan and David Raines were good friends?"

Pitman shrugged. "They work the same clubs not always on the same night and not always at the same venue, they work on a rota system, so yes they would know each other in conjunction with their work, beyond that I wouldn't have a clue what they did in their spare time, that's got nothing to do with me."

Toller pressed on regardless. "So would you know if they were both working on Wednesday night or if it was their night off?"

"It's not something I would know. As I said, you'd need to speak to either Pentangle or …"

Toller cut Pitman off. "Yes I've got that thank you."

"So why are you so interested in those two men?"

"My understanding is, all three are good friends and I need to know their whereabouts for Wednesday night, just the same as I did for you."

"And this is in connection with the death of Johnnie yes?"

"Yes."

"And you think I may have had something to do with that, do you?" Pitman felt Morgan lightly tap on his sleeve.

"I'm just saying we need to speak to you all in connection with an ongoing enquiry."

"Mm," was all that Pitman had to offer in response.

Morgan addressed Toller. "My client has given a full account of his whereabouts for Wednesday evening, all of which can be readily verified and furthermore he has told you of his scant knowledge of the other men apart from infrequent meetings via their places of employment. Now if there's nothing further you need to ask, I think we've done all we can to assist you." Morgan stood and gestured for Pitman to follow suit.

Toller laid his pen down neatly in line with the edge of his notes and stood. "Thank you for coming in gentlemen it's very much appreciated." He watched them troop out of the room and then whipped his hand along the desk and flung his notes and pen across the room. "Fuck it all!" he said and jabbed his finger at the buttons stopping the tape from any further recording.

Chapter Forty-Six

The caravan site wasn't exactly what you'd call posh; it had twenty-seven static vans on it and twenty caravans that they let out, usually in the summer months. But the man who had enquired about a partial winter let had informed him that he was a writer and he had a deadline to meet on his latest book and that he was looking for somewhere quiet to write. So Mr Hindley who owned the site had agreed to tow one of the holiday-let vans further away from the rest of the site down nearer the trees and away from the facilities on the site, where the writer hoped it would be peaceful enough to overcome his current bout of writer's block. Mr Hindley had been happy to do so when the man insisted on paying three months' rental up front in *cash* and Mr Hindley grateful for the unexpected lengthy out-of-season booking, had readily given him a ten percent discount and assured him that he wouldn't be bothered during his stay.

That was almost two weeks ago and Finch was becoming stir-crazy. He hadn't shaved in that time and had also let his hair grow, so in essence he had made a lazy attempt to disguise himself a little. The inside of the caravan stunk of cigarettes, which wasn't surprising when you looked at the overflowing ashtrays and the dog ends that had been cast into the grubby sink that itself was clogged with dirty crockery. The thin curtains were pulled closed and they stayed that way day and night regardless. Finch lay back on the bed propped up with pillows watching a small colour television that had a very poor reception that made the picture all fuzzy round the edges. He had a can of lager in one hand and a half-smoked cigarette in the other.

Further down the room sitting at the table were two other men playing cards, they too were both smoking. One was a Romanian, Anton Buscan, formerly from Bucharest who had fled his native country after killing a policeman in an aborted burglary in the town centre. Luckily for him, although he had basically made his living from stealing since he was eleven years old, he'd never been caught, so there was nothing known about him. He'd managed to get a job aboard a cruise ship and when the ship docked at Southampton, he decamped and made his way to London and had never set foot in his own country again. He was a hard man, as adept with a knife as he was with a gun. Both of which he carried with him at all times. He wasn't afraid or reluctant to kill, if the money was right he'd do just about anything for anyone and right now he was bodyguarding the pathetic little English man lying on his bed who shit bricks every time he heard a car door slam or a dog barked.

The other man was English, John Deacon, he had worked with Buscan twice before and he too was not backwards in coming forward when things got heavy. Unlike Buscan, he had a record as long as his arm and was currently wanted for manslaughter. If you asked him about the charge he'd laugh in your face and tell you it wasn't manslaughter, it was murder, he'd wanted to kill the man and he had, slicing through his neck with the knife he usually wore strapped to his ankle that was so sharp it could cut through a sheet of paper if you just dropped it across the blade. The knife was his favourite because you had to get up close and personal to use it and he liked the buzz he got from that. He too carried a gun and he sure as hell wouldn't hesitate to use it. He'd currently skipped bail whilst waiting to be tried for the manslaughter case.

Both men had been with Finch for just over a week. The two bodyguards took it in turns to leave the caravan to buy provisions, they always left at different times and they also took a different route on each trip. Caution was the byword; it helped to keep you alive.

Finch still had funds to pay the two men but he knew his money wouldn't last indefinitely and he also knew that Pitman wouldn't stop searching for him and that sooner or later there'd be a showdown and only one of them would walk away from it. Neither Buscan or Deacon knew Pitman like Finch did so they weren't unduly worried by the prospect and were more than willing if the price was right to take him out and earn a fuck-off bonus for doing so, trouble was, Finch had been unable to come up with a foolproof plan as yet and the clock was ticking and now that Toke was dead, Pitman and his boys would be spending all their efforts in tracking him down.

Chapter Forty-Seven

Pitman pulled into the driveway of his house and cut the engine. He was tired, he hadn't been sleeping too well lately and the stress of the last few weeks had started to take their toll. He rubbed the knuckles of his hands into the corners of his eyes trying to ease the tension. What he could do with was a full massage with some slinky smooth-skinned Thai bird with amazing hands that would go in deep and hard and work all the knots out. It was a nice thought and he was still thinking of the prospect when he climbed out of the car and that's when he thought he caught a movement to the side of his house. That side of the house was partially in shadow, the security lights had come on automatically as he drove into his driveway but not every nook and cranny was covered and some of the shrubs that grew alongside that side of the house could have done with a trim. It provided a perfect place to hide.

Pitman stopped and made out he'd forgotten something in the car and turned back and clicked open the boot. He ducked inside and pretended to be searching for something whilst continually checking through the gap between the boot lid and the car's rear bodywork. There it was again! There was definitely someone there. Easiest thing to do was to get back in the car and drive away, but

Pitman had never taken the easy route before in his life. If there was someone waiting there, if it didn't happen today it would only happen another day, at least now he had seen the danger and could prepare for it. He picked up the extension bar for unscrewing the wheel nuts on his tyres and held it so the bar was running upwards along his wrist and lower arm out of sight. He closed the boot lid down and clicked the key fob securing the vehicle. He started to walk towards the front door, his pulse had started to quicken and his senses were on full alert. He just hoped that whoever it was they didn't just start blasting away with a gun - that would certainly change the tide in their favour.

He was almost at the steps the led up to the front door when he heard a noise from the opposite side to where he had first seen movement. He stopped and waited, he doubted the person he had originally seen could have moved without him seeing, so that meant that there was more than one of them ... OK. It was what it was, bring it on then and let's get it over with.

Pitman turned towards the sound and tensed ready for action. But it wasn't Finch as he had first suspected. It was the big black guy from Carson's office, and he'd brought a friend with him. The man Pitman had first caught a glimpse of joined the other two and they fanned out making a semi-circle in front of Pitman. Pitman wondered if he could make it to the front door and get inside where he kept a licensed and loaded firearm in the desk drawer, but he doubted he could run up the steps, get the key in the lock at the first attempt, open the door and hold off the advance of three guys thirsting for blood whilst he opened the drawer and cocked the weapon. No, it would happen here and now, this was it.

The big black stepped forward, "Remember me, Pitman?" he asked, curling back his lip.

"Yeah course I do," Pitman replied lightly still not revealing the extension bar, "you're the big tub of lard that Carson employed to protect him that was as much use as a fucking chocolate teapot. I see you've come back with your mates for another lesson then, have you?" Pitman spread his legs and balanced his weight evenly.

"Yeah well, times is changed white boy, now I'm gonna carve you up good and proper!" He slashed the knife he held around in the air to show he meant business.

That's it you fucking amateur, always telegraph your intention and leave yourself wide open Pitman observed, good start.

Pitman burst out laughing which momentarily threw his waiting attackers; that was the last thing they had been expecting. All three of them exchanged glances; Pitman meanwhile was biding his time. He knew that the security lights came on as soon as he entered the drive but only stayed on for three minutes, which gave him enough time to park the car and walk up the steps and unlock the door, any second now the lights would go off and he would be ready.

As soon as the lights went off Pitman hurled himself at Marvin Reid, the large black man. He swung the extension bar round with his full force behind it and it smashed the black man across the side of his head and he crashed down onto the floor, Pitman was already moving before the other two had even realised what was happening or the danger that was coming at them.

Pitman hit the nearest man across the side of his face with the bar and he screamed, the force of the blow knocked him into the third man. The third man was different he was tooled up and he raised the gun and fired. The sound was deafening close up but he hadn't had time to aim and the shot went high. He didn't have time for a second shot Pitman grabbed the second man and used him as a shield and slammed him into the gunman and then unable to use the bar effectively lashed out with his foot and slammed it into his attackers' left knee. The force was such that the kneecap twisted to the side and the man's leg gave way, the pain sent shockwaves through his body and he dropped the gun and screamed in agony clutching at his useless leg.

Pitman picked up the gun and covered the three men, slowly moving the gun across them one at a time. "Eeny, meeny, miny, mo. Now who do I shoot first? You?" he asked standing over the second man who lay on the floor still dazed but not enough to realise how much shit he was in. He curled up into a ball and covered his head with his arms. "Or how about you, Hopalong?" Pitman asked aiming the gun at the man whose face was contorted in agony still grasping his damaged knee. Pitman turned his attention to Reid and kicked the big black man who was just coming round and he grunted and stirred. Pitman bent down and held the gun against the man's temple. "Listen up you piece of shit, I can't think of one good reason not to smear your brains all over my driveway. You've had two chances now and you blew them both. Now you ever come anywhere near me or my crew in the future and I will kill you. And that ain't a threat that's a fucking promise!" Pitman rammed the barrel of the gun hard into the man's temple. Reid's head had already started to swell and was bleeding quite badly. Marvin groaned and sagged back. "And I'll tell you something else for nothing as well, as soon as I get indoors I shall be on the blower and

I'll have your address. I'll also know very quickly if you're married, how many kids you've got and how often you change your fucking socks and I'll be watching you. Now pick up the rest of your pussy garbage and get your fat arse off my driveway … now!" Pitman barked and the three injured men helped each other up and together they limped back down the driveway. Pitman watched them leave and then put the extension bar back into the boot together with the gun; he'd get rid of the gun in the morning it wasn't worth hanging on to it you never knew its history.

What a fucking day Pitman thought as he cast another look down his lit driveway before he climbed the steps to his home and temporary sanctuary.

Chapter Forty-Eight

Both Reardon and Talbot had been brought in for questioning. Reardon had played dumb and pretended not to know either Finch or Toke and had a ready list to hand of all the people that worked for him both on a regular basis and on a casual cash-in-hand basis. As he said, he had nothing to hide and wasn't connected in any way, shape, or form with the murder of Mrs Calder and indeed brought along proof that he had been out of the country when she was murdered and was most aggrieved that his good reputation had been brought into question especially as soon as he had heard he had sent a large bouquet of flowers.

That left Steven Talbot, who openly produced duplicate paperwork offering to buy the properties belonging to John Calder. He had further explained about the alternative plans he'd had drawn up if Mr Calder didn't want to sell and he had produced them and left the officers with a copy. If in the event his business friend decided not to sell, then the development would still go ahead but with slightly altered plans. In essence although there was a connection, and in Talbot's case, a motive, there was no actual evidence that could be brought against either man at this time and both were released without charge. Nevertheless, the investigation would continue with both of them sitting firmly in the frame.

Chapter Forty-Nine

Dave Wicks had his own little business called 'Handy Van.' It was a one-man business and he was proud that he could make a living from it. Nothing fancy or grand like, but he could pay his bills and he was never skint and he could still manage to put a bit by and save a bob or two. No two days were ever the same and that was one of the things he liked about it. One day he could be cleaning out a house for a letting agency, the next day he could be doing a garden rubbish clearance. Another day he might be delivering a parcel for someone or a small furniture removal. If he could lift it and he could fit it in the van, he'd deliver it for you, provided you didn't want it carried up fourteen fucking flights of stairs when he got to the other end!

Dave lived about a mile from the caravan site, this time of year it was fine, he didn't like it quite so much in the summer though, it brought extra traffic into the narrow roads close to where he lived and twice he'd had a wing mirror knocked off, but he just got on with things and life rarely got Dave down. Now he wrapped a hi-vis vest around the offside mirror when he parked his van up for the night and touch wood, since he'd started doing that no one else had knocked his mirror off.

Most mornings Dave popped into the local Tesco Express to grab a sandwich and a drink to carry him through the morning and then he dropped in again on the way home to grab a pie or a microwave dinner to finish off the day with. He'd just grabbed a newspaper and was coming out of the aisle and heading towards the tills when he heard someone talking with a foreign accent. He looked up and recognised the man doing the talking. Dave was good with faces, he never forgot one. Names he was crap with but faces he never forgot.

He'd seen the man three times now in the last six or seven days and he'd just supposed he'd recently moved in somewhere close by. Like most areas nowadays they were all getting their share of immigrants and there was nothing anyone could do about it so you just had to accept it and get on with your own life. The man was at the till and as usual he had a full basket. He pulled some notes out of his pocket and dropped a fiver on the floor, as he bent down to pick it up Dave noticed the handgun stuck down the waistband of his trousers. Instinct and the need for self-preservation took over and he edged back into the aisle and suddenly faked an avid interest in the pet foods piled up on the shelves whilst he kept obs on the foreign man curious as to what he would do next.

Dave thought that maybe he was going to rob the store and that the previous times he'd been in he'd merely been casing the place and that today was the day he was going to do it. It didn't seem worth it to Dave, it was too early in the morning for there to be much money in the tills and he knew for a fact that once the money started to build up, for security reasons it was taken out of the tills and locked in the safe. He watched as the man paid for his groceries and then walked towards the exit carrying his shopping bags. Dave walked up to the till and put his basket down and explained he'd left his money in his van and would be straight back in. Dave followed the man out of the shop keeping a safe distance behind him. Dave unclipped his mobile and clicked on the memo icon looking to all intents and purposes that he was texting someone, when in actual fact he was noting down a description of the man whilst watching what car he was heading towards. The foreigner opened up the boot to a black Renault and put the groceries in the boot and slammed the lid shut and climbed into the car and drove away. Dave wrote down the registration number in his memo and then unlocked his van and climbed in and started the engine.

Dave dithered for a few moments, should he make the call or not? He knew people, OK? And yes, when he had first started he had done a couple of dodgy deals. One in particular sprang to mind regarding a building site in the dead of night where a brand new fitted kitchen that had only recently been installed in the show-house two days before, had miraculously disappeared overnight thanks to Dave and a couple of chums looking to make a few quid. But that was a few years ago and Dave was pretty straight now. Dave decided that it was worth a call especially as he knew there was ten grand up for grabs if the info led to someone getting fingered, no names and no pack drill, he had nothing to lose. So it might be worth it, besides he wasn't happy about someone out and about in broad daylight carrying a gun. It might be something it might not, but for the price of one small phone call, you just never knew ...

Chapter Fifty

Kenny was lined up on the black and just about to take the shot when his phone rang. "Shit!" he exploded, his concentration lost. He straightened up, laid the cue across the table and pulled out his mobile.

"Hey!" Andy cried out, "Whatcha doing? Take the shot man we gotta game going here; it ain't 'phone a friend time!'"

Kenny grinned back at the man and took the call walking away from the table. "Yeah hi Dave, you alright? Long time no hear mate, how are things?"

"We got a game going on here!" Andy called out after him and leant back on the table and took a slow deep drink of his beer.

"Yeah," Kenny said interested, "the money's still up for grabs as far as I know. You got something then?" Kenny pulled out a slim notebook with a pen attached and clicked the pen and opened the book. He listened. "So you've seen this foreign guy a few times yeah? Three or four. OK so what makes you think there maybe something going on then?" Kenny listened. He was a good listener. He moved further away from the table. "Tooled up yeah. And you clocked the motor? That's brilliant, yeah go ahead I've got a pen."

Dave gave him the vehicle reg and Kenny noted it down. "And you followed him? Shit, did you? So where'd he go then?"

Dave told Kenny that he had trailed the guy for about a mile keeping well back but that was no problem as it was home ground to Dave and he saw him drive onto Meadow View Caravan Park.

"It's a static mobile home park but it has caravans to let as well throughout the year. I was just thinking that maybe Finch was holed up there and he'd hired a minder to protect him?" Dave said.

"You could be right, no one's seen hide nor hair of Finch for getting on for two weeks so he's gone to ground somewhere and from what you're saying that could be the perfect place. If he's staying put, there's no passing traffic and no one's likely to just clock him if he stays in the van waiting for the heat to die down. Good one mate, I'll pass it on and keep you in the loop. This is the place off Bury Avenue, isn't it?"

"Yeah that's the one," Dave replied.

"Sweet, I'll get back to you and thanks mate, Tone will be pleased if it comes through and he'll see you alright, don't worry. Later." Kenny disconnected the call and stood there for a moment digesting the information. It sounded good to him and pretty viable. Kenny scrolled down his list of contacts and hit the number for Tony Pitman.

"Oi we playing or not you wanker!" Andy yelled out.

Kenny made his way back to the table and flipped a tenner onto the table. "I'll give you that one, double or quits next time yeah, I've gotta split. Sorry mate business calls." Kenny turned away and headed for the exit as Tony answered the call.

"You'd have lost anyway!" Andy yelled after him pocketing the note. Kenny gave him the finger and left the snooker club grinning as Tony spoke to him.

Kenny explained what Dave had told him and Tony agreed that he could well be onto something. It was decided that Kenny would go down to the caravan park and see if they had an office or get a phone number for the site manager and make enquiries about hiring a caravan for the Easter break, that would give him an opportunity to take a look around the site and keep his eye out for the black Renault. Kenny said he'd go down around lunchtime when there might be more chance of someone being there who could show him some caravans and better still show him around the site.

Chapter Fifty-One

Marvin Reid's head was killing him and that's exactly what he wanted to do to Pitman: kill the bastard. Reid had lost face in front of two of his 'brothers' and what little street cred he had had vanished overnight. Now it felt like even little fourteen year old jive-asses on the street were taking the piss and laughing at him. Not to his face exactly but he knew it was going on. He had to take Pitman down or die trying or he'd never be worth shit in this town ever again.

Reid now carried a gun, it had been stupid not to have been more prepared the last time they'd met up but he figured three to one was good odds in his favour and he'd used both the 'brothers' before and the result had been sensational! They'd knocked over a bookie's together and got away with thousands. It had been a one-off chance thing where a cousin of a friend who had a window cleaning round had been cleaning the windows of a house next to a bookmaker's for a first time customer, and he'd noticed that members of staff would come out of the back door of the premises, prop the door open and have a cigarette. He'd also noticed that there were no cameras around the back of the building. That little nugget of information had earned him a century when Reid and Co pulled the job two days later.

It had been a piece of piss; Reid and Smarts, aptly named because he only ever wore designer gear, had been waiting at the rear of the building just before five o'clock and Darren had been sitting in the service road out the back in a stolen Beemer with the engine running. There had been three big race meetings that day and they figured it being a Thursday, that they would probably bank the takings for the week on the Friday before the weekend punters tried their luck. Smarts had just put a gun to the head of the terrified woman who'd popped out for a quick fag and then the two men wearing 'Scream' masks had walked her back into the building and created havoc. They'd copped just over twenty-seven grand on that little job and both his boys had stayed cool and done exactly as he'd asked, so he knew they were sound.

Next time he'd plan it better and then he'd fucking take Pitman down ... third time lucky man, bring it on. So with planning in mind, Paine had organised some young brothers on bikes and others with their own cars to keep a low profile not to get involved but just to watch Pitman and see where he went and what he did and see if there was a pattern on certain days or nights etc. Reid suspected he probably had some bitch he saw from time to time and once a man's dick was hard he wouldn't be concentrating on anything else, that would be insulting to the bitch and even a bitch had feelings and that would be the best time to take him out.

Chapter Fifty-Two

Kenny drove up and parked outside the wooden shack-type office on the Meadow View Caravan Park. It was a quarter to one. The windows to the office were covered in flyers and fluorescent out-of-date adverts and Kenny couldn't even be sure it was open or if there was anyone in there. He got out of his car and had a brief glance around before he walked up and opened the door; he didn't want to alert Finch if he was watching the comings and goings of the office. The wooden door creaked as Kenny pushed it open, he guessed it had slightly swollen with all the rain they'd had lately. Inside it smelt slightly musty probably because out of season the door was always shut to keep the cold out.

A woman in an old grey cardigan was tapping away behind an old-fashioned computer and seemed surprised at his intrusion.

"Can I help you?" she offered stopping what she was doing and standing.

"Yeah hi," Kenny said amiably, "I was thinking about booking a van for the Easter break for six of us for a week. I didn't know if it was possible to have a look at a couple of the vans just to get an idea like you know?"

"Oh," she said apologetically, "well Mr Hindley's not here at the present. We don't see much of him during the winter months. It's out of season you see."

"Oh that's a shame," Kenny said acting out the role, "I've made a special journey down I've got a wedding tomorrow and I thought I could kill two birds with one stone." He tutted and frowned.

"You just want to look at a couple of vans you said?" Kenny nodded.

She didn't really want to risk losing a potential customer; bookings had been dropping off for years. So many other sites had so much more to offer nowadays, so unless you liked hiking through the woods or fishing in the large lake, apart from the beautiful setting, the site didn't really have much else to offer.

"I could show you if you like?" she offered.

"Well if it's no trouble," Kenny replied giving her his best, smooth smile.

She pulled an old anorak off the coat stand and as she went to put it on Kenny stepped in and held it for her.

"Oh, that's very kind of you," she gushed not used to being treated so formally. She grabbed a couple of sets of keys off a large board and headed towards the door. "I'd better lock up, you just can't afford to trust anyone these days I'm afraid."

"I know what you mean," Kenny agreed as he held the door open for her and then she closed it and locked it shut behind them.

"I can show you one of our premier range. It sleeps eight and it has all mod cons as they say," she giggled and led the way down the tarmac drive.

"You said about out-of-season. I can see you've got some static vans here, so do many people stay in the winter months then?"

"No not really, we sometimes get a few stragglers in late September time but not many." The woman lowered her voice a little. "We do have someone staying here at the moment though; he's a writer, quite famous by all accounts. He needed somewhere quiet to finish off his latest book. I haven't met him, Mr Hindley has of course, he said he seemed like one of those people that liked to keep himself to himself if you know what I mean. He never goes out he just keeps working away. I suppose that's what you have to do to meet your deadlines. I wouldn't really know I don't know much about writing. He's got a secretary who does his shopping and things for him. He's foreign, I've met him. He doesn't speak English very well; I had to show him how to change the gas bottle. Anyway, Mr Hindley moved one of the vans right down next to the woods to give him some extra privacy so he's out of harm's way down there. And it's nice and quiet for him which I suppose is what he was after for his writing. Right this is the Regent then," she said climbing up the short flight of steps that led to the door of the garish pink-painted caravan.

But Kenny wasn't paying attention; he was more interested in the caravan parked right down the end away from the road and the other caravans, because lo and behold, there was a black car parked alongside it. It was too far away to see what the make was but it was black and the man renting it had asked to be moved away for extra privacy and he had a 'secretary' with him that just happened to be foreign! It had to be him. And the only writing that Finch should be concentrating on was his last will and testament because the net was drawing in.

Chapter Fifty-Three

If there was one thing Tony Pitman wasn't, and that was stupid. And it wasn't long before he began to notice youngsters on push bikes who seemed to be up and down his road all the time, stopping and chatting into mobiles whilst clocking him as he drove past. He'd also noticed and old dark blue Fiesta that popped up quite regularly and a red Golf. He didn't have to be Brain of Britain to realise that people were following him and reporting back to someone. Tony suspected that someone was Marvin Reid, and he'd grab one of the little shits and find out for himself very soon.

Tony pulled over to the side of the road and turned off the engine and waited. It wasn't long before a young black guy materialised out of the adjoining road and stopped his bike and reported it in. Pitman slid down in his seat so he was no longer visible through the window. He'd long ago removed the interior light and he opened the passenger door and slid out onto the pavement. He kept very still, all he had to do now was wait and sooner or later the lad would get curious and cycle over to see what had happened.

Seven minutes later Tony heard the swish of tyres and when he looked under his car he could see a cycle wheel. He moved up into a crouch and then sped around the front of the car and surprised the youth who was so taken aback he dropped his mobile. Pitman grabbed the boy and yanked him off his bike.

"What the fuck you doing!" Pitman demanded, holding the youth in a powerful wrist lock and ramming the boys arm up his back.

"Get off me you fucking Paedo!" The boy yelled trying to break free. Pitman applied a little more pressure and the boy stopped moving.

"Keep very still and very quiet or I'll snap your arm. D'you understand?" Pitman gave the lad's arm a tweak and he cried out and nodded his head. "Right, so I don't want to hear any shit, I just need you to tell me who's paying you to keep obs on me. Tell me the truth and I'll let you go. Lie to me and you'll be trying to call for an ambulance with two broken arms. Might be a little bit tricky."

The fight drained out of the boy and he realised that all he'd heard about the man was true; he *was* one tough evil motherfucker!

"It's a friend of a friend man, that's the truth," he gushed.

"That's not very helpful to me though, is it? A friend of a friend," Pitman replied calmly, bending the boy's arm a little further up his back. The boy winced and stood on his toes trying to take some of the pressure off.

"Reid! Marvin Reid! He's the one doing the asking, straight up man that's all I know. He said you set on him with your gang and done him, so he's looking to wipe you out man. That's it, that's it man! There ain't no more to tell!"

Pitman replied calmly. "There now, that wasn't so difficult, was it? So has he got any plans?"

"I dunno!" The boy said irritably hoping that now he'd told the man what he wanted to hear he'd just let him go like he'd said he would. Typical white man, nothing but fucking dirty liars all of 'em! "We'd just been told to follow ya and see where you go. He was hoping you got some bitch tucked away so then he could ram-raid your arse and take you out whilst you was in the middle of dirty dancing!"

Pitman smiled. So Reid wasn't going to let it go then. He wanted to try for a hat trick of getting himself battered, well so be it then. It needed to be put to rest; Pitman did not relish having to keep looking over his shoulder for evermore. Pitman released the boy and shoved him forward and he fell awkwardly onto the pavement. "If I see you again we'll find out how many bits of your bike I can fit up your arse. Now piss off before I change my mind."

The boy scrambled forwards and yanked his bike up and jumped on it. "I hope he fucking gets you, you fucking sicko!" The boy gave Pitman the finger and cycled off as fast as his legs could carry him forever turning round to make sure Pitman wasn't in hot pursuit, his heart pumping fit to burst. He couldn't wait to report it in and then he stopped. He didn't have his mobile, he'd dropped it when Pitman had dashed around the car. "Fucking hell!" The boy yelled to himself. That was a cracking phone that was. That was part of a haul he'd got with Kane when they'd turned over a house in Miller's Lane that had left a side window open as an invitation to visit and they'd made quite a killing from there. The phone was part of Delroy's cut and now he'd lost it, it wasn't so much the phone, he could soon get another one, it was the numbers on it he'd have a job to replace and there were some stunning little chicks on there, damn the man, damn him all the way to hell and back!

Pitman picked up the phone and shoved it in his pocket. He'd trawl through the list of contacts later when he had more time. You never know there might be some interesting connections in there. Pitman got back in his car and drove away. The black youth was nowhere to be seen.

Chapter Fifty-Four

Pitman was sat in the small downstairs bedroom that served as his office. Davey-Boy was leaning against the wall and Steve was sat in one of the other vacant chairs.

"So," Pitman said, "as I said it's up to you guys. You want to walk away now, it's no big deal, I'll just get some other guys in. I appreciate all you've done and so does Mr C and it has got pretty heavy but there again, if we don't come down hard on people then slowly but surely we'll lose our grip and other teams will start muscling in on our patch and I won't stand by and see that happen. Not while I can still deal with it anyway, but I sure as hell ain't getting any younger," he added with a smile.

"I'm in boss," Stevie said, "No one cuts me and shoots at me, they have to go down and I kinda owe it to Mrs Calder, she was always lovely to me. Let's just get it done."

Pitman nodded. "OK, thanks Stevie."

Davey-Boy looked across at Stevie. "Oh well if he's in, I'm in, Christ knows how he'd avoid fucking it up if I'm not there looking after him!"

Stevie flung his arm out and slapped Davey-Boy on the arm and Davey-Boy growled back at him good-naturedly.

Pitman continued. "Brilliant ... thank you. Right, so from what Kenny's said, we're ninety-nine percent certain that Finch along with some foreign bloke are holed up in a caravan on Meadow View Caravan Site. We do know the foreign guy's a big lad and that he's tooled up, and going on what's been happening I think it's fair to assume that Finch will be carrying now as well. They're parked right down the far end of the site. Finch apparently told the site manager he was a writer and that he needed peace and quiet, so the manager towed the caravan right down to the edge of the forest. So in one way, that makes it easy for us to come up through the woods behind the van where we can't really be seen, unless he's rigged up some security lights or something but I don't think Finch is that clever. Now we do know the layout of the caravan, Kenny had a good look round an identical van so I can tell you there's only the one door and the windows are all double-glazed. There's two windows on each side and a large picture window at the rear. I haven't figured out how we're going to get in yet. The windows are metal framed and so's the door, so once we start making any kind of noise they're liable to hear us and start blasting away."

Tony paused and then carried on. "I have come up with one idea. I phoned up the site myself after Kenny had dropped into see me and said that my friend was staying with me due to the wedding tomorrow ..." Stevie and Davey exchanged looks.

"What wedding?" Davey-Boy asked interrupting.

"The fictional one that Kenny was telling them about as to why he was down here."

"Oh right, you had me worried for a moment then, I thought I might have to put me hand in me pocket to buy you something!" They all laughed at the thought.

Pitman continued. "Anyway, I said my friend forgot to ask about the power to the caravans. And the very helpful lady said there was a mains hook up to every van and that every van had their own RCD board …"

"What the fuck's that?" Davey-Boy asked.

"Ah," Pitman said trying to remember. "I can't remember what the initials stand for, but it's basically a device that cuts off the electrical supply to the caravan if there's a fault or the system gets overloaded."

"So where we going with all this then Tone? You gonna wire up the van as it's metal and electrocute the bastards? That'll be a good un that would! Yeah I'd like to see that!" They all enjoyed the thought and then Pitman picked up where he'd left off.

"No, but you're on the right lines. Right, so I've spoken to Billy Scott, he's a sparky and told him what I want and this is what I've decided to do. You two will make your way through the woods and you'll be in constant contact with me so I know exactly where you are at all times. Once you get within sight of the caravan you need to hang fire, no pun intended." All three cracked up at the memory of the burning shed. "So soon as I know you're there, Billy will cut the power to the main generator that supplies electricity to the whole of the site. Hopefully they won't just start shooting but will realise that the power has gone off and either look out their windows or better still come out to investigate and they'll see that it's not just their van that's gone off, it's the whole site and that hopefully will give us a way in."

"Why can't we just unplug their hook-up then?" Davey-Boy asked.

"Because if they look out and everyone else's power is still on, they're going to realise that something's going on and all hell will break lose. No, it's got to be everyone off and then as soon as one of them leaves the van to check things out," Pitman reached down and picked up a large round metal unit and swung it round towards the two men and switched it on. The Dragon light illuminated the whole room. Stevie and Davey-Boy yelled and shielded their eyes turning away from the dazzling bright light.

"Fucking hell!" Davey said, "It's like being in the blitz and being hit by a searchlight!"

"Turn it off!" Stevie shouted walking across the room to get away from the light. "It's setting fire to my clothes. Shit that's bright."

Pitman turned the light off. Both men were still having trouble letting their eyes adjust to the light. Davey-Boy especially kept blinking and rubbing at his eyes.

"Sorry about that guys," Pitman said putting the lamp back on the floor. "That's what you'll do when you see them; it'll momentarily blind them …"

Danny cut in, "It momentarily blinded me! I still can't see properly!"

"It'll be alright don't worry. Your retina gets smaller to protect your eye and stop too much light from entering," Pitman explained.

"It's a bit late for that!" Stevie said wiping the tears away. "Christ that works a bloody treat that does."

"That's what I'm hoping for. I don't want any more dead bodies. We just need to get Finch away from there so Mr C can have a word and get the full story and then he can go on a little holiday courtesy of the NHS!" All three of them laughed. Tony always had a good way of putting things.

"So when you planning on going in then boss?" Stevie asked, "Provided you haven't done me eyes any permanent damage."

"And me!" Davey-Boy chorused in.

"Yeah alright, alright children," Pitman grinned at them. "Tomorrow, I'll make sure it's alright with Billy because without him we can't do it. And then we'll get together at mine about half-eight and talk it all through. It'll take you about twenty minutes or so to walk through the woods from the cut-in on Gravel Road, that's provided you don't get lost! I know what you two losers are like!"

"Fucking cheek!" Stevie said. "I love it; he blinds us and then expects us to find our way through Hundred Acre Wood in the dead of night!"

"Yeah well the bear would have more chance of finding his way there than you two will ever have!" Pitman replied and all three broke up laughing.

Chapter Fifty-Five

Darren had parked the Fiesta further up the road and had walked closer to Pitman's house. He'd clocked one of Pitman's regular crew driving past him and had phoned it in and now Smarts had seen another one turn up at the house. They were getting ready for something and they wondered if it had anything to do with a revenge attack on Marvin.

Marvin was organising his troops, this was gonna be one big fuck-off battle to settle things once and for all and Darren wanted to be part of it. He'd been moving up and gaining favour for the last few months and this could be the day to really prove his worth and progress in the crew. He reassured himself by tapping the butt of the gun he had in his pocket. He'd never actually fired the gun yet, he'd only ever threatened people with it, but he was big enough and mean enough *not* to have actually fired it, the mere fact he had one and pointed it at you had always been enough so far, he was one mad fucker when he wanted to be.

Inside Pitman's house the three of them were going over the final plans whilst Chrissie sat in the corner playing on her iPad. Tony had called her over early and he'd sent her round to Pat's with a bottle of wine to apologise for parking partly across her drive the other night and said she'd parked properly tonight and giggled like girls do to show what kind of evening she had lined up. Pat had smiled and taken the bottle, she wouldn't have minded spending the night with Tony herself she thought as she watched the woman sashay back down her driveway on impossible high heels.

Billy would make his own way to the caravan park and had already checked the place out and knew where everything was and what he had to do. Once Pitman gave him the go-ahead he would do his bit and then scarper, he didn't want to know anything more than he'd already been told. Mr Calder put a lot of work his way when he was restoring old houses that needed rewiring or building new ones and OK so if the odd dodgy job came up, it was all part of it as far as Billy was concerned. He was getting a couple of hundred quid for ten minute's work and jobs like that didn't come along very often. It beat climbing about in dirty old lofts and running in new cables at his age. Let's just get it done so I can get back home and put me feet up he thought to himself as he waited for Pitman to phone and start the ball rolling.

Reid on the other hand had nine boys. Four were in their early to mid-twenties but the rest were all in their late teens wanting to move up and make a name for themselves and who was he to deny them the chance. The more the merrier he thought, he was determined not to lose face in front of Pitman again and this time he would take him down. Three of his crew had hand guns and the rest carried an assortment of knives, machetes and baseball bats, plus he himself had a Magnum and he wasn't talking about the fucking ice cream either!

It was time to go to war. As soon as Pitman was mobile he would know and they'd be ready to follow in a trio of cars and then let war commence. Reid touched the side of his head. It was still swollen and still hurt like hell to touch, but that was nothing compared to what was coming Pitman's way, after this he'd be dead.

Chapter Fifty-Six

Tony called Billy and told him it was a go, Billy said he'd leave right away. Davey-Boy and Steve left the house a few minutes later and Tony followed in the Astra with the set of false number plates in place.

Darren called it in and Reid told him to stick with Pitman and said Kane would tag the other car.

"Just don't blow it," Reid said, "if something's going down and we gotta chance to bag that motherfucker then I want to be the one that does it, Pitman's mine. Update me all the time. When he gets to where he's going let me know and I'll send the troops in." Reid cut the call and allowed himself a little smile. "Vengeance is mine sayeth the Lord, yeah well he ain't the only bringer of bad news!" He grinned and held the rolled up note to his nose and inhaled. He sniffed up the lines, gasped and shook his head and his fingers flicked around the opening to his nostrils. "Shit!" He exclaimed shaking his head again. "Shit that's good shit!" He laughed at his joke and pulled on his jacket.

Kane phoned Reid. "Yeah what's happening?" Reid said continuing to sniff and wrinkle his nose.

"The other two they's parked up in Gravel Road and I kept eyes on 'em. Then they got out and they's got some big weird looking round thing with 'em."

"Jesus!" Reid said a note of concern creeping in. Pitman was a nutter and Reid wouldn't put anything past him. "D'you think it could be some kind of bomb?"

"No, it don't look like a bomb type bomb, it's like you know round and silver with a handle on it an' that."

"Fuck knows what that is then," Reid said, "so where'd they at now then?"

"They's in the woods."

"Whatcha mean in the woods? What fucking woods?"

"There's a gate in Gravel Road leads to the woods. Jessie my brother's cuz takes her dog in there, that's how I know. Them woods is big man."

Reid racked his brain. None of this made any sense. Reid's phone beeped he had a call waiting. "Hang on," Reid said and took the other call, it was Darren. "What cha got?" Reid asked.

"Pitman parked up and he's gone walkabout on some caravan park. Too easy to get seen, I'm still on the road. He ain't gonna go for the quick escape tho man, I done his tyres, slit 'em deep. That fucker's sitting on its rims man, it ain't going no place!" he said pleased with what he'd done.

Reid nodded in appreciation. That Darren was a cut above the rest. He could work on his own initiative and not many could. "Good work man yeah. So what's at the caravan park then?"

"Dunno, there's no posters or nothing saying there's a thing on and the man want dressed to party. The man's all in black."

"Go gentle but keep your distance. See where the man goes and see what he's doing yeah?"

"Yeah man I'm on it." Darren pocketed his phone, looked all around and then walked twenty yards down the road, checked again and then ducked under the fence into the caravan park.

Reid took Kane off hold. "I'm back. Darren's just clocked Pitman going onto some caravan park …"

Kane cut in, "them woods is part of it man, they lead to the caravans."

"That so. Could it be drugs? I heard tell one time some dude was dealing outta some caravan site. Maybe Pitman's gonna hit him. Can you track 'em, see where they go. I'm bringing the crew down; this could be 'Showtime!" He laughed loudly causing Kane to pull the phone away from his ear.

"OK yeah. I'll let ya know." Kane opened the gate and followed the path that he'd seen Pitman's men take earlier. He smiled to himself, 'Showtime' Reid had said, yeah bring it on. His hand felt the familiar butt of the gun and he picked up his pace.

Twenty minutes later Reid and his crew were on site. They swarmed like ants down between the vans keeping to the shadows out of sight, honing in on where Darren had seen Pitman go.

Chapter Fifty-Seven

Tony was crouched down alongside the last caravan before the open ground and the path that led down to the woods and the fishing lake and the caravan that they suspected that Finch was hiding out in. Tony checked his watch and then his phone vibrated.

"Yeah go ahead," Pitman whispered.

"We're here," Stevie said sounding a little breathless. "It's bloody boggy through there some of it. It's all the rain we've had me shoes are caked in it, they're totally fucked. I went in almost up to me knees in one part it's like fucking quicksand! There's like all these little swamps coming off the main lake, we've had a hell of job to get through some of it in the frigging dark."

"OK, OK, don't stress it. So where exactly are you now then?" Pitman asked straining his eyes towards the caravan.

"Just to the side of the van about twelve feet away. We can hear voices so there's definitely people in there and the Renault's parked outside."

"Yeah I can see it. Right if you're ready then, I'll tell Billy to cut the power, so as soon as he does you move into the side of the van cos somehow, you've got to hit him with the light as soon as they come out to check what's going on. We want to try and avoid any shooting; I don't want any more of you guys getting hurt. Right here we go then, good luck and don't take any risks, if it starts going pear-shaped duck out and we'll meet up later, it's not worth anyone else ending up in the morgue."

"Yeah well, thanks for that," Stevie said soberly, "we'll wait for the lights to go out then. Later." Stevie cut the call and explained what was about to happen to Davey-Boy who just grinned and pulled the slide back on his gun. He was born ready. Stevie hefted up the Dragon lamp and settled it on his thigh ready for when they made their move.

Billy worked fast, he'd dismantled the terminals and disconnected the main feed and then he pulled the power arm down shutting off the supply. The sudden change in light was total. He still held the torch between his teeth and he transferred it to his hand as he left the small brick building that housed the power generator taking care to wipe the door handle when he left. He slipped as quickly as he could down the main path towards the entrance and a well-deserved pint of something when he arrived back home.

Somewhere on the site alarms went off triggered by the loss of power and people began to emerge from their vans wondering what the problem could be. Some fiddled with their supply inputs connecting and re-connecting them hoping to restore power but all to no avail. Here and there the more prepared residents lit candles, whilst others started searching for torches, batteries and matches.

Stevie and Davey-Boy moved into position. They heard a chair scrape inside and voices were raised, moments later the door opened.

"Everywhere's dark, no lights no place," Buscan said over his shoulder.

Deacon joined him at the door and looked around. "It must be a mains power cut there's not a light anywhere. Fucking hell what we supposed to do now then?"

Stevie hit the switch and the Dragon light burst into life as he and Davey-Boy rounded the corner of the van. Davey leapt up the stairs and pistol-whipped Buscan across the face and Buscan fell off the steps down onto the path. Davey sped forward and head-butted Deacon sending him flying backwards into the caravan entrance. Tony had started running towards the caravan as soon as he'd seen the Dragon light come on and he was about half way across when he caught movement to his left and he could just make out the shape of an outstretched arm holding a gun. He hit the ground and rolled as the gun fired and the shots went high.

Suddenly more shots rang out towards the caravan and Deacon clutched at his chest as two bullets ripped through him. Davey-Boy dived over the hand rail of the stairs and ran for the safety of the darkness and the woods. "Stevie come on!" he yelled.

Stevie spun the light in an arc in front of the van and illuminated Reid and his crew running forwards across the open ground. He threw the light down and it turned onto its back and sent a brilliant shaft of light up into the night sky. Bullets ricocheted off the van and Stevie ducked down under the stairs and returned fire hitting one of Reid's crew in the face and throat, he crashed down hard and shook twice and lay still.

When Stevie had swung the light around Pitman had taken advantage of the confusion and run back to the nearest van and rolled underneath it. He pulled out the gun. Although he kept a firearm in the drawer of the hall unit which was registered and licensed he'd never used it.

He'd carried it when he did close-protection work for a foreign diplomat and when the job ended the gun went back into the drawer. This was the first time he'd ever taken a gun with him on a job and this one was untraceable. This one he'd bought off Agile a year before when they'd had a few problems with some foreign guys who were bringing drugs and prostitutes into the area and making waves. He thanked his foresight now for bringing it as it might mean the difference between getting out of here alive or not.

There seemed to be a concerted effort concentrated towards the caravan and more shots were fired and then Pitman could make out the outlines of about six or seven people moving forward from both sides towards the van, amongst them standing head and shoulders above the rest was Marvin Reid. "Bastard," Pitman said to himself, now of all times he chooses to shake me down. Pitman took aim and then squeezed the trigger letting fly with a short burst. Reid threw his arms up in the air and spun round and crashed to the ground and another member of his crew was also hit in the leg and screamed and fell down clutching his shattered and bleeding limb. He was sixteen years old. The butterfly knife he'd been holding seconds before now lay discarded by the side of him as he held his leg and cried.

Stevie saw the big man fall and decided to make a run for it and join Davey-Boy. He fired a quick burst and stood ready to run when Darren crept round the side of the van and shot him through the back of his head. He plunged forwards and Darren stepped over to him and shot him twice more in the back. Darren wished one of the crew had filmed him in action. If you put that on YouTube, it would go fucking viral overnight he thought!

He was so fuelled up with adrenalin that he never heard Finch come out of the van. Finch was shaking with fear and just opened fire, and never having fired a gun before was unprepared for the recoil and although he hit Darren twice, the barrel of the gun dropped and sprayed closer to the ground. It was unfortunate that Buscan had chosen that moment to stand even though he was still having difficulty focusing, partly because of the effect of the Dragon light but more so due to the pistol-whipping that Davey-Boy had given him that had broken his nose and torn a gouge across his left eye almost leaving him blind in the one eye. One of Finch's bullets passed clean through his trachea and he died instantly.

Kane had to admit he'd been shit scared the moment all the guns had opened up and he'd thrown himself down on the ground and cowered half-hidden under the car that was parked alongside the target caravan. It wasn't like you could detach yourself from it like in the films and games he played at home on his computer. No, this was real and people he knew had been ripped apart by bullets and now lay dead. He still wanted to make his mark though and if he could only control the shakes that were wracking his body he'd do what he came here to do, and prove himself. And then the opportunity presented itself. Whitey-Boy was there, standing almost directly in front of him.

Jesus, he thought this is it. I can do this, Marvin will be so proud of me. He took a firmer grip on the gun and slid out from under cover. He held the gun out in front of him, pointed it at the man and pulled the trigger. Nothing happened. He turned the gun on its side and stared at it desperately and then held it back out in front, took aim and pulled the trigger again. Nothing happened again, it must have jammed. There was still too much noise and confusion going on all around for Whitey-Boy to have noticed him and the boy with the shattered leg was still screaming his head off.

Kane shoved the gun back into his pocket and pulled out the large kitchen knife he had tucked into the waistband of his trousers and moved forwards fast and drove the knife deep into the man's side using all the force he could muster. The man arched his back and cried out and Kane managed to retrieve the knife and as the man started to turn towards him, Kane slammed the blade deep into the man's stomach where it lodged and Kane couldn't pull the knife back out as his hand kept losing its grip with all the blood running down across the handle, so Kane shoulder barged the man and sent him flying.

Kane nodded down at his handiwork. So this was Pitman was it, mister fucking hard man. Kane spat on the body as the man's feet rubbed across the ground a few times and then he made a spluttering sound and lay still.

"Gotcha!" Kane whispered loudly and then he fumbled out his mobile and quickly took a photo of his handiwork to prove what he'd done in case another crew member tried to steal his moment of glory and then he turned and ran into the woods to make his way home. He knew he'd have to take it easy though as there'd been some very swampy parts he'd had to try and avoid on the way in, which had proved very difficult as it was so dark in there, the last thing he wanted was to get stuck in the swamp knowing the feds wouldn't be too far behind him.

Leaderless and suddenly aware of how serious the whole business of guns and violence had become, two of Reid's crew turned and ran back between the caravans seeking the way out. Several residents had already phoned the police and told of the ongoing gun battle that was raging on their quiet little caravan park. The dispatcher had alerted the relevant departments as she herself could hear the sounds of gunfire in the background and a team was already getting assembled to attend the scene. A few brave residents had ventured out of their homes to see what was going on and Gerald Croad, who was either braver than most or more stupid than most depending on your viewpoint, had ventured away from the relative safety of his caravan wondering what the bright light shining up into the sky and all the noise meant. He told his wife it was probably a film company making a film and that Mr Hindley had probably forgotten to let them know about.

Croad crept closer, it all sounded rather effective he had to admit, and then suddenly someone ran almost full pelt into him knocking him backwards into the side of number twenty-eight, Mrs Humphries caravan, and the pair of them landed in a heap on the ground. Mr Croad only just had time to realise that the person that had knocked him flying was a young black teenager and then before he had a chance to do or say anything he was aware of the air being knocked out of him and then the youth was scrambling to his feet and running away. Mr Croad felt suddenly faint and his hands reached down to his stomach, it was then he realised he had been stabbed and that was about the same time his eyes rolled up into his head and he slumped back down onto the ground, his life's blood pooling out of the massive wound and soaking into the ground.

Suddenly sirens could be heard in the distance and the remainder of Reid's crew began to disperse in all directions just desperate not to get caught. Tony rolled out from under the van. He knew he only had a few minutes before the feds roared in but he had to check and see if Stevie was still alive.

Pitman ran at a half-crouch and covered the ground to the caravan quickly. Christ there were bodies everywhere. He recognised Finch. He lay where Kane had left him with the large kitchen knife still protruding from his stomach. There were two other white men near the steps to the van, neither one Pitman knew, and he guessed one must have been the foreign man that Kenny had mentioned and he suspected that Finch must have had two minders looking out for him and not one. Too late to ask for a refund now he thought to himself. C'est la vie.

Pitman saw Stevie; he lay flat on his stomach. There was no need to check for signs of life; the back of his head had been blown apart and there were two other holes in the back of his jacket. Pitman knelt down beside him and gently touched Stevie's arm.

"I'm so sorry mate I never wanted this to happen. You've been a great mate ... I'm gonna miss you." Pitman was aware the sirens were very close now and he could see the revolving blue and red lights of the vehicles in the distance. He decided to leave Stevie's gun behind to further confuse the feds or help the investigation, anything that would take the pressure off him when they matched the bullets up. Either way would be a result.

Pitman patted Stevie's arm and then jogged back towards the security of the shadows and began tracking his way back towards the entrance. He needed to get in his car and get the hell out of there.

A line of officers were approaching cautiously forwards, strong-beamed torches lighting their way. Luckily it appeared they hadn't brought any dogs with them, they may be en route but for now it made escape easier without those fuckers sniffing you out. Pitman moved parallel with the officers each moving in a different direction. He came to the perimeter fence and crouched down and waited, making sure the coast was clear, not only from the feds but also from any of Reid's crew who he knew were also trying to hightail it away from the scenes of carnage they'd created minutes before.

Pitman rose up and ducked down under the fence and was just about to enter onto the road when he heard more sirens very close by and he ducked back and waited. Moments later two ambulances and another police car sped into the park, sirens wailing and lights flashing and slammed to a halt by the wooden office. Pitman ducked under the fence and walked as fast as he dared towards his parked car. By the time he'd almost reached it, there were cars and people making their way down the pavements and roads towards the caravan site to see what all the excitement was about. Fucking ghouls he thought to himself as he neared his car. He slowed down, his car didn't look right, it looked lopsided. As he drew closer he could see what the problem was, someone had slashed all the tyres, "Shit!" he hissed to himself. He thought about ripping off the false plates and taking them with him and then thought better of it. If he did get a pull on the way home or if the feds were waiting for him when he got there, there was no way he could explain what he was doing carrying a set of false number plates. No, there was only one thing to do. He pressed the fob and the lights flashed on and he opened the car door and leant inside. He took the duster he used to wipe the windscreen with and cleaned the steering wheel and the gear stick and all the controls and door handles and the boot lid. There was an old newspaper on the back seat and he scattered it around on the driver and passenger seat and then he opened the petrol cap and stuffed the duster partially down inside the tank. He could smell the fumes rising. After a few moments, he retrieved the duster, it was dripping with petrol. He left the petrol cap open and lit the duster and threw it inside the car onto the newspaper. It ignited immediately and he slammed the door shut with his foot and walked away from the car, pressing the key fob to lock the doors as he went. He risked a backwards glance when he was a few hundred yards away. He could see the flames and smoke raging inside the vehicle and he bent down pretending to tie his shoelace and dropped the car keys down a drain then tucked his hands deep into the pockets of his jacket and started to make his way home.

Chapter Fifty-Eight

Davey-Boy was running as fast as he could through the forest, all the while casting fearful glances over his shoulder, thinking that at any moment shots would ring out and he'd feel bullets ripping through him as they had through the men at the caravan.

Branches slapped at his face and body as he blundered forwards in the darkness. Part of him wanted to get his mobile out, he had an app on there for a flashlight but he daren't use it in case his followers saw the light and his position would be revealed and they would hone in on him and finish him off. His shoes slid in the mud and he almost lost his balance but he raced on, his breathing ragged and a stitch had started to build up in his side. He heard a noise and spun round bringing his gun up to face where he'd heard the twig snap but he still kept on moving. Suddenly his foot squelched into deeper muddy water and the suction ripped his shoe off and he stumbled forward into a bog losing the grip on his gun which quickly sank down out of sight. He swished his hands about in the water that was rising up his legs desperate to arm himself from his would-be attackers who Danny was convinced were hot on his heels. He couldn't find the gun and Davey-Boy was suddenly aware that whilst he'd been splashing about searching for the weapon he had sunk almost up to his waist and he was now stuck in the oozing, rising muddy water.

"Oh fuck no!" he cried out frantically trying to extricate himself from the grip and the pull of the muddy swamp. He felt his other shoe come off and then he found he couldn't touch the bottom, there was no bottom and he was sinking, deeper fast. Davey-Boy flayed his arms about trying to get some sort of traction going or to reach a branch or a bush or something but there was nothing within reach and the water was rising and the cold and wet had started to make him shiver. He fiddled frantically in his pocket and pulled out his phone but his hands were slippery and the phone flipped out of his hand and sunk under the rising water.

"Tony! Tony!" Davey-Boy screamed no longer caring who heard him. He was sinking in the swamp and there was nothing he could do to save himself. Davey-Boy then did something he hadn't done in years, he started to cry. He couldn't help himself, his eyes just filled up with tears and they ran cutting lines through his grubby face as he cried for a wasted life and a life that he knew was ending much too soon. Slightly to Davey-Boy's right was a sign warning of the danger of the swampy ground and instructing people to stay on the path. The sign was the last thing Davey saw as he coughed and spluttered and cried out as he sank beneath the muddy surface of the bog.

Tony meanwhile had been breaking down his gun piece by piece and dropping the parts down various drains as he made his way home. What a God Almighty fuck up. Stevie was dead and he had no idea where Davey-Boy was or if he was still alive. He'd tried phoning him but it went straight to voicemail which didn't sound very promising. Tony phoned Chrissie and told her to shove a change of clothes into a holdall and leave them down by the side of the house for him. He also told her to turn the lights off and keep obs out of the upstairs window and see if she could see anyone hanging about. She said she couldn't see anyone so he told her to go out to her car and get a CD or something and check outside and make sure the coast was clear and then go back inside. She did as she was told and said as far as she could see there were no cars there that hadn't been there before she'd arrived. He thanked her and said he wouldn't be long.

Shortly afterwards Pitman collected the change of clothing and walked back up the road to a small parade of shops. He slipped down the alleyway at the side of the shops and stripped off; shoving his used clothes and shoes into the holdall. Chrissie, bless her had even put in a pack off clean-wipes that she used for removing her make-up and he'd cleaned his hands and face with them and then pushed the used wipes down a drain. He left the holdall on the Cancer Research doorstep knowing full well that the bag would be long gone before the shop opened in the morning and then he turned and made his way back home.

Chapter Fifty-Nine

More police were arriving and the police helicopter was circling above the caravan site, its powerful spotlight illuminated the bodies lying sprawled on the ground. Someone had picked up the Dragon lamp and was now using it as a searchlight to scan the immediate area. Residents were being guided back into their caravans and an Inspector using a loud hailer had warned residents to stay inside their caravans and not to venture out. Police and ambulance crews were attending to the dead and injured and armed officers were making a slow sweep of the grounds.

PC Sam Holt let his dog have her head around the Finch's caravan and she began to pull towards the back fence and the woods. Sam told two armed officers that Jessie had picked up a trail and the small group started to make their way into the woods.

Kane heard the dog bark in the distance and could make out the beams of light coming towards him. He threw caution to the wind and ran faster. His feet slipped in the mud and he barged his way through the closely packed trees and shrubs keeping off the main path, thinking it would make it harder for the dog to track him and slow his pursuers down. His left leg suddenly slid along the mud and as he was running so his momentum carried his body forward and he fell head first into the boggy pool. He flailed his arms and body around desperately trying to right himself and by sheer force of will managed to break the surface of the muddy water. He coughed and spluttered, spitting the foul water from his mouth and he rubbed frantically at his eyes trying to clear his vision. He became aware of the fact that he couldn't move; he was stuck and there was nothing within reach except a few spindly shrubs that he could grab hold of to pull himself out with.

He grabbed a handful of the shrubs and tried to extricate himself from the bog but the shrubs just came away in his hands, it was useless, he was sinking deeper and deeper. Fear gripped him and he realised his only hope were the police who were already searching for him. He began to yell for help at the top of his voice, aware that as he did, so he was slipping further and further down into the slimy, oozing mud.

He carried on yelling and he could hear the dog closer now and see the torches cutting through the trees and bushes in his direction but the police were cautious and it looked like the lights had separated and were coming from different directions. Kane was desperate, the water had pinned his arms under the water and had risen up to his neck, he tried throwing his whole body weight upwards to stave off the rising mud and give him some additional time, the lights were getting closer, but the added movement did more harm than good and he lurched to the side and the water rose and started to creep up his face. Kane tilted his head back and yelled for help as loud as he could and then his foot felt something, he tried to make purchase on it and get a foothold to lift him up but whatever it was moved away and suddenly Kane sunk completely under the water. Davey-Boy's body rolled away as if to make room for the other man who sank alongside him, both of them sharing the same watery grave.

Two minutes later Jessie and PC Holt entered the start of the swamp. "Stay!" Holt yelled causing Jessie to jump; she moved back a few feet conscious of the water that had risen over her paws. Holt turned to his fellow officers. "Take it easy guys it's very muddy here, it's one of the swamps. There's quite a few of them in this area it's the overflow from the lake when it gets a lot of rain. They're pretty dangerous and some of them are really deep. Jessie tracked him to here, so I'm going to walk her round the edge and see if he's skirted the pond, so hold back till I say, it's pretty boggy."

PC Holt let Jessie have her head but kept her lead short, he didn't want her sinking into the bog. Last year a young lad had drowned in one of them when he'd been racing through the woods on his dirt bike and had literally just sunk beneath the water in a matter of seconds. When the swamp had been drained down, apart from the young lad and his bike, they found a deer, two foxes and an array of smaller animals that had all become victims of the boggy swamp. There were warning signs in place and fences had been erected but there would always be people that choose to ignore the signs and check things out for themselves.

The trail had ended and PC Holt retraced his steps and joined the other officers. "There's nothing heading away," he said as he crouched down. There were footprints leading almost up to the edge of the bog and then it looked like a swathe had been made in the mud. "I've got a rotten feeling, looking at these footprints that they slid and went into the bog headfirst, God help them. But there's some other footprints here as well. Christ don't tell me there's more than one person gone in there. We'll have to mark it and see about getting it drained in the morning. We'll move on there's nothing more we can do here and there maybe others making their way through the woods. Jessie's keening in that direction so we need to take a look. This side of the woods comes out on Gravel Road, Ken can you call it in and see if you can get a unit to the entrance of the woods in case someone beats us to it and they make it through?"

"Roger that," the officer said switching to transmit on his radio to make the call.

Chapter Sixty

Inspector White mirrored his name, he looked pale and drawn, he'd been up most of the night and still hadn't had a chance to shave or put on a clean shirt. Sergeant Willis had just written the last few details on the white boards and it was now the Inspector's job to update the detectives in the room and try and help them make some sense of it all.

"Right so what do we know?" he said starting off, "Well we have the equivalent of 'Gunfight at the OK Corral' that's what we've got!" he said without humour. A few tecs started to laugh then stopped abruptly when they realised it wasn't really meant in a humorous way. "We have ten dead bodies ladies and gentlemen, TEN! Never in my nineteen years' experience on the force have I witnessed such a tragic loss of life in one night as this and we're in England not in some tin-pot town in South America! So what the hell went on last night? We have another person injured, shot in the leg, who's just sixteen years old! So in case you're not aware, all leave has been cancelled and any officer not actually away from home has been recalled to duty. Meadow View Caravan Park is now completely sealed off, no one comes in and no one goes out, not until we're completely satisfied that everyone has been spoken to and every scrap of evidence no matter how small has been recovered. Uniform are down there now together with Detective Sergeant Briar and his team taking statements and obviously SOCO are up to their armpits in it. PC Holt, the dog handler was right and the bog where he thought one of the fugitives may have ended up proved to be correct and having drained back the water from the swamp first thing this morning, two bodies in fact were discovered." The Inspector used his pointer to illustrate on the boards. "One, David Raine, who as you know worked for Calder and has been in and interviewed on a number of occasions regarding both the disappearance of Mrs Calder and the beating of Martin Conner, not to mention the shooting of Harry Toke. A handgun was found in the swamp which we suspect may belong to Raine. This weapon is currently with the forensics team. The other body recovered alongside Raine, was this man here," he pointed to a photo of Kane. "This is Kane Miller twenty-four years old. A handgun was found in the pocket of his jacket, as yet we haven't determined whether or not it's been fired recently, but what is interesting, Kane's phone was recovered and surprise, surprise it was still working and on there was a photograph taken last evening we assume by Kane of a male we know to be, Kevin Finch who was lying dead on the ground with a large carving knife protruding from his stomach. Prints found on the knife confirm that they belong to Kane. Finch was lying outside this caravan," the Inspector pointed to a large colour photograph, "and Finch's prints are all over the inside and outside of the caravan. Uniform showed the site owner, Mr Hindley, photographs and he confirmed that he'd let the caravan to Mr Finch two weeks ago for three months. There were four other bodies outside of the caravan.

Steven Morgan, again someone who worked for Calder and with whom we've had dealings over the last few weeks, he'd been shot in the back of the head and twice more in his spine for good measure. A gun was found alongside him which bore his fingerprints. Two other white men were close by; I use the term 'white' not in a racial way and you'll see why later. The first was John Deacon who is well known to police forces around the country and was currently at large having jumped bail awaiting trial on a manslaughter charge. He was shot twice. The other white male was," the Inspector checked his notes for the pronunciation, "Anton Buscan, wanted in his home town of Bucharest for the murder of a police officer three years ago. He was shot and also sustained a serious facial injury suggesting that he was attacked first and shot a short time later." The Inspector was interrupted by one of the detectives.

"Excuse me sir, do we know who shot him? Was it Raines or Morgan?"

"It's too soon to say just yet, forensics have got their work cut out at the moment and are still gathering spent cartridges from around the site. Hopefully we'll know soon enough. So, where were we? Ah yes, now there is clear evidence to suggest that the two men were living in the caravan with Finch, primarily we suspect to protect him. Now moving on to this area here," the Inspector pointed to a photo where two other bodies lay on the ground. "We have two bodies quite close together here; we can tell you they were shot by different weapons. This man, who has sustained quite a few injuries of late, is Marvin Reid, who was hired by Dave Carson to help run things for him whilst Carson's site manager is recovering from a hernia operation. Now we can't prove it, but we suspect that Pitman was responsible for a beating that Carson and Reid received a short while ago although they claimed it was done by a gang of youths. Carson's car lot, Top Class Cars has since gone into receivership following the vandalisation of most of his cars shortly after he was admitted to hospital. Reid was armed at the time of his death. The other youth with him, who was also black, was Byron Cave, a nineteen year old with a lot of previous convictions, he was carrying a machete. Carrying on with the toll of black bodies, also outside Finch's caravan was Darren Brewer, Brewer was shot by Finch and Brewer we believe was responsible for shooting Steven Raine."

The Inspector paused and took a sip of water. "So is it about drugs? Reid we know has been responsible for bringing drugs into the area lately, although as you're all fully aware, there's a vast difference between knowing something and proving something. So was Finch dealing in drugs as well or was he just lying low following the murder of Elizabeth Calder which it's believed he had a hand in? Were Reid and his crew there to wipe out the opposition if it was about drugs? I do know that apart from a small amount of cannabis, no other drugs were found in the caravan or in Finch's car, which was parked at the scene. A search is being conducted later on today at both Finch's home address and Marvin Reid's, so we'll see what, if anything turns up from that. So again, if it is about drugs, what were two of Calder's men doing there, one of them Morgan, carrying a torch that wasn't far short of resembling a world war two searchlight! To date there's never been any evidence of drugs at any of Calders' clubs nor has any of his staff ever been involved to the best of our knowledge in anything to do with drugs, so it just doesn't make sense."

"Excuse me sir?" A young female detective asked. "You said there were ten dead bodies. You've only mentioned nine, sir."

The Inspector was thrown for a moment, he was tired and he felt the waves of fatigue wash over him. Sergeant Willis stood. "It's Mr Croad sir," he offered and then resumed his seat.

"Yes, yes it is. Thank you, Sergeant. Right well the tenth body belongs to a Mr Gerald Croad who has lived on the site for the last fifteen years, who, by all accounts was an innocent bystander, who according to his wife, said her husband was convinced someone was making a film and he'd gone to take a look. Mr Croad was fatally stabbed by person or persons unknown, he, sadly is our tenth victim."

"Thank you, sir," the female Detective said.

"Well team, your mission, should you accept it, is to find out what the merry hell is going on and let me know because I haven't got a bloody clue!" He smiled to let them know he realised what a very difficult job they had ahead of them putting all the pieces of the jigsaw together and hopefully coming up with some answers that led to some arrests and answered all the un-answered questions that he was currently being bombarded with by the top brass. "I'm convinced Tony Pitman's involved in this saga somewhere, bring him in and let's see what he has to say for himself. Sergeant take over will you please I have a meeting *upstairs*. Good hunting people and keep me informed." The Inspector nodded at Sergeant Willis and left the room.

Willis stood and picked up his notes from the table, "Right, well as the Inspector said, 'we've got a hell of a lot of work to do.' Barry," Willis said addressing a tall detective, "I want you to send someone to speak to Carson; he may know something more about Reid that we don't know about. Anything maybe useful."

"Yes Sarge," Barry replied.

"Reid had quite a number of local people working for him," he checked his notes, "mostly from one of the local gangs, The Stripes. Delroy Phillips, Kane Miller, Byron Case & Darren Brewer were all members. I want someone to visit the youngster, Delroy in hospital, he's scared and he might feel like talking. Check it out. We've also got a burnt-out car less than a quarter of a mile away from the scene which was set alight from the inside and then locked back up. It's been towed away and is currently being examined, chances are, it's connected in some way, it's too much of a coincidence to think it's not. I want CCTV cameras checked in the area leading to the caravan park; something's got to flag up somewhere. Also, I want a check done on anyone on file who has any electrical background. The mains supply was cut off to the park at the time of the incident and it couldn't have been done by anyone without the necessary knowledge. It wasn't like they just turned a switch off. SOCO are checking for prints, you never know, we might get lucky, God knows we could do with some. I also want to know Calder's whereabouts last night and I want both Talbot and Reardon checked out as well. Someone somewhere must know what the hell last night was all about. Right any questions?"

There were a few mumbles and brief words uttered but no one proposed anything.

"Right then let's get to it and give me results people, we've got a Super coming down at lunchtime and I want to have something concrete to tell him. Chop-chop let's go!" He clapped his hands twice and then gathered up his notes and joined his colleagues as they all started making for the door and their relative tasks.

Chapter Sixty-One
Epilogue

The caravan site was locked down for close on two weeks with all the residents' movements being logged and documented, and despite SOCO finding a large amount of evidence, no clear motive could be established for the massive outbreak of violence, nor was the person responsible for the fatal stabbing of Gerald Croad apprehended, although the case is still open and still being investigated. Nor were any charges brought against anyone else for the murders on the site.

Tony Pitman was interviewed on two further occasions and released without charge, his alibi stood up together with the neighbour's statement and there was no sighting of Pitman's BMW anywhere within five miles of the caravan park before or after the incident and apart from the fact that two of the dead victims were employees of Calder's and Pitman knew them, there was nothing else to link Pitman to the incident.

The burnt-out car had had the VIN number removed and the engine chassis number had been ground off leaving nothing to identify the vehicle with, and as such, no actual connection could be made to the incident.

John Calder, Steven Talbot and Tommy Reardon were all brought in and interviewed but there was nothing of any note that could link any of them to the massacre at Meadow View Caravan Park and they were all released without charge.

Both the murders of Elizabeth Calder and Clive Russell remain open but as yet there are no new leads to follow despite repeated coverage via the press and television. The police firmly believe that Harry Toke and Kevin Finch were responsible for the abduction and murder of Elizabeth Calder but as yet there has been no real proof to substantiate this and with both men now deceased the likelihood of a definite connection becomes more remote with each passing day.

In the months that followed, the new shopping complex started to take shape despite the fact that John Calder still refused to sell his small block of shops and flats.

Kevin Doyle had an operation on his eye that restored his sight and he started work for his brother and to all intents and purposes he seemed fairly content in his new role as a law-abiding citizen. To date he hasn't been fishing again and his tackle remains locked in his garden shed.

Martin Conner was sentenced to four years' imprisonment for assaulting a police officer and the handling of stolen property. The judge explained to him the leniency of the sentence was due to the fact he attended court on crutches and was still suffering from his injuries and was having ongoing surgery to his hands.

Dave the van driver received an envelope through his letterbox in the dead of night containing five thousand pounds in cash and Sue the practise nurse had her kitchen steam cleaned and an all-inclusive holiday in Madeira with her girl-friend paid for as a way of saying thank you.

Sonia despite earning four thousand pounds for less than an hour's work still had her carpet cleaned, and she texted Tony to let him know there was still a freebie waiting for him whenever he wanted.

Dave Carson returned to his car lot but despite trying to re-establish his business, without the necessary funding the business never really got started and he gave up and went to work managing a small garage for an old friend that also had a car valeting service attached. It wasn't what he was used to, but he didn't have to keep looking over his shoulder every five minutes any more. And there was a lot to be said for that peace of mind.

Kenny maintained a low profile, but he did receive a brand new jet ski that arrived at his house one Saturday morning that he couldn't wait to try out.

And with the publicity surrounding the Meadow View Caravan Park which never seemed to be off the television or out of the papers for weeks after the bloodshed, the site took on a new lease of life, with bookings up sixty percent which enabled Mr Hindley to get planning permission to erect a swimming pool and bar area, which boosted the bookings even more. It's an ill wind ...

And as for Tony Pitman? Well Tony would always be Tony ...